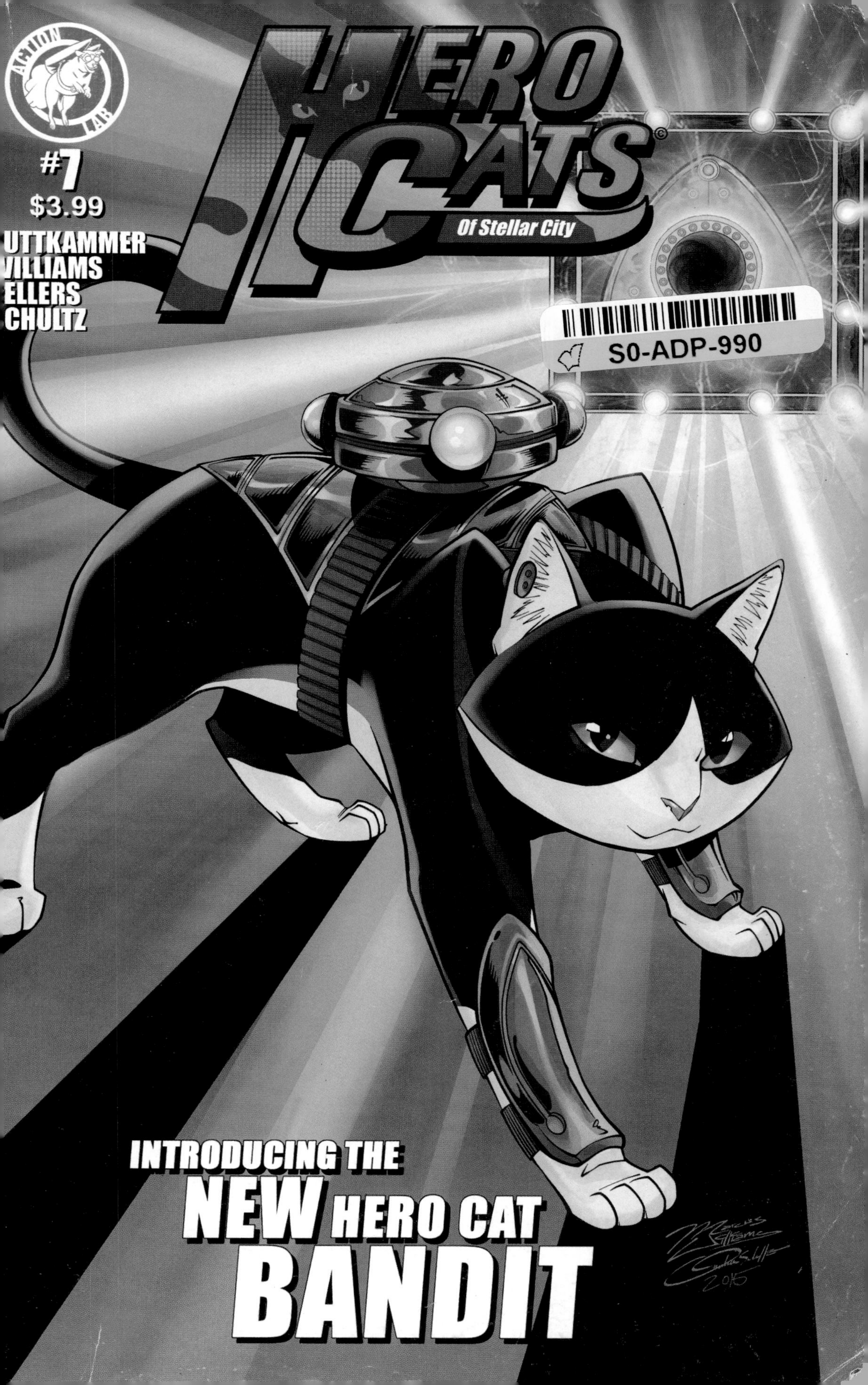
ACTION LAB
HERO CATS
Of Stellar City
#7
$3.99
UTTKAMMER
VILLIAMS
ELLERS
CHULTZ
S0-ADP-990
INTRODUCING THE
NEW HERO CAT
BANDIT

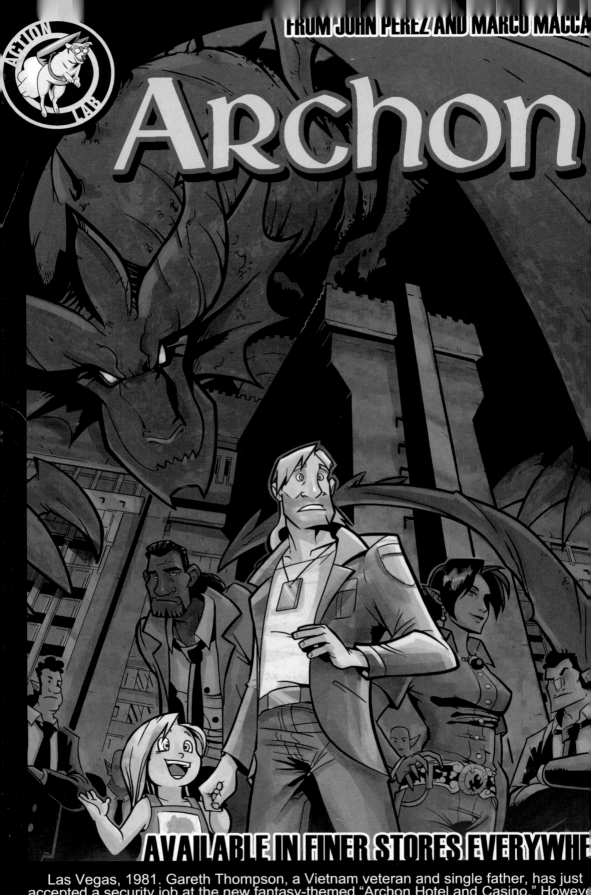

FROM JOHN PEREZ AND MARCO MACCA

Archon

AVAILABLE IN FINER STORES EVERYWHE

Las Vegas, 1981. Gareth Thompson, a Vietnam veteran and single father, has just accepted a security job at the new fantasy-themed "Archon Hotel and Casino." Howeve he'll soon discover all the Orcs, Elves and Dragons at the Resort are not people in costumes, but actual creatures of myth and legend.

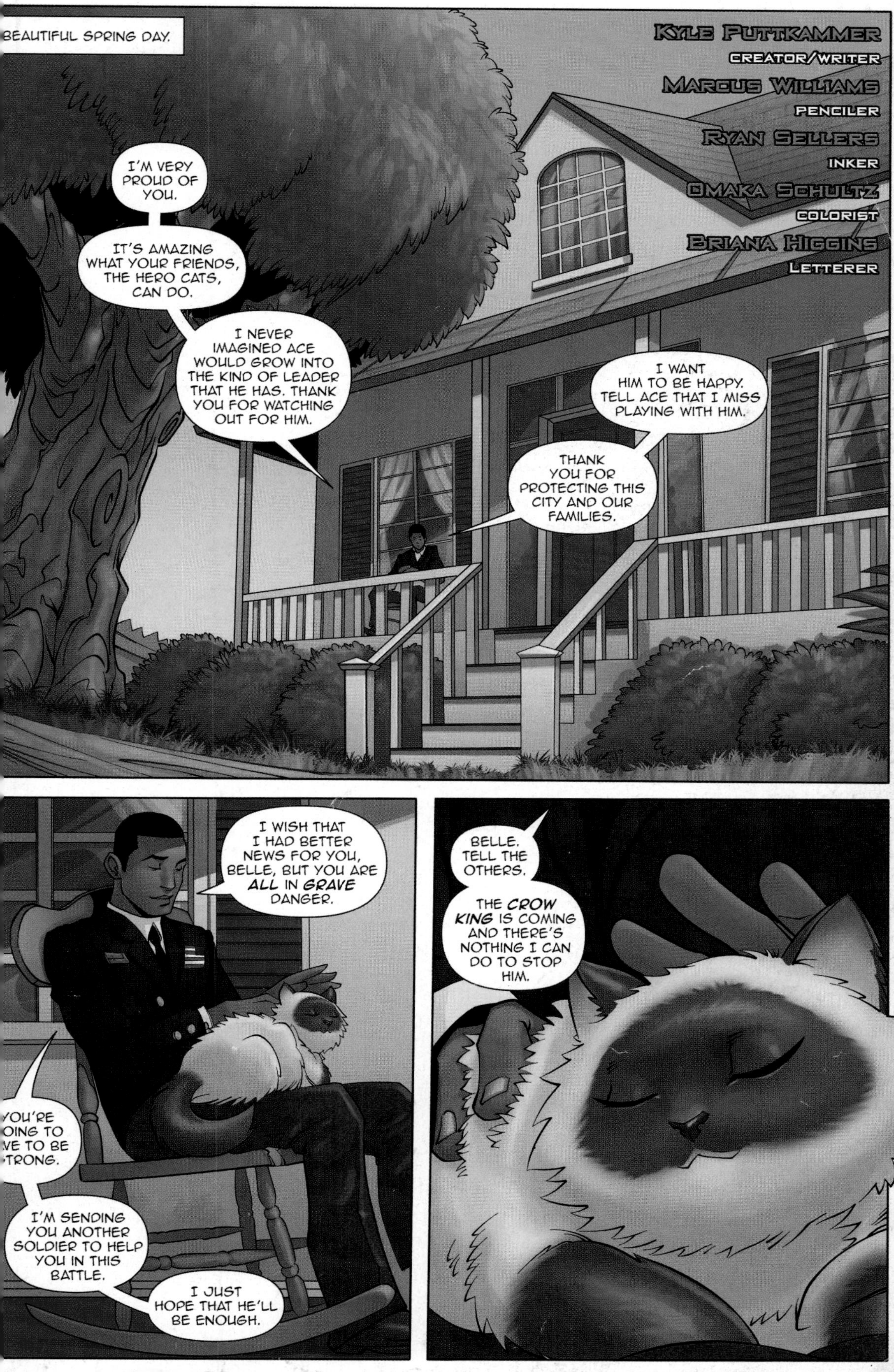

BEAUTIFUL SPRING DAY.
KYLE PUTTKAMMER
CREATOR/WRITER
MARCUS WILLIAMS
PENCILER
RYAN SELLERS
INKER
OMAKA SCHULTZ
COLORIST
BRIANA HIGGINS
LETTERER
I'M VERY PROUD OF YOU.
IT'S AMAZING WHAT YOUR FRIENDS, THE HERO CATS, CAN DO.
I NEVER IMAGINED ACE WOULD GROW INTO THE KIND OF LEADER THAT HE HAS. THANK YOU FOR WATCHING OUT FOR HIM.
I WANT HIM TO BE HAPPY. TELL ACE THAT I MISS PLAYING WITH HIM.
THANK YOU FOR PROTECTING THIS CITY AND OUR FAMILIES.
I WISH THAT I HAD BETTER NEWS FOR YOU, BELLE, BUT YOU ARE ALL IN GRAVE DANGER.
YOU'RE OING TO VE TO BE TRONG.
I'M SENDING YOU ANOTHER SOLDIER TO HELP YOU IN THIS BATTLE.
I JUST HOPE THAT HE'LL BE ENOUGH.
BELLE. TELL THE OTHERS.
THE CROW KING IS COMING AND THERE'S NOTHING I CAN DO TO STOP HIM.

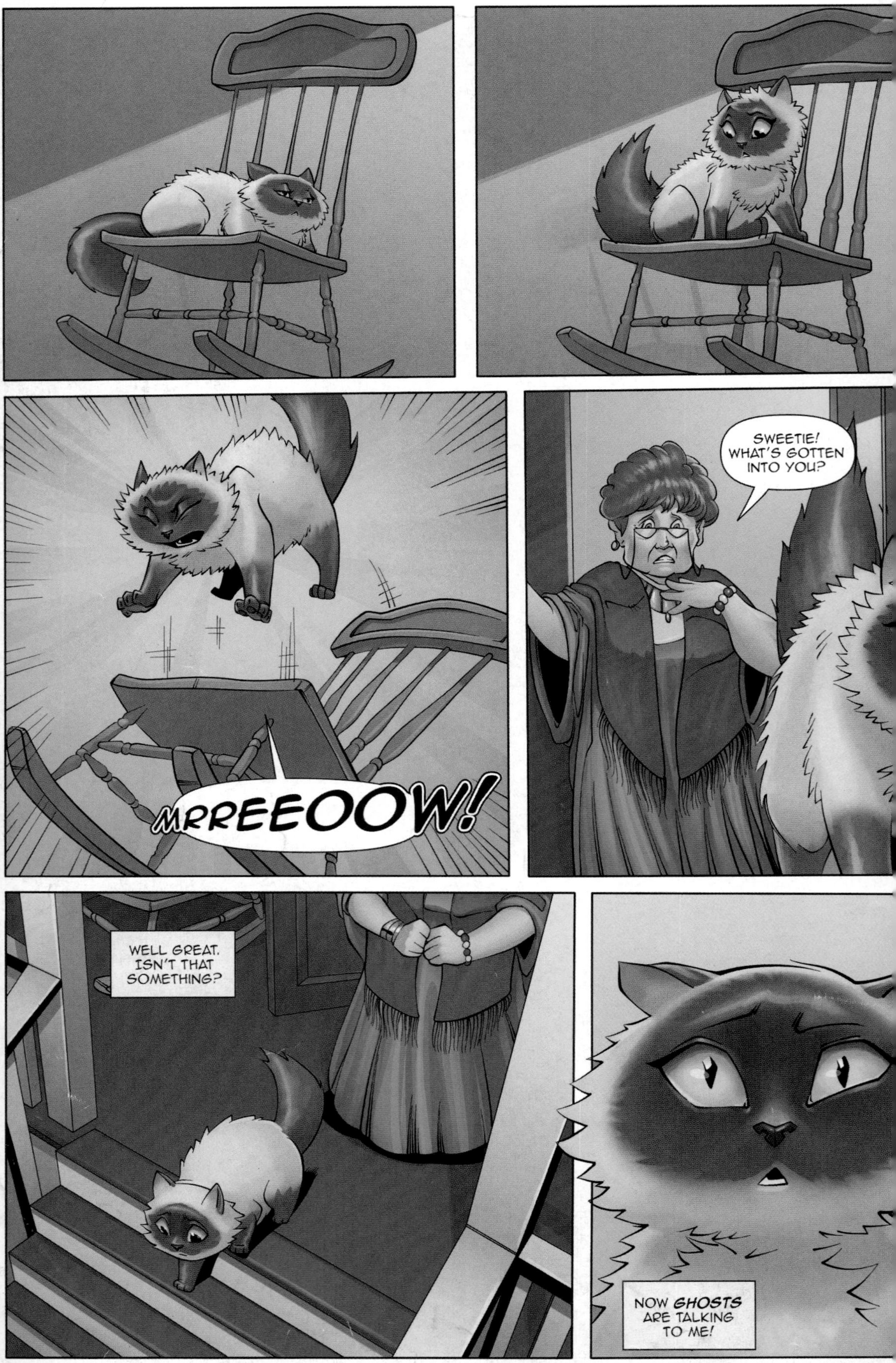
MRREEOOW!
SWEETIE! WHAT'S GOTTEN INTO YOU?
WELL GREAT. ISN'T THAT SOMETHING?
NOW GHOSTS ARE TALKING TO ME!

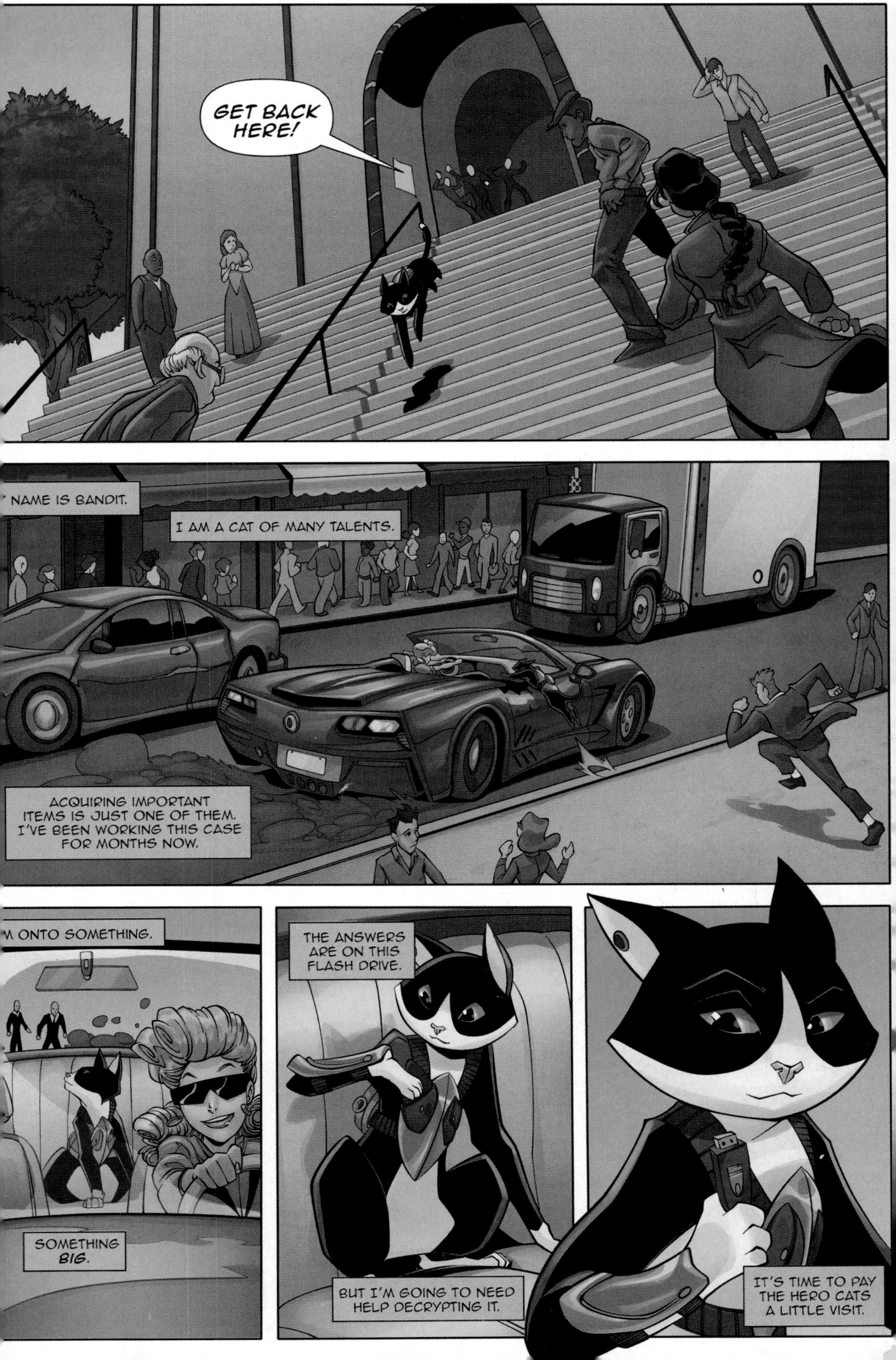
GET BACK HERE!
NAME IS BANDIT.
I AM A CAT OF MANY TALENTS.
ACQUIRING IMPORTANT ITEMS IS JUST ONE OF THEM. I'VE BEEN WORKING THIS CASE FOR MONTHS NOW.
M ONTO SOMETHING.
SOMETHING BIG.
THE ANSWERS ARE ON THIS FLASH DRIVE.
BUT I'M GOING TO NEED HELP DECRYPTING IT.
IT'S TIME TO PAY THE HERO CATS A LITTLE VISIT.

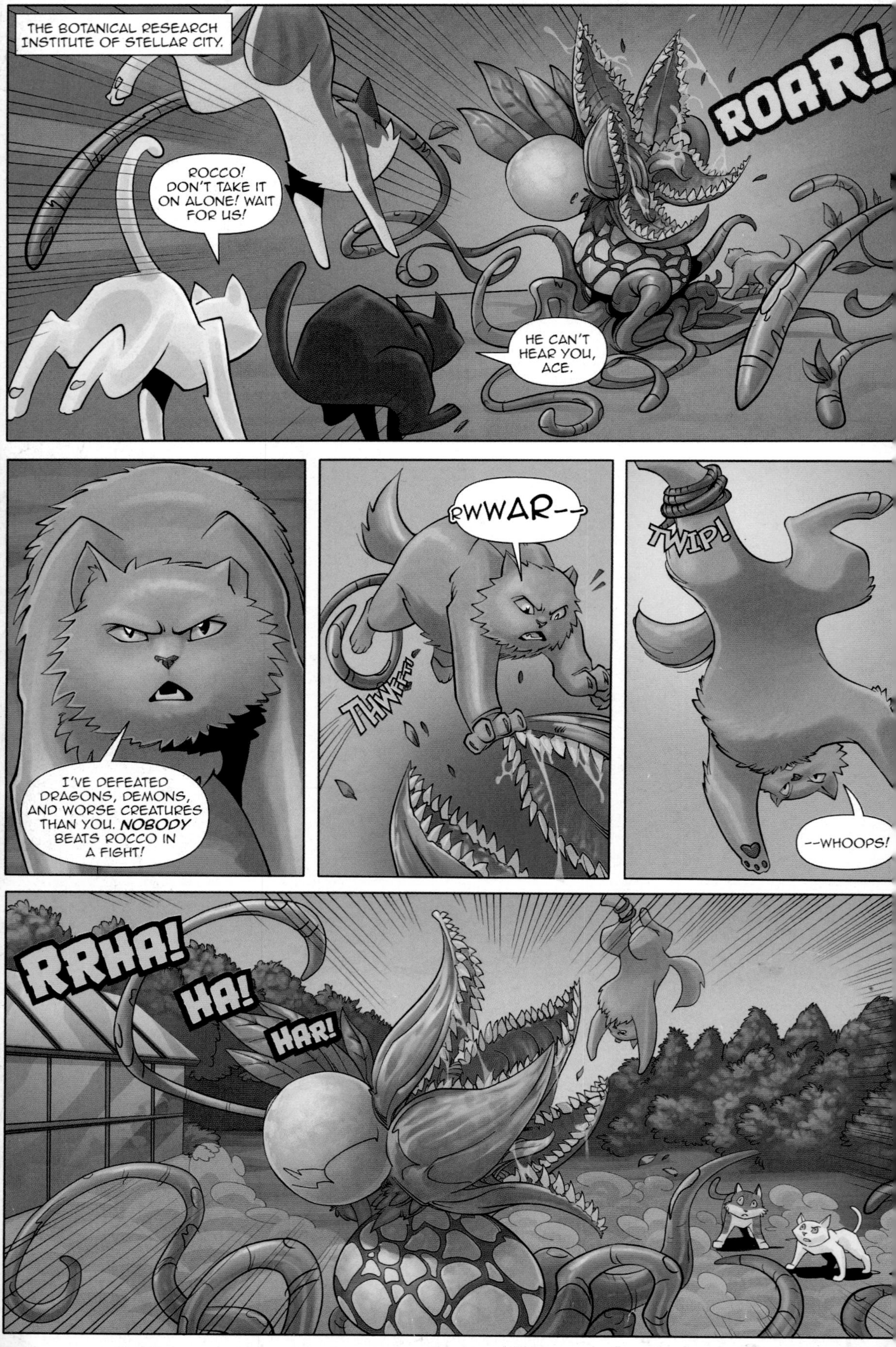
THE BOTANICAL RESEARCH INSTITUTE OF STELLAR CITY.
ROCCO! DON'T TAKE IT ON ALONE! WAIT FOR US!
ROAR!
HE CAN'T HEAR YOU, ACE.
I'VE DEFEATED DRAGONS, DEMONS, AND WORSE CREATURES THAN YOU. NOBODY BEATS ROCCO IN A FIGHT!
RWWAR--
THWEET!
TWIP!
--WHOOPS!
RRHA!
HA!
HAR!

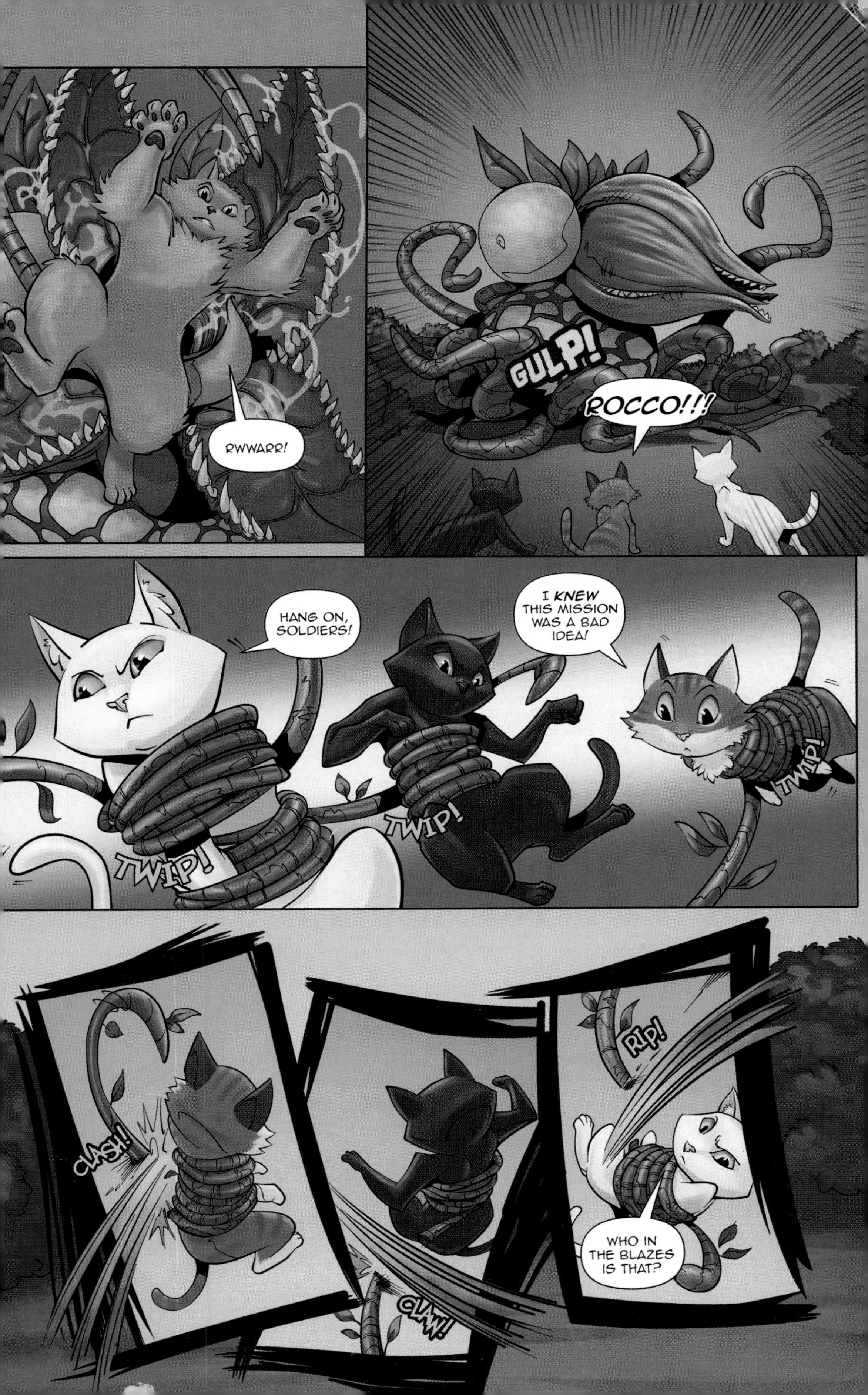
RWWARR!
GULP!
ROCCO!!!
HANG ON, SOLDIERS!
I KNEW THIS MISSION WAS A BAD IDEA!
TWIP!
TWIP!
TWIP!
CLASH!
CLAW!
RIP!
WHO IN THE BLAZES IS THAT?

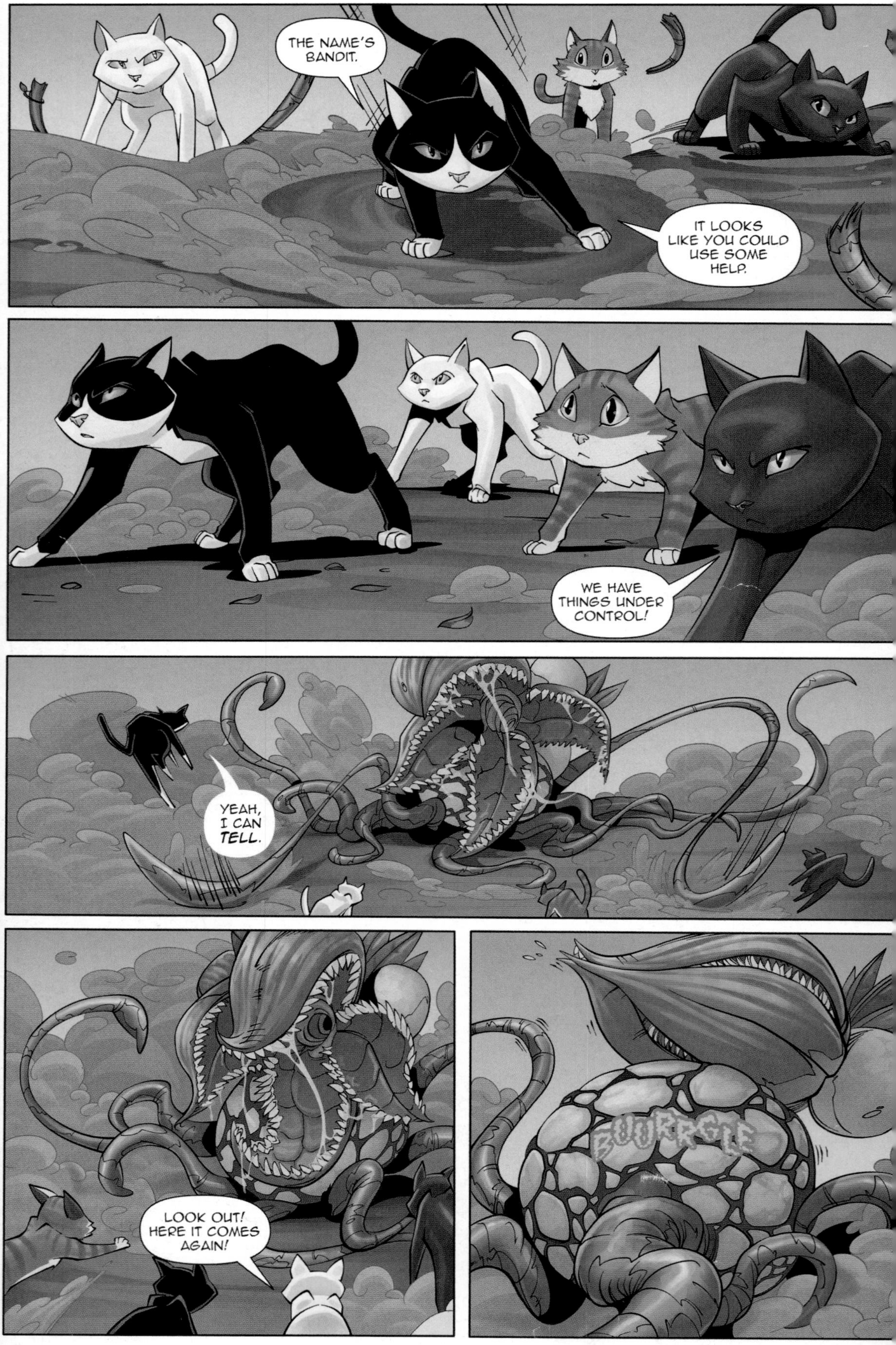
THE NAME'S BANDIT.
IT LOOKS LIKE YOU COULD USE SOME HELP.
WE HAVE THINGS UNDER CONTROL!
YEAH, I CAN TELL.
LOOK OUT! HERE IT COMES AGAIN!
BUURRGLE

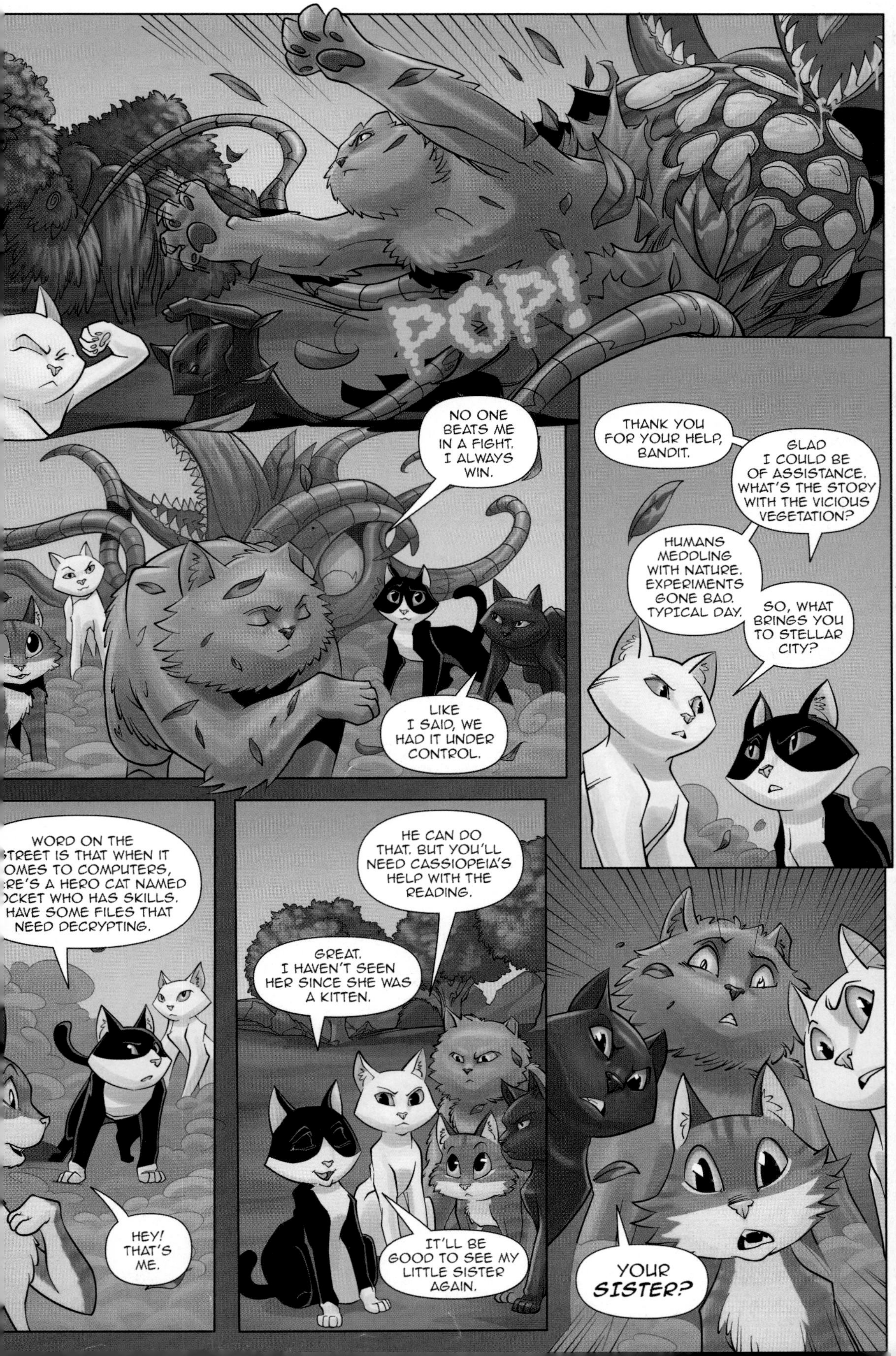
POP!
NO ONE BEATS ME IN A FIGHT. I ALWAYS WIN.
LIKE I SAID, WE HAD IT UNDER CONTROL.
THANK YOU FOR YOUR HELP, BANDIT.
GLAD I COULD BE OF ASSISTANCE. WHAT'S THE STORY WITH THE VICIOUS VEGETATION?
HUMANS MEDDLING WITH NATURE. EXPERIMENTS GONE BAD. TYPICAL DAY.
SO, WHAT BRINGS YOU TO STELLAR CITY?
WORD ON THE STREET IS THAT WHEN IT OMES TO COMPUTERS, RE'S A HERO CAT NAMED OCKET WHO HAS SKILLS. HAVE SOME FILES THAT NEED DECRYPTING.
HEY! THAT'S ME.
HE CAN DO THAT. BUT YOU'LL NEED CASSIOPEIA'S HELP WITH THE READING.
GREAT. I HAVEN'T SEEN HER SINCE SHE WAS A KITTEN.
IT'LL BE GOOD TO SEE MY LITTLE SISTER AGAIN.
YOUR SISTER?

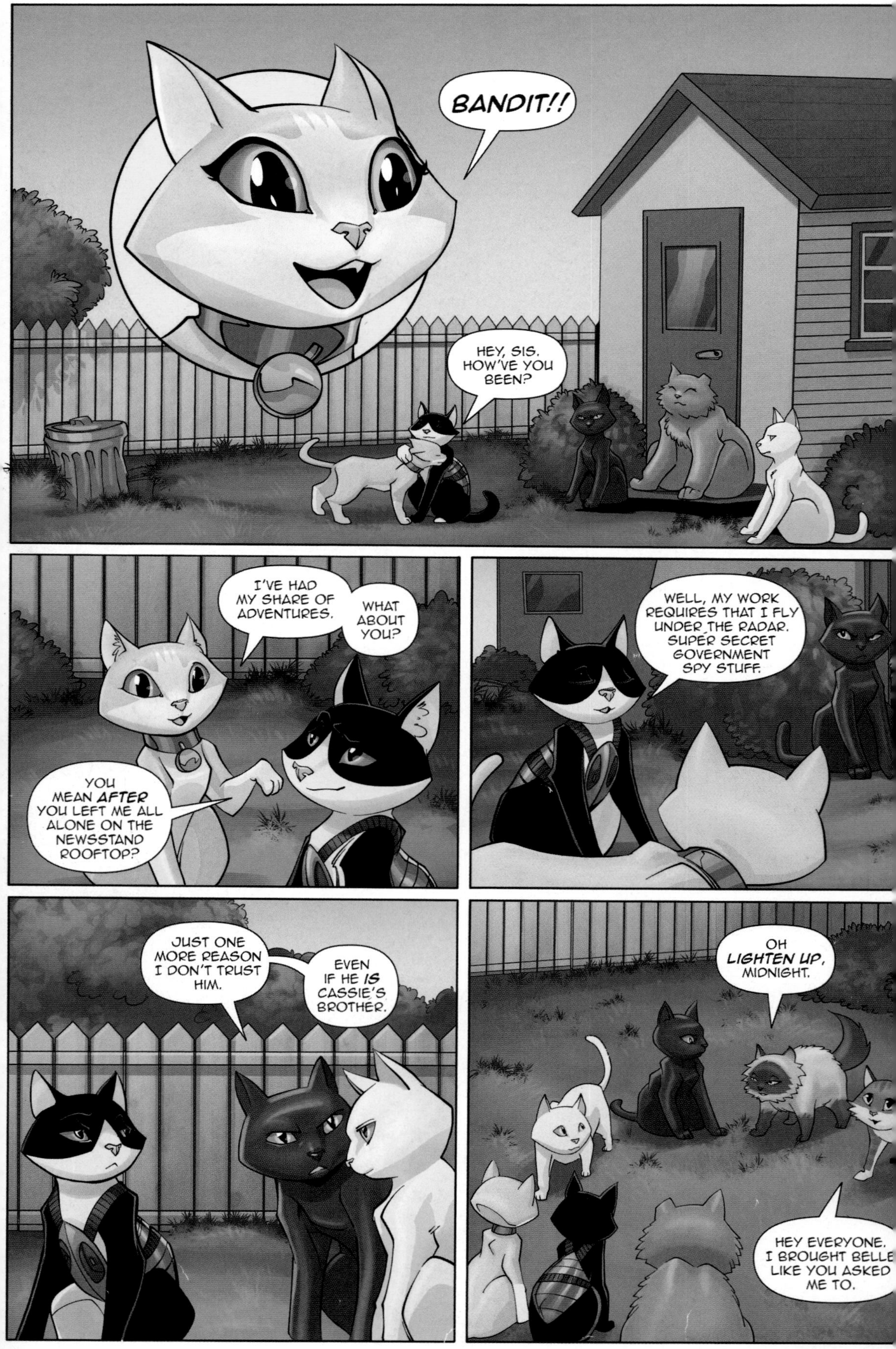
BANDIT!!
HEY, SIS. HOW'VE YOU BEEN?
I'VE HAD MY SHARE OF ADVENTURES.
WHAT ABOUT YOU?
YOU MEAN *AFTER* YOU LEFT ME ALL ALONE ON THE NEWSSTAND ROOFTOP?
WELL, MY WORK REQUIRES THAT I FLY UNDER THE RADAR. SUPER SECRET GOVERNMENT SPY STUFF.
JUST ONE MORE REASON I DON'T TRUST HIM.
EVEN IF HE *IS* CASSIE'S BROTHER.
OH *LIGHTEN UP,* MIDNIGHT.
HEY EVERYONE. I BROUGHT BELLE LIKE YOU ASKED ME TO.

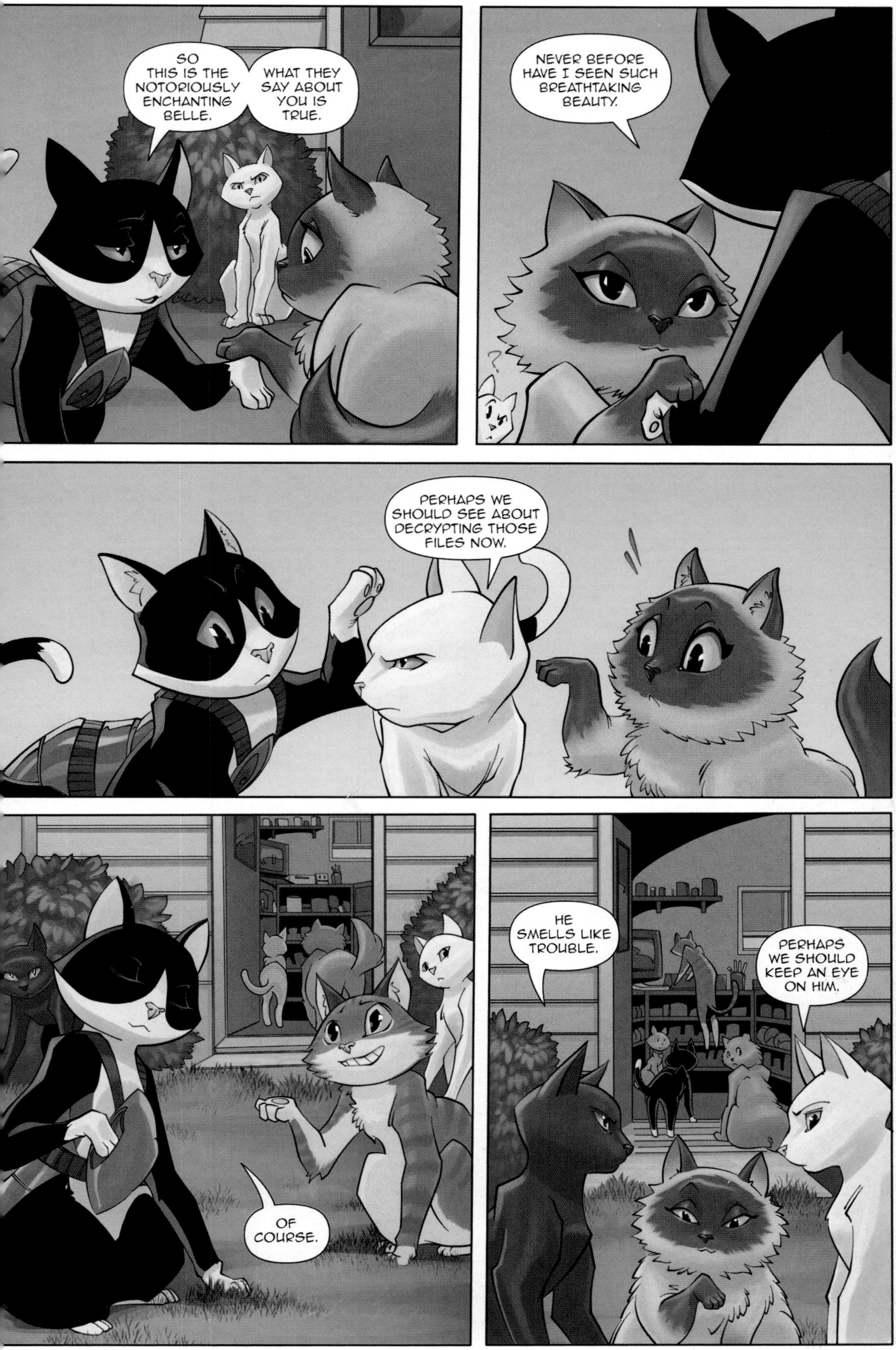
SO THIS IS THE NOTORIOUSLY ENCHANTING BELLE.
WHAT THEY SAY ABOUT YOU IS TRUE.
NEVER BEFORE HAVE I SEEN SUCH BREATHTAKING BEAUTY.
?
PERHAPS WE SHOULD SEE ABOUT DECRYPTING THOSE FILES NOW.
!
OF COURSE.
HE SMELLS LIKE TROUBLE.
PERHAPS WE SHOULD KEEP AN EYE ON HIM.

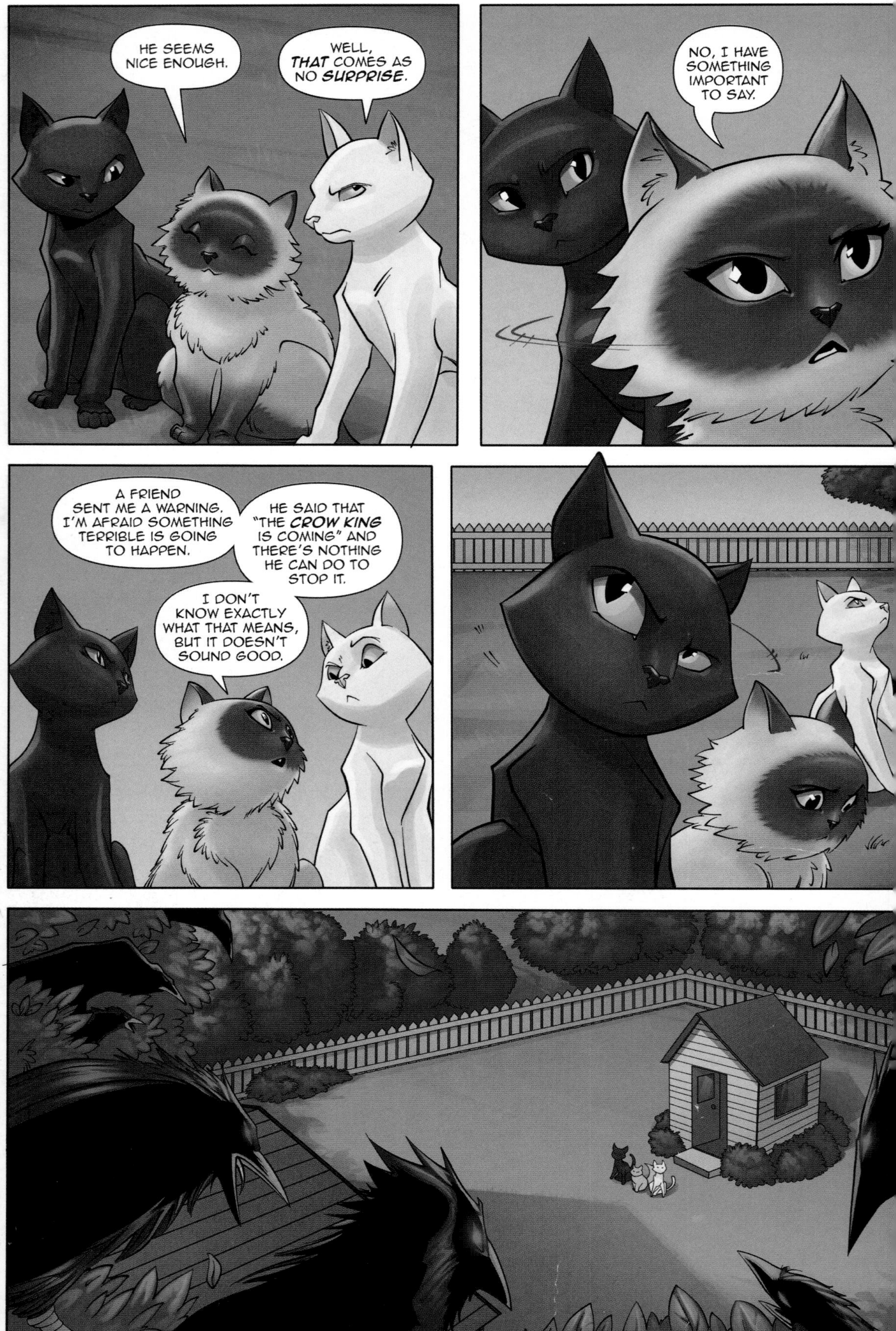
HE SEEMS NICE ENOUGH.
WELL, THAT COMES AS NO SURPRISE.
NO, I HAVE SOMETHING IMPORTANT TO SAY.
A FRIEND SENT ME A WARNING. I'M AFRAID SOMETHING TERRIBLE IS GOING TO HAPPEN.
HE SAID THAT "THE CROW KING IS COMING" AND THERE'S NOTHING HE CAN DO TO STOP IT.
I DON'T KNOW EXACTLY WHAT THAT MEANS, BUT IT DOESN'T SOUND GOOD.

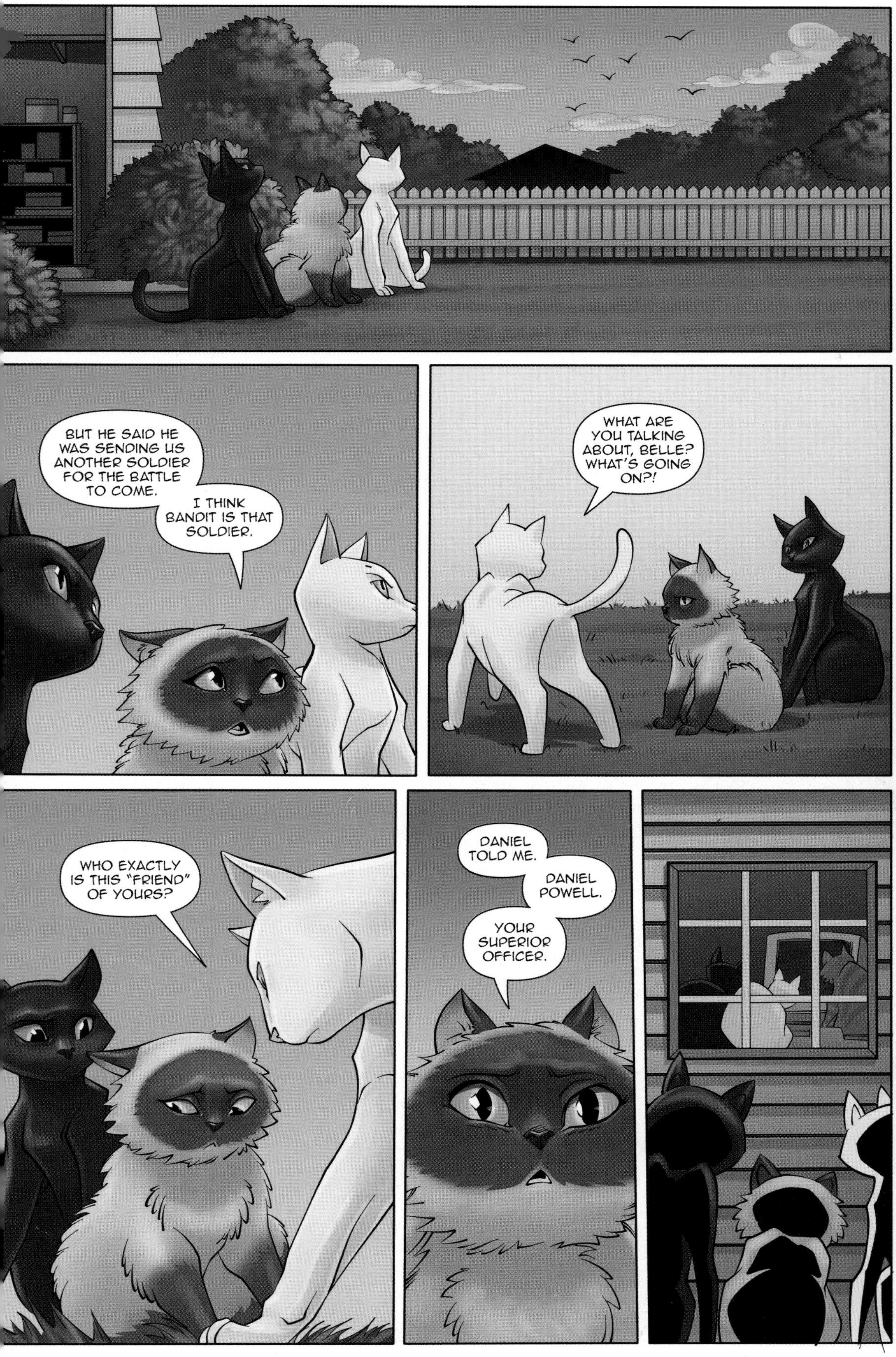
BUT HE SAID HE WAS SENDING US ANOTHER SOLDIER FOR THE BATTLE TO COME.
I THINK BANDIT IS THAT SOLDIER.
WHAT ARE YOU TALKING ABOUT, BELLE? WHAT'S GOING ON?!
WHO EXACTLY IS THIS "FRIEND" OF YOURS?
DANIEL TOLD ME.
DANIEL POWELL.
YOUR SUPERIOR OFFICER.

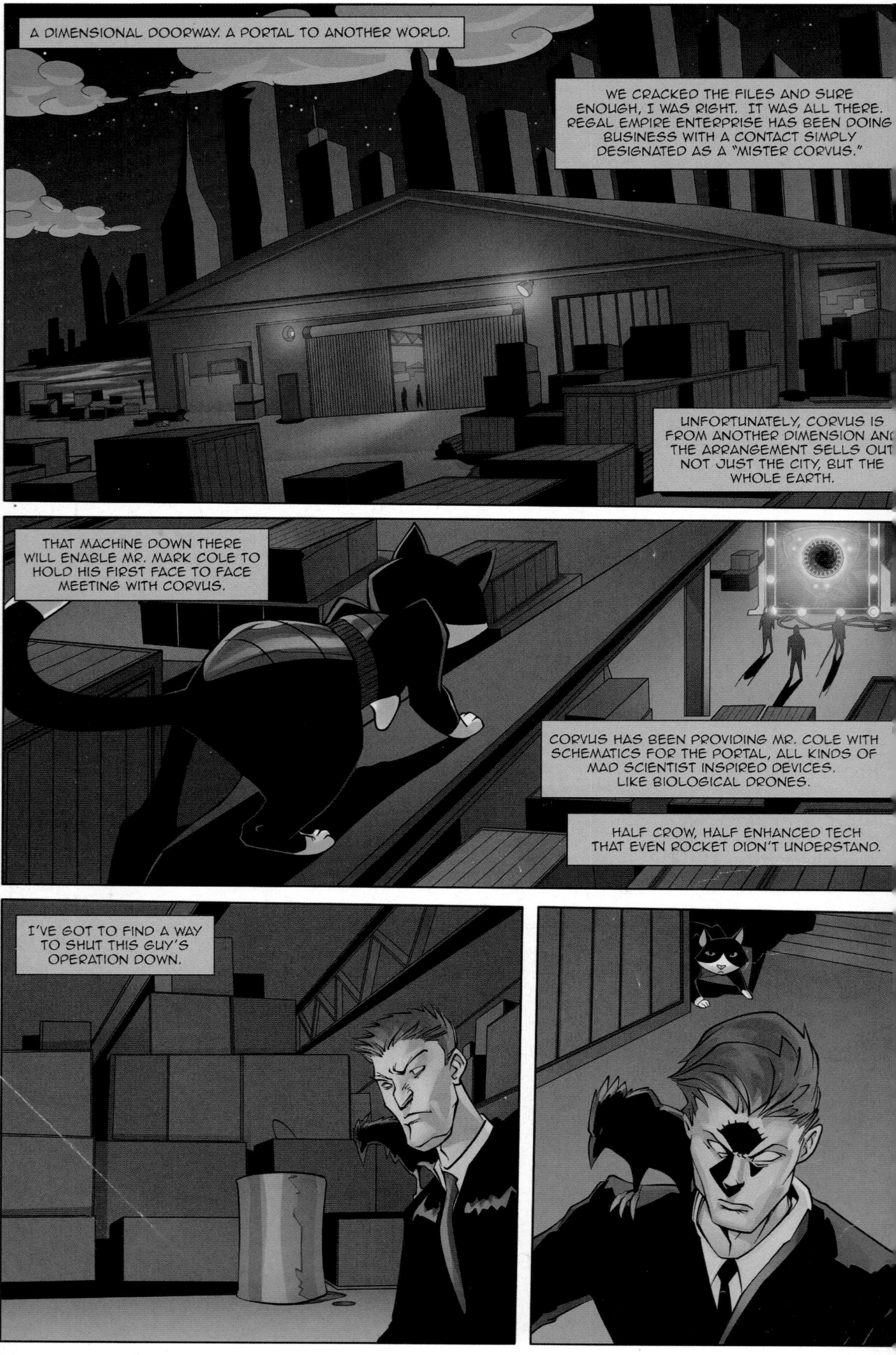
A DIMENSIONAL DOORWAY. A PORTAL TO ANOTHER WORLD.
WE CRACKED THE FILES AND SURE ENOUGH, I WAS RIGHT. IT WAS ALL THERE. REGAL EMPIRE ENTERPRISE HAS BEEN DOING BUSINESS WITH A CONTACT SIMPLY DESIGNATED AS A "MISTER CORVUS."
UNFORTUNATELY, CORVUS IS FROM ANOTHER DIMENSION AND THE ARRANGEMENT SELLS OUT NOT JUST THE CITY, BUT THE WHOLE EARTH.
THAT MACHINE DOWN THERE WILL ENABLE MR. MARK COLE TO HOLD HIS FIRST FACE TO FACE MEETING WITH CORVUS.
CORVUS HAS BEEN PROVIDING MR. COLE WITH SCHEMATICS FOR THE PORTAL, ALL KINDS OF MAD SCIENTIST INSPIRED DEVICES. LIKE BIOLOGICAL DRONES.
HALF CROW, HALF ENHANCED TECH THAT EVEN ROCKET DIDN'T UNDERSTAND.
I'VE GOT TO FIND A WAY TO SHUT THIS GUY'S OPERATION DOWN.

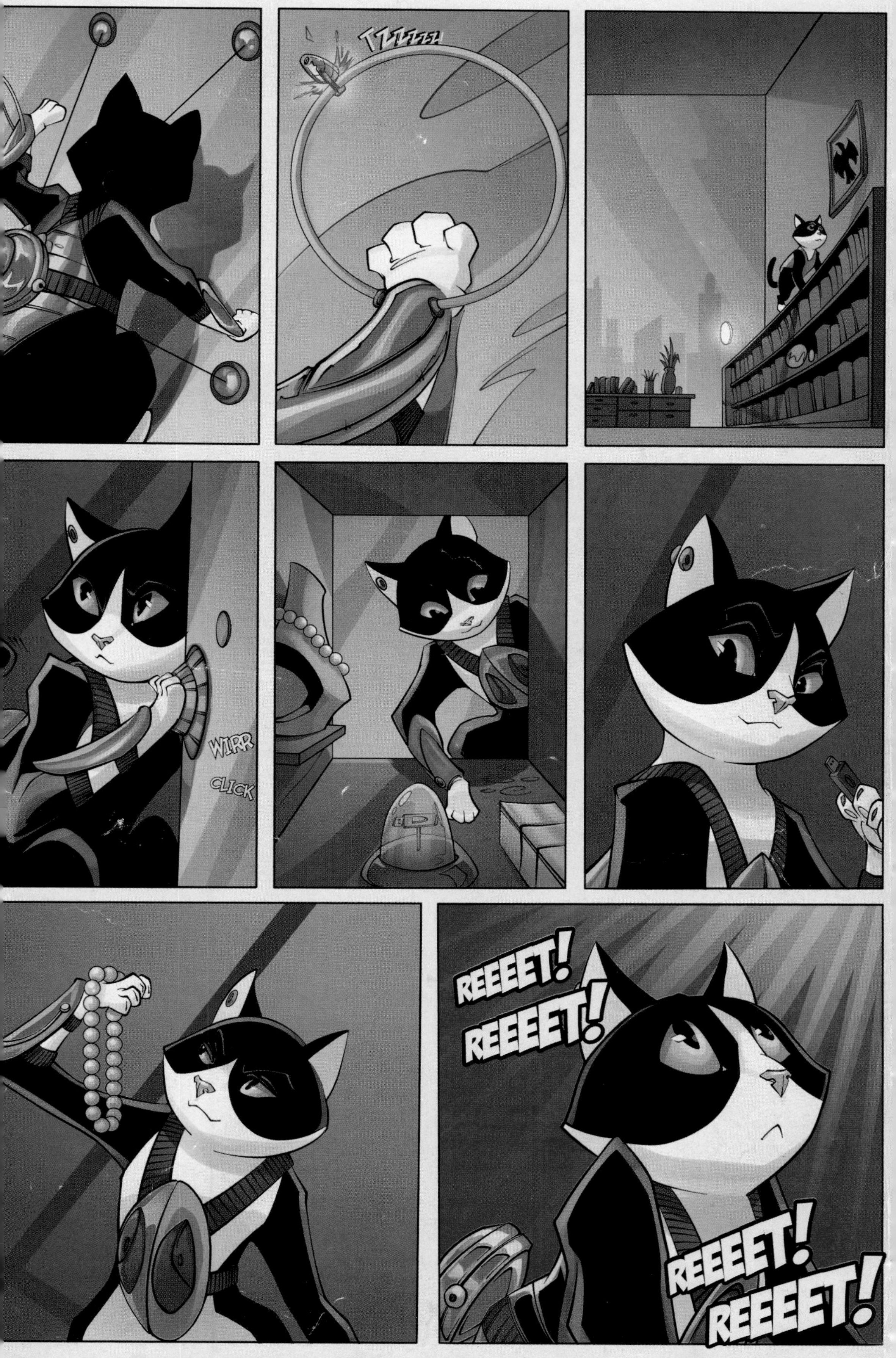
TZZZZZZH
WIRR
CLICK
REEEET!
REEEET!
REEEET!
REEEET!

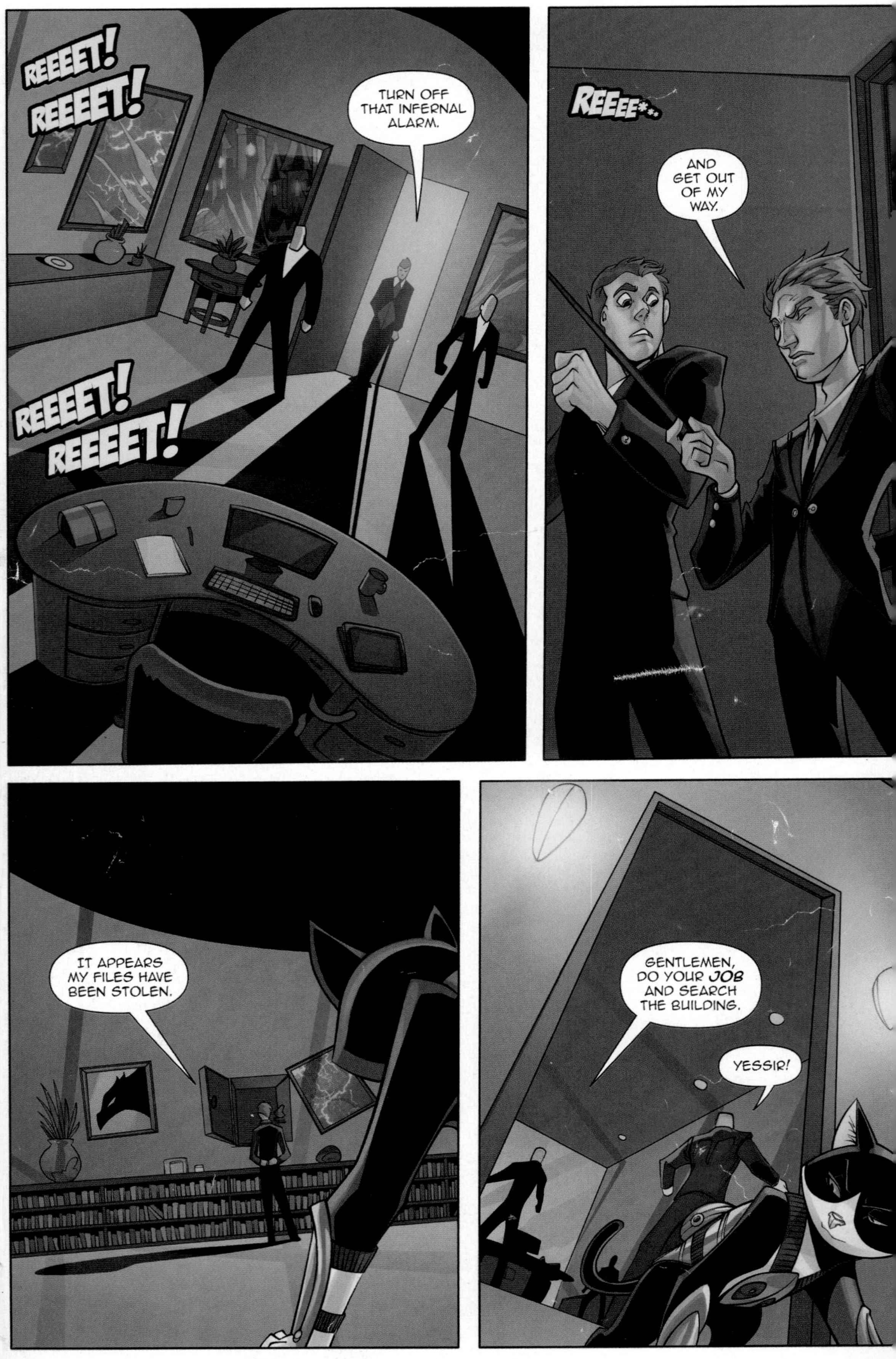
REEEET!
REEEET!
TURN OFF THAT INFERNAL ALARM.
REEEET!
REEEET!
REEEE*..
AND GET OUT OF MY WAY.
IT APPEARS MY FILES HAVE BEEN STOLEN.
GENTLEMEN, DO YOUR JOB AND SEARCH THE BUILDING.
YESSIR!

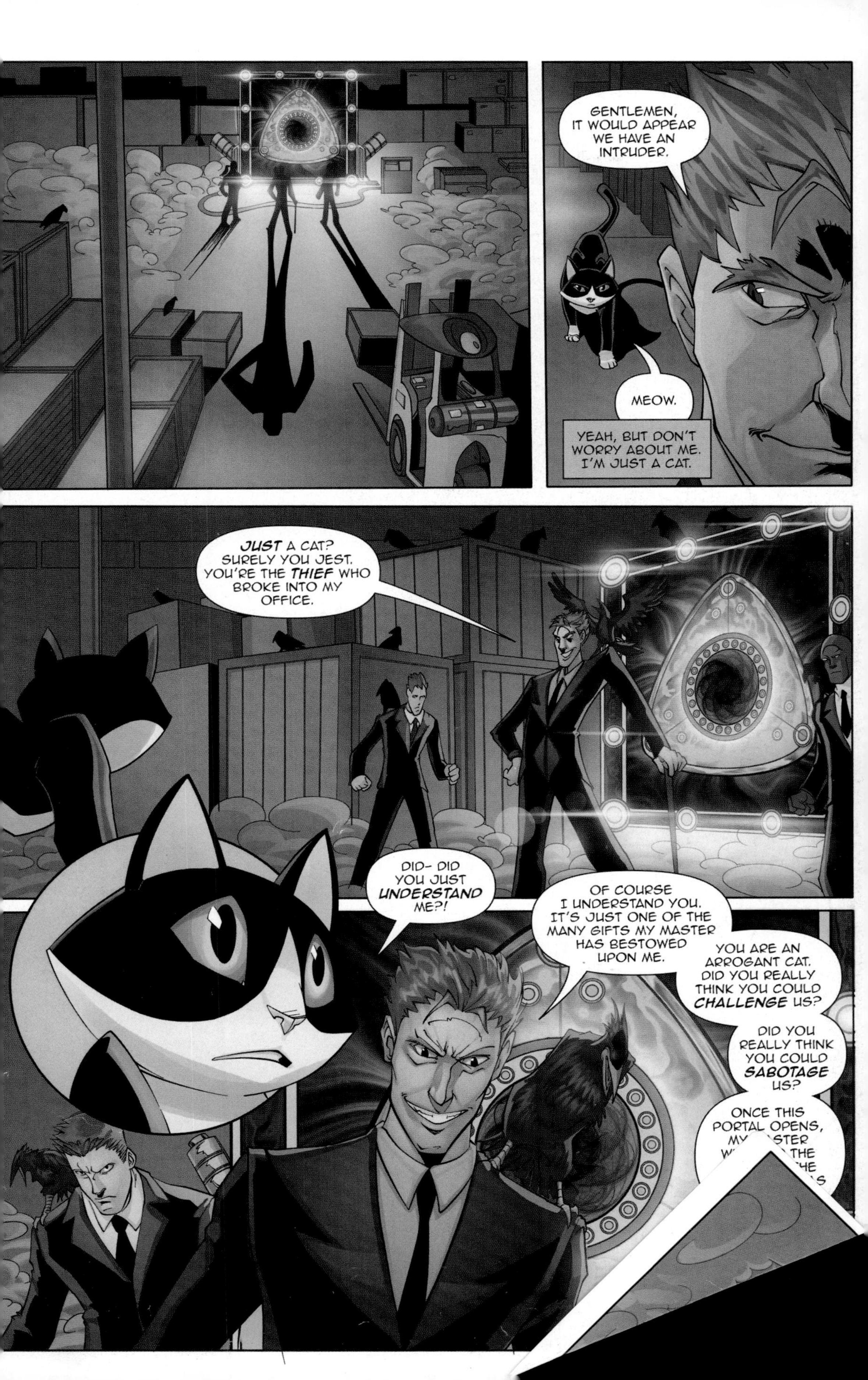
GENTLEMEN, IT WOULD APPEAR WE HAVE AN INTRUDER.
MEOW.
YEAH, BUT DON'T WORRY ABOUT ME. I'M JUST A CAT.
JUST A CAT? SURELY YOU JEST. YOU'RE THE THIEF WHO BROKE INTO MY OFFICE.
DID- DID YOU JUST UNDERSTAND ME?!
OF COURSE I UNDERSTAND YOU. IT'S JUST ONE OF THE MANY GIFTS MY MASTER HAS BESTOWED UPON ME.
YOU ARE AN ARROGANT CAT. DID YOU REALLY THINK YOU COULD CHALLENGE US?
DID YOU REALLY THINK YOU COULD SABOTAGE US?
ONCE THIS PORTAL OPENS,

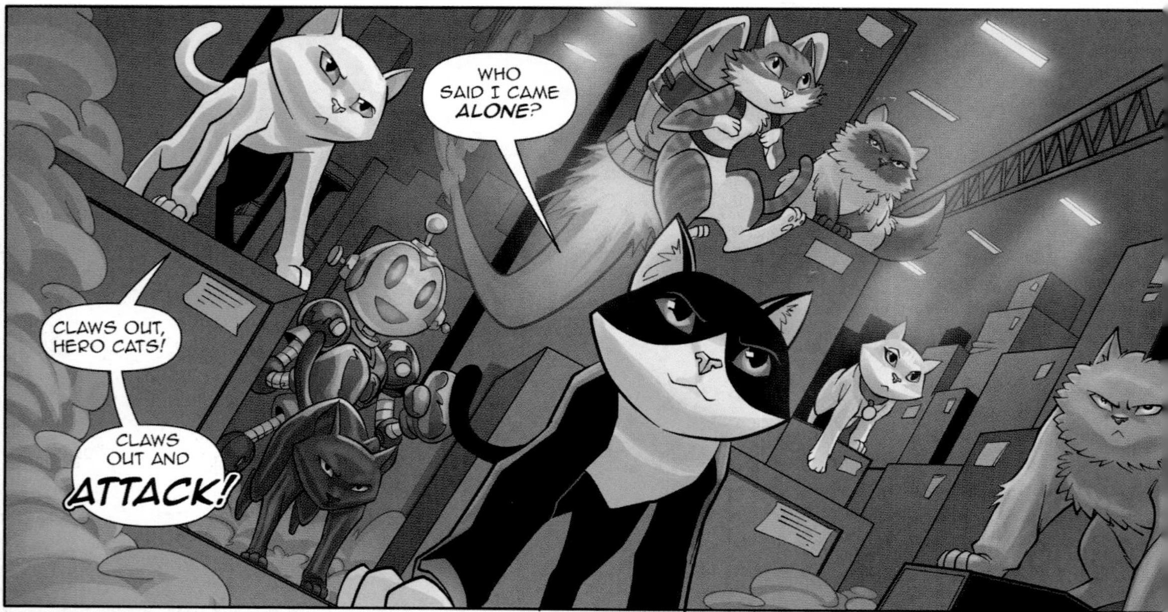
WHO SAID I CAME ALONE?
CLAWS OUT, HERO CATS!
CLAWS OUT AND ATTACK!

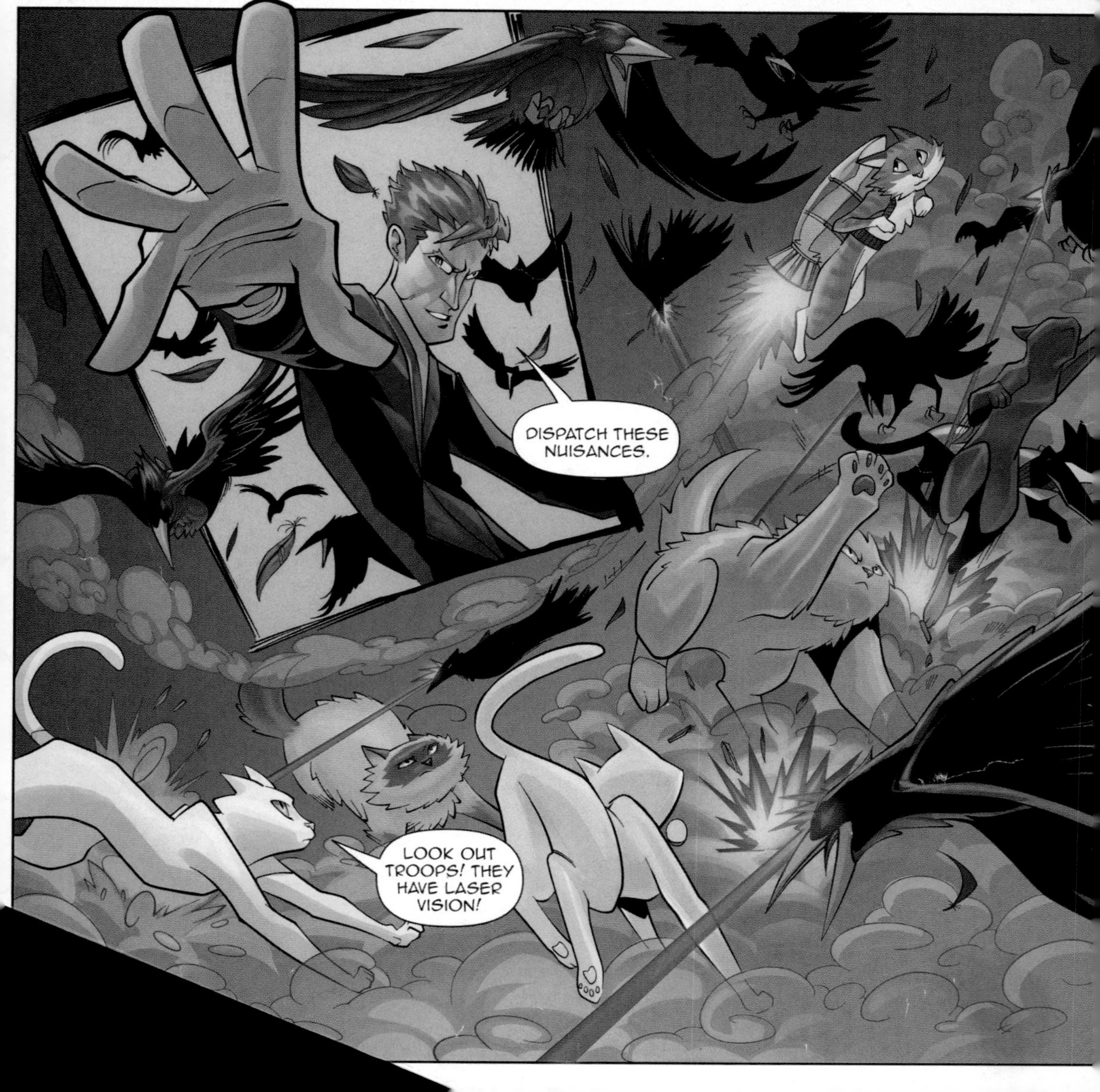
DISPATCH THESE NUISANCES.
LOOK OUT TROOPS! THEY HAVE LASER VISION!

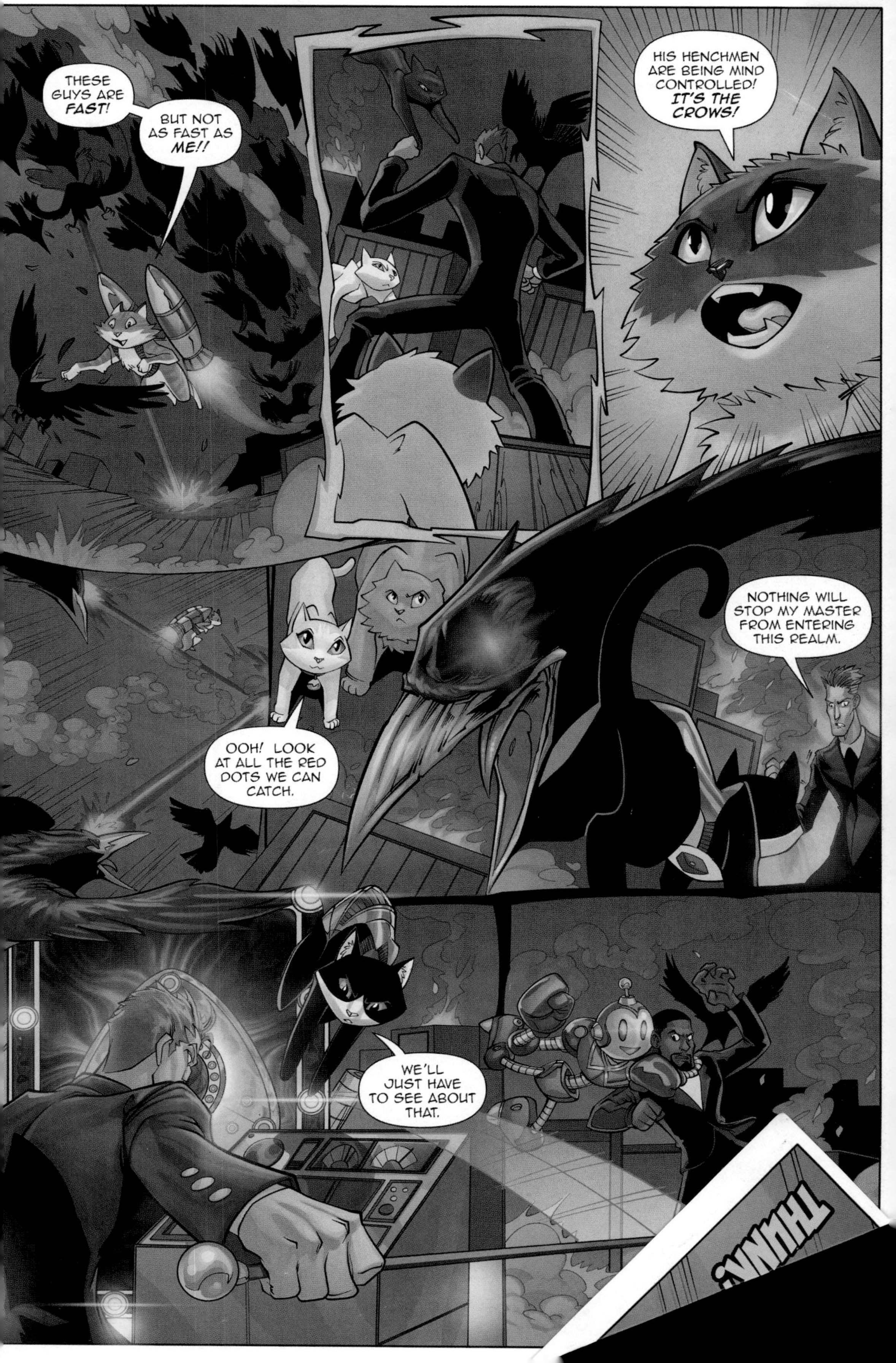
THESE GUYS ARE *FAST*!
BUT NOT AS FAST AS *ME!!*
HIS HENCHMEN ARE BEING MIND CONTROLLED! *IT'S THE CROWS!*
OOH! LOOK AT ALL THE RED DOTS WE CAN CATCH.
NOTHING WILL STOP MY MASTER FROM ENTERING THIS REALM.
WE'LL JUST HAVE TO SEE ABOUT THAT.
THUNK!

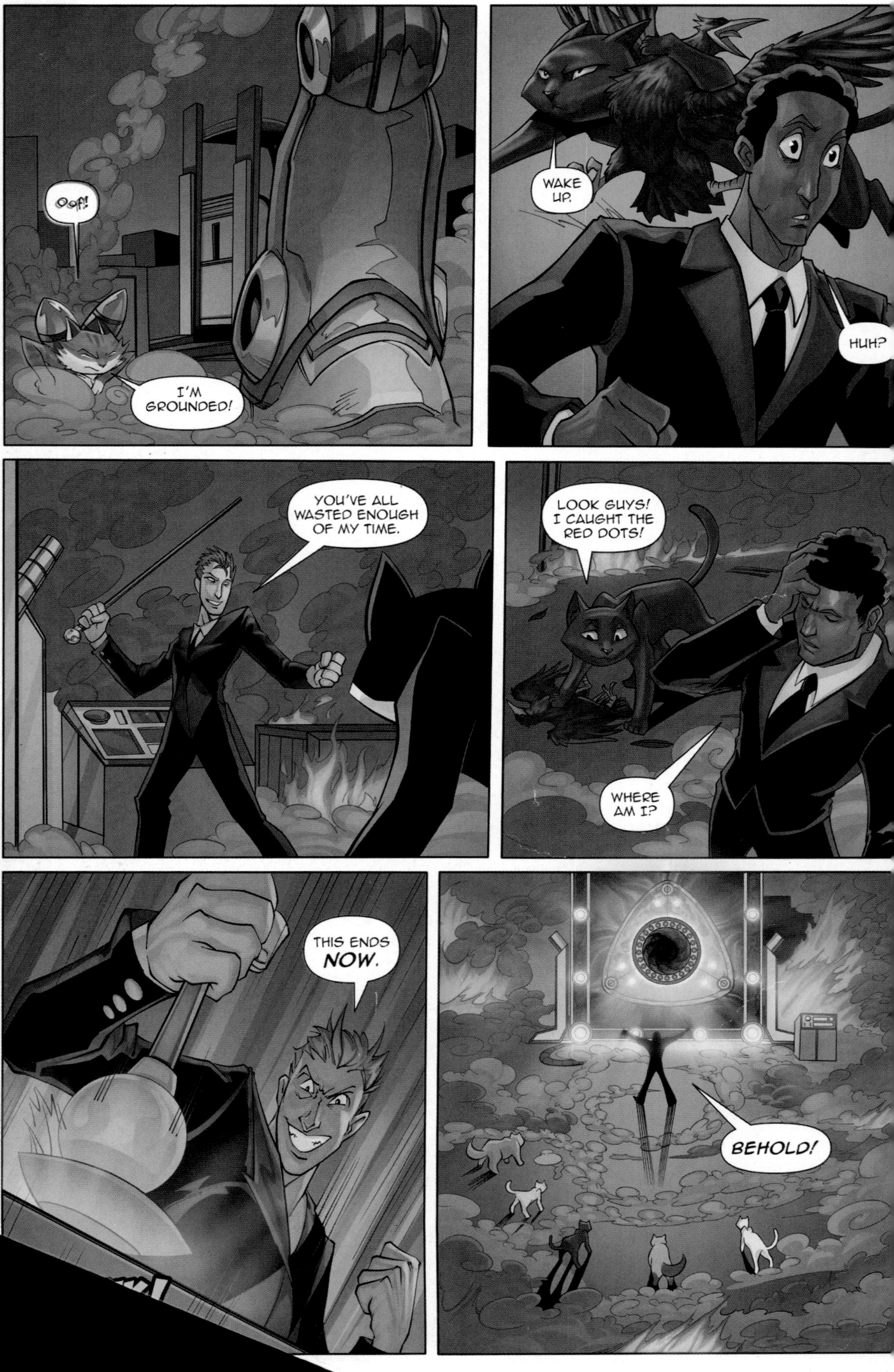
OOF!
I'M GROUNDED!
WAKE UP.
HUH?
YOU'VE ALL WASTED ENOUGH OF MY TIME.
LOOK GUYS! I CAUGHT THE RED DOTS!
WHERE AM I?
THIS ENDS *NOW*.
BEHOLD!

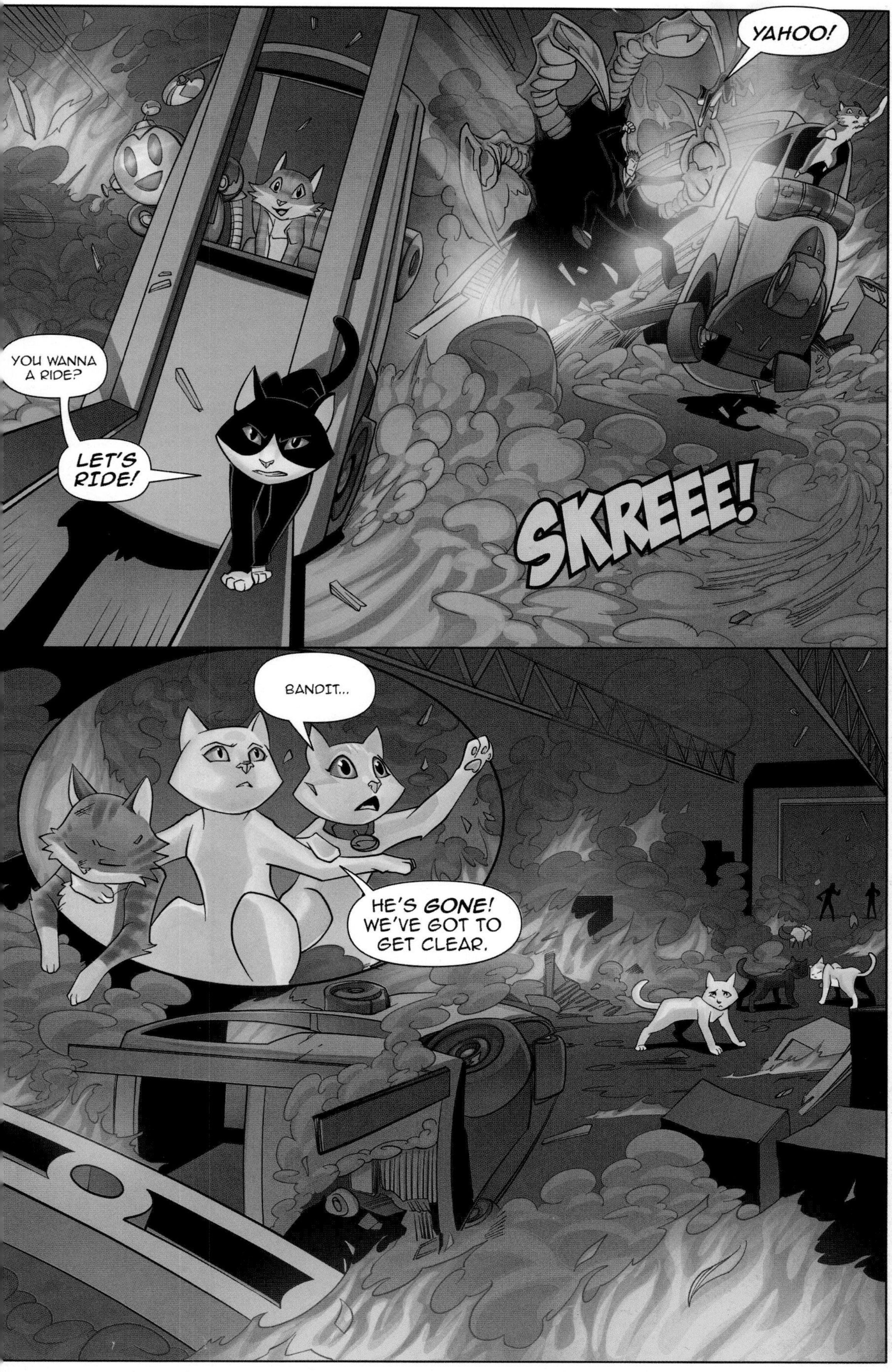
YAHOO!
YOU WANNA A RIDE?
LET'S RIDE!
SKREEE!
BANDIT...
HE'S GONE! WE'VE GOT TO GET CLEAR.

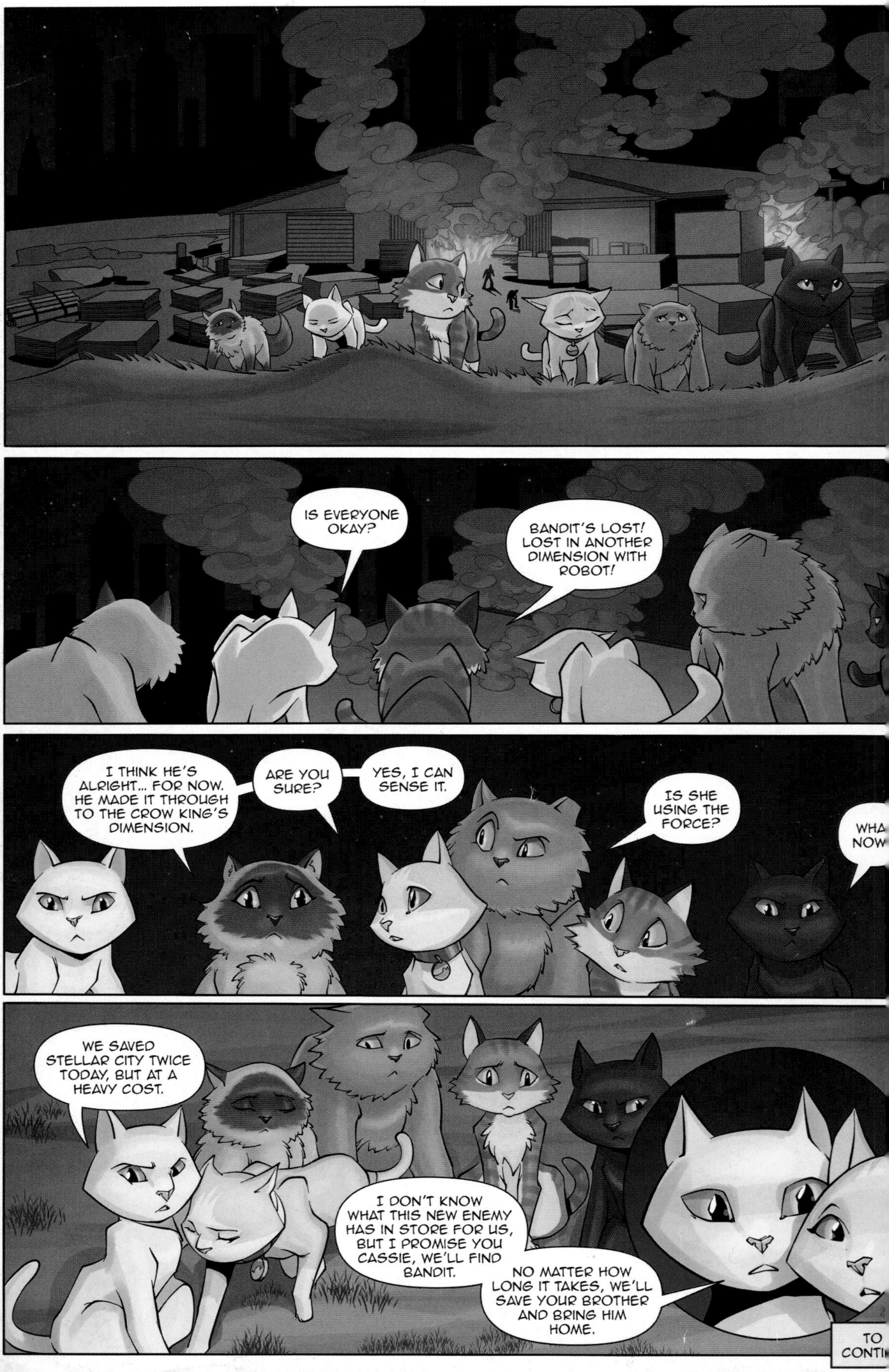

IS EVERYONE OKAY?
BANDIT'S LOST! LOST IN ANOTHER DIMENSION WITH ROBOT!
I THINK HE'S ALRIGHT... FOR NOW. HE MADE IT THROUGH TO THE CROW KING'S DIMENSION.
ARE YOU SURE?
YES, I CAN SENSE IT.
IS SHE USING THE FORCE?
WE SAVED STELLAR CITY TWICE TODAY, BUT AT A HEAVY COST.
I DON'T KNOW WHAT THIS NEW ENEMY HAS IN STORE FOR US, BUT I PROMISE YOU CASSIE, WE'LL FIND BANDIT.
NO MATTER HOW LONG IT TAKES, WE'LL SAVE YOUR BROTHER AND BRING HIM HOME.

HEROCHAT

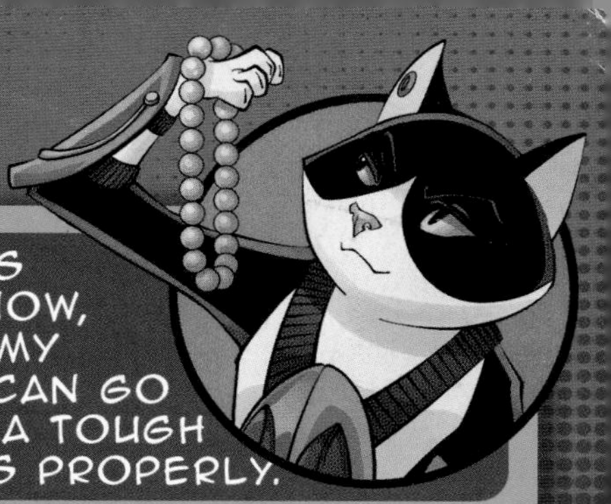

HEY KIDS & CATS. THE TRUTH ABOUT YOURS TRULY IS OUT, I'M A SECRET AGENT CAT! NOW, I CAN'T GO INTO ALL THE DETAILS ABOUT MY EMPLOYER (SPY LAWS AND SUCH), BUT I CAN GO THROUGH THE TOOLS OF THE TRADE. IT'S A TOUGH JOB, AND ONE HAS TO EQUIP THEMSELVES PROPERLY.

SPY CAT GEAR

HEATED GEL GRAPPLING HOOK

With this awesome tech, I can scale virtually any surface vertically using four quick-heating gel pads. Once armed, the pads are rapidly heated causing them to become super sticky which allows them to adhere to just about any surface. If needed, I can even use this to swing from one spot to another continuously.

LASER CUTTER ARM BRACE

When armed, this arm brace exposes a small but very powerful laser that can slice through almost anything. I can use this to escape lots of tight spots.

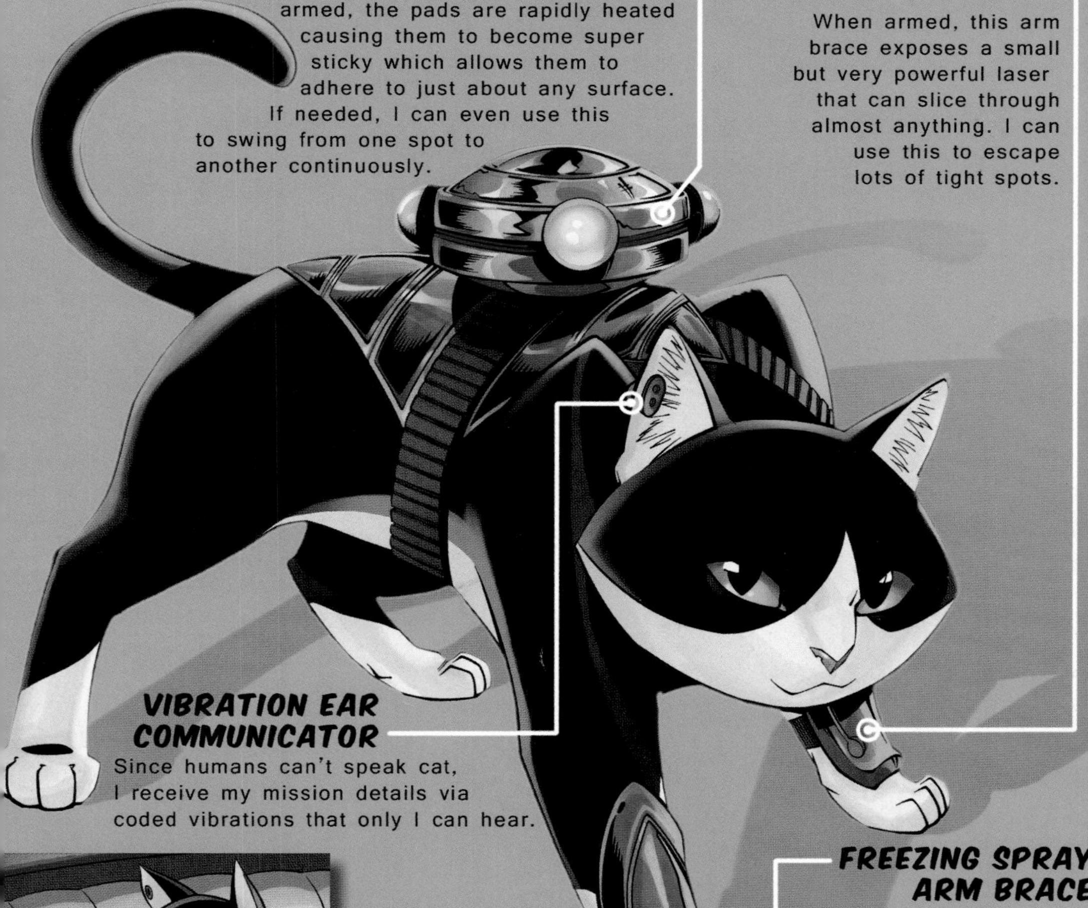

VIBRATION EAR COMMUNICATOR

Since humans can't speak cat, I receive my mission details via coded vibrations that only I can hear.

FREEZING SPRAY ARM BRACE

When armed, this arm brace houses a chemical that can quickly freeze just about anything. With a small amount of liquid nitrogen, I can freeze locks, door handles, chains, and more within seconds to gain access to certain restricted areas.

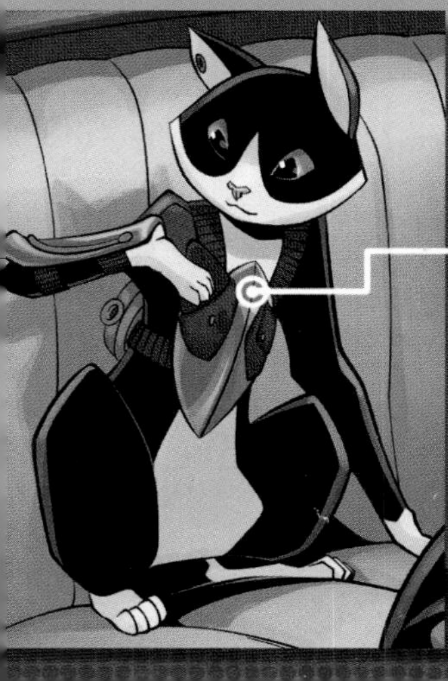

ARMORED STORAGE PLATE

This tough chest plate has two storage pockets to hold onto any special items I come across. It also protects me from impact if I fall from up high.

HEATED GEL GRAPPLING HOOK

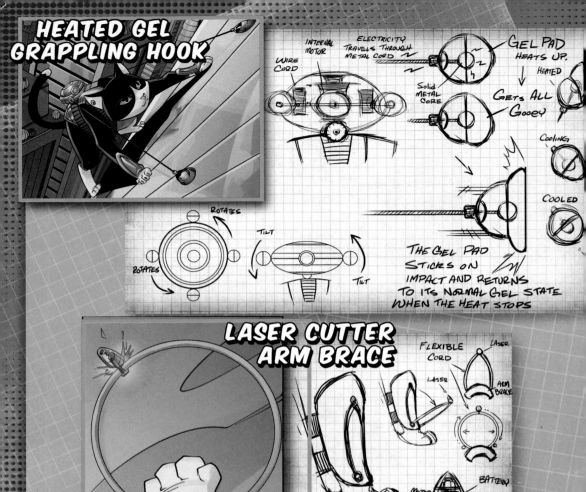

WIRE CORD

INTERNAL MOTOR

ELECTRICITY TRAVELS THROUGH METAL CORD

SOLID METAL CORE

GEL PAD HEATS UP.

HEATED

GETS ALL GOOEY

COOLING

COOLED

ROTATES

TILT

ROTATES

TILT

THE GEL PAD STICKS ON IMPACT AND RETURNS TO ITS NORMAL GEL STATE WHEN THE HEAT STOPS

LASER CUTTER ARM BRACE

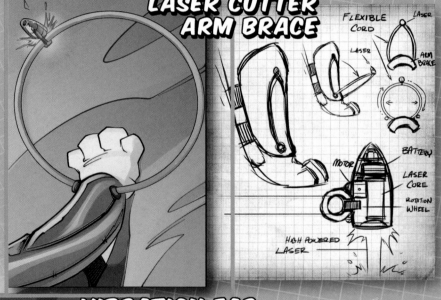

FLEXIBLE CORD

LASER

LASER

ARM BRACE

MOTOR

BATTERY

LASER CORE

ROTATION WHEEL

HIGH POWERED LASER

VIBRATION EAR COMMUNICATOR

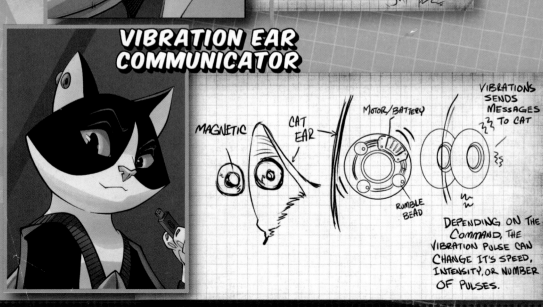

MAGNETIC

CAT EAR

MOTOR/BATTERY

VIBRATIONS SENDS MESSAGES TO CAT

RUMBLE BEAD

DEPENDING ON THE COMMAND, THE VIBRATION PULSE CAN CHANGE IT'S SPEED, INTENSITY, OR NUMBER OF PULSES.

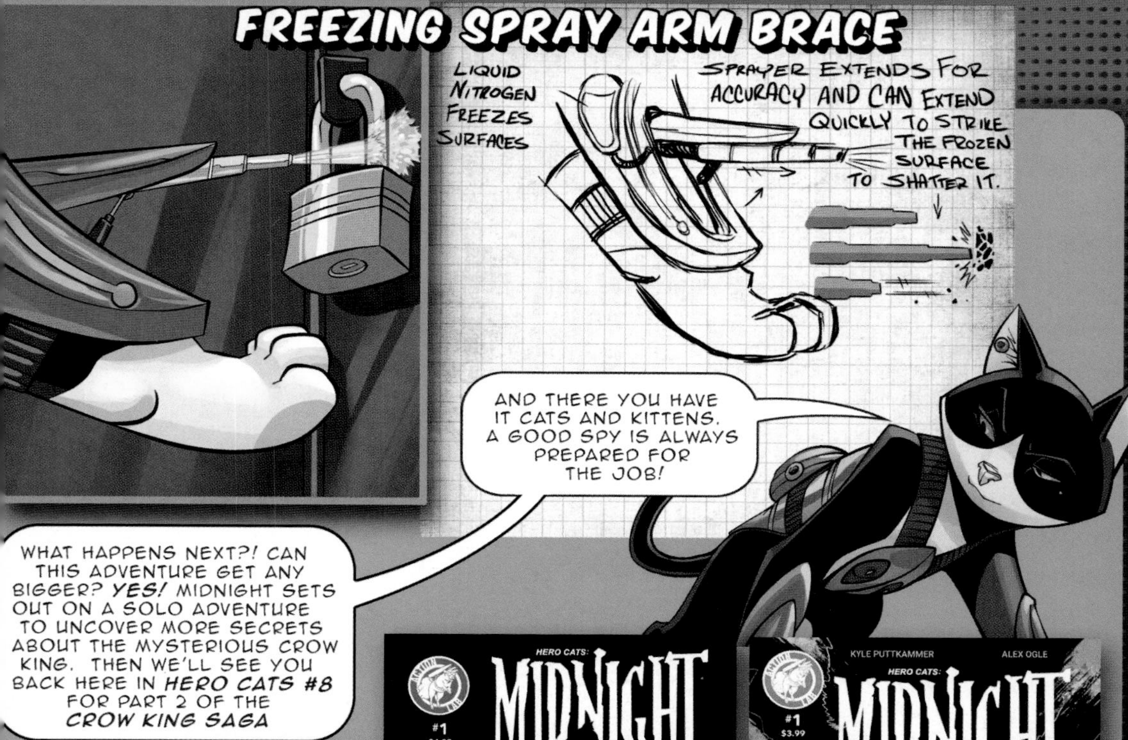
FREEZING SPRAY ARM BRACE
LIQUID NITROGEN FREEZES SURFACES
SPRAYER EXTENDS FOR ACCURACY AND CAN EXTEND QUICKLY TO STRIKE THE FROZEN SURFACE TO SHATTER IT.
AND THERE YOU HAVE IT CATS AND KITTENS. A GOOD SPY IS ALWAYS PREPARED FOR THE JOB!
WHAT HAPPENS NEXT?! CAN THIS ADVENTURE GET ANY BIGGER? *YES!* MIDNIGHT SETS OUT ON A SOLO ADVENTURE TO UNCOVER MORE SECRETS ABOUT THE MYSTERIOUS CROW KING. THEN WE'LL SEE YOU BACK HERE IN *HERO CATS #8* FOR PART 2 OF THE *CROW KING SAGA*

FOLLOW MIDNIGHT'S MISSION

A NEW BOOK!

STORY BY KYLE PUTTKAMMER

ART BY ALEX OGLE

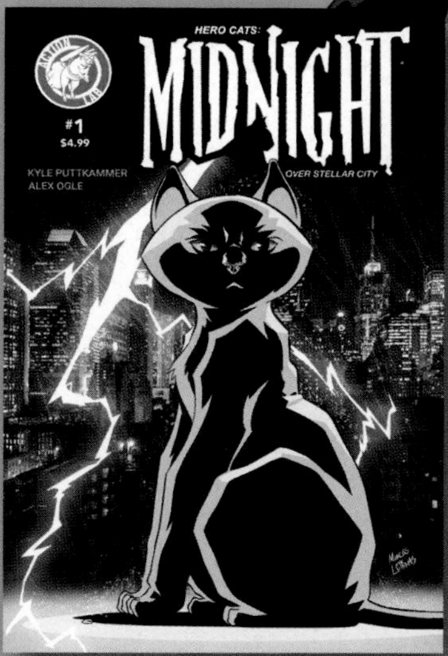
HERO CATS:
MIDNIGHT
#1
$4.99
KYLE PUTTKAMMER
ALEX OGLE
OVER STELLAR CITY

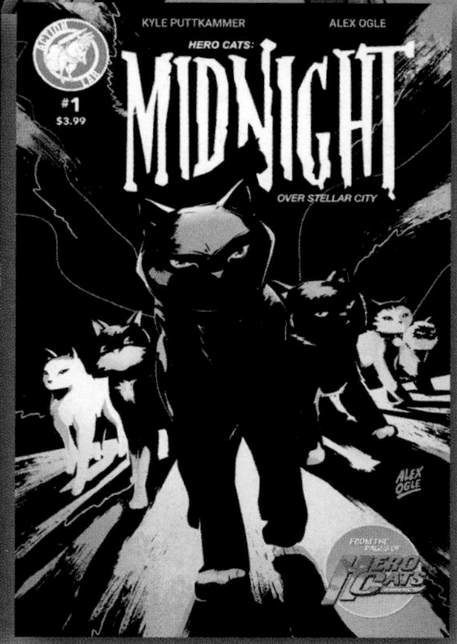
KYLE PUTTKAMMER
ALEX OGLE
HERO CATS:
MIDNIGHT
#1
$3.99
OVER STELLAR CITY

NEXT UP: THE CROW KING SAGA

write to us @ kyle@galacticquest.com

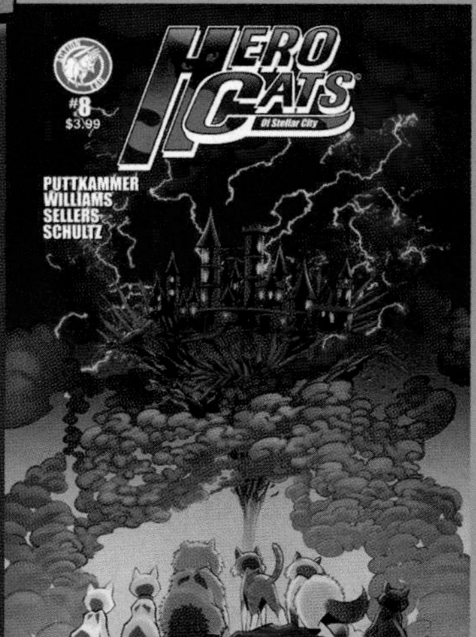
HERO CATS
of Stellar City
#8
$3.99
PUTTKAMMER
WILLIAMS
SELLERS
SCHULTZ

ryan Seaton - Publisher
evin Freeman - President
ave Dwench - Creative Director
hawn Gabborin - Editor in Chief
mal Igle & Vito Delsante - o-Directors of Marketing
m Dietz - Social Media Director
eremy Whitley - Education Outreach irector
had Cicconi & Colleen Boyd Associate Editors

ERO CATS #7, August 2015

rinted in Canada.

rst Printing.

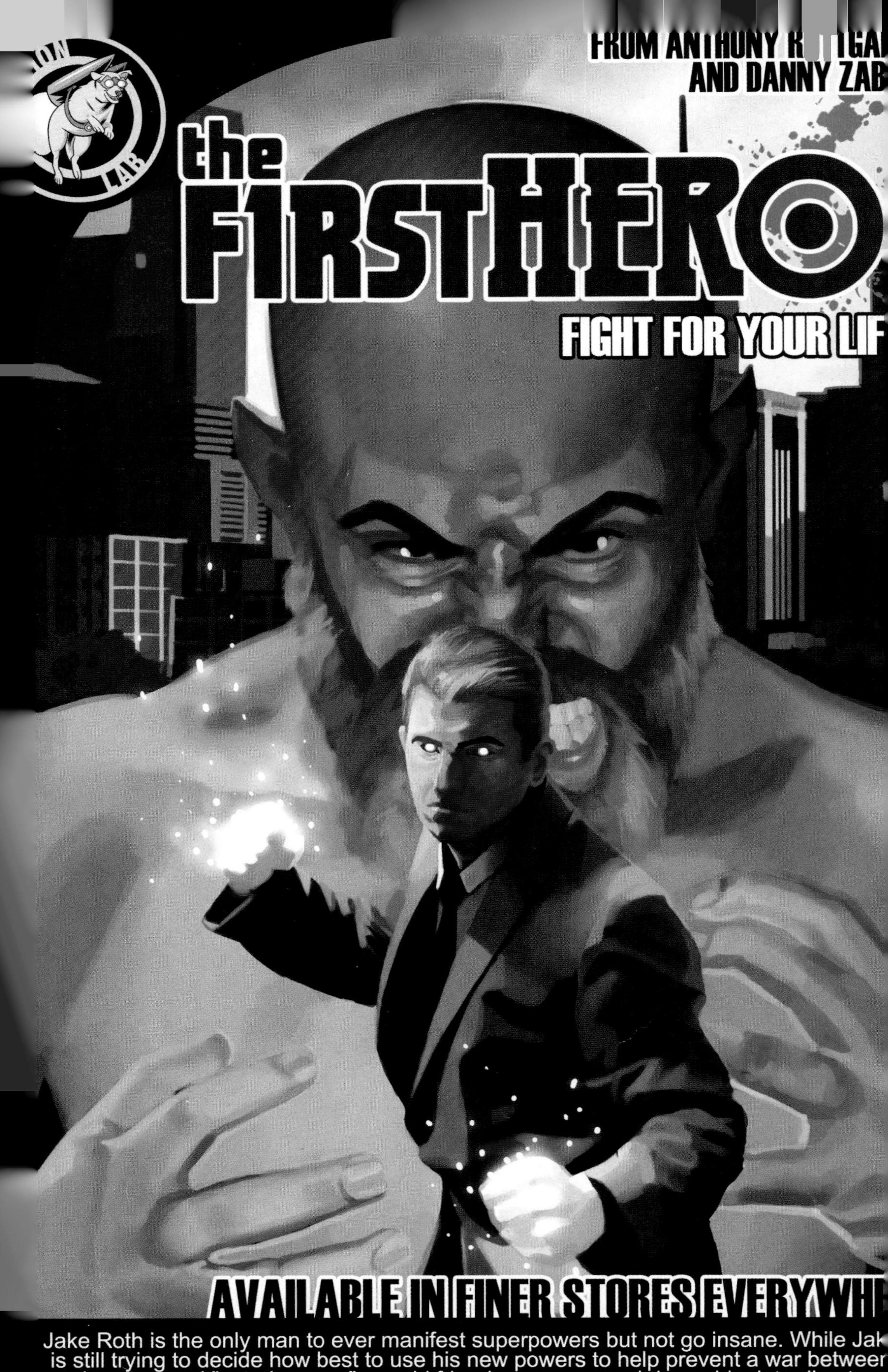

FROM ANTHONY R
AND DANNY ZAB
the FIRST HERO
FIGHT FOR YOUR LIF
AVAILABLE IN FINER STORES EVERYWH

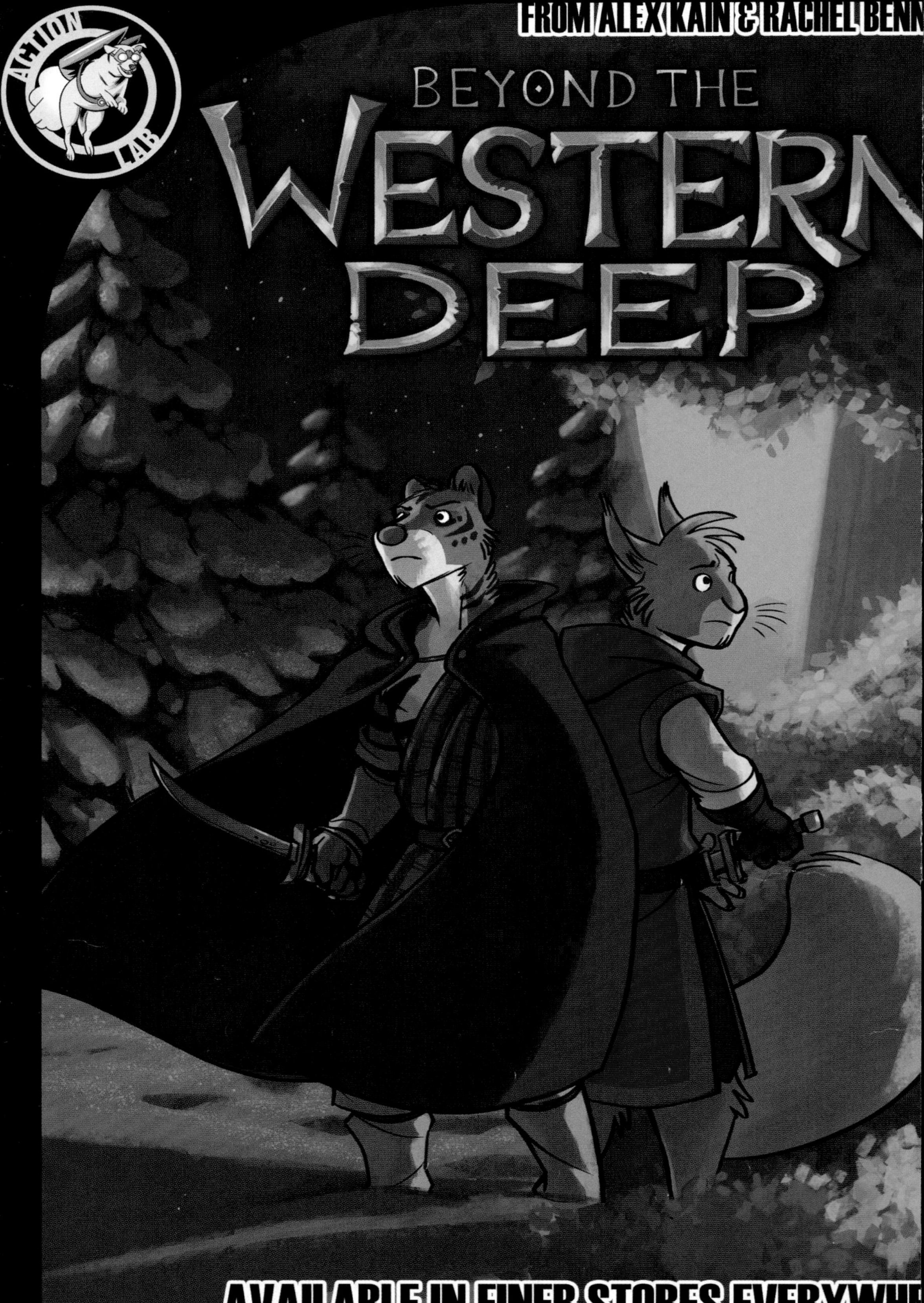
ACTION LAB
FROM ALEX KAIN & RACHEL BENN
BEYOND THE
WESTERN
DEEP
AVAILABLE IN FINER STORES EVERYWH

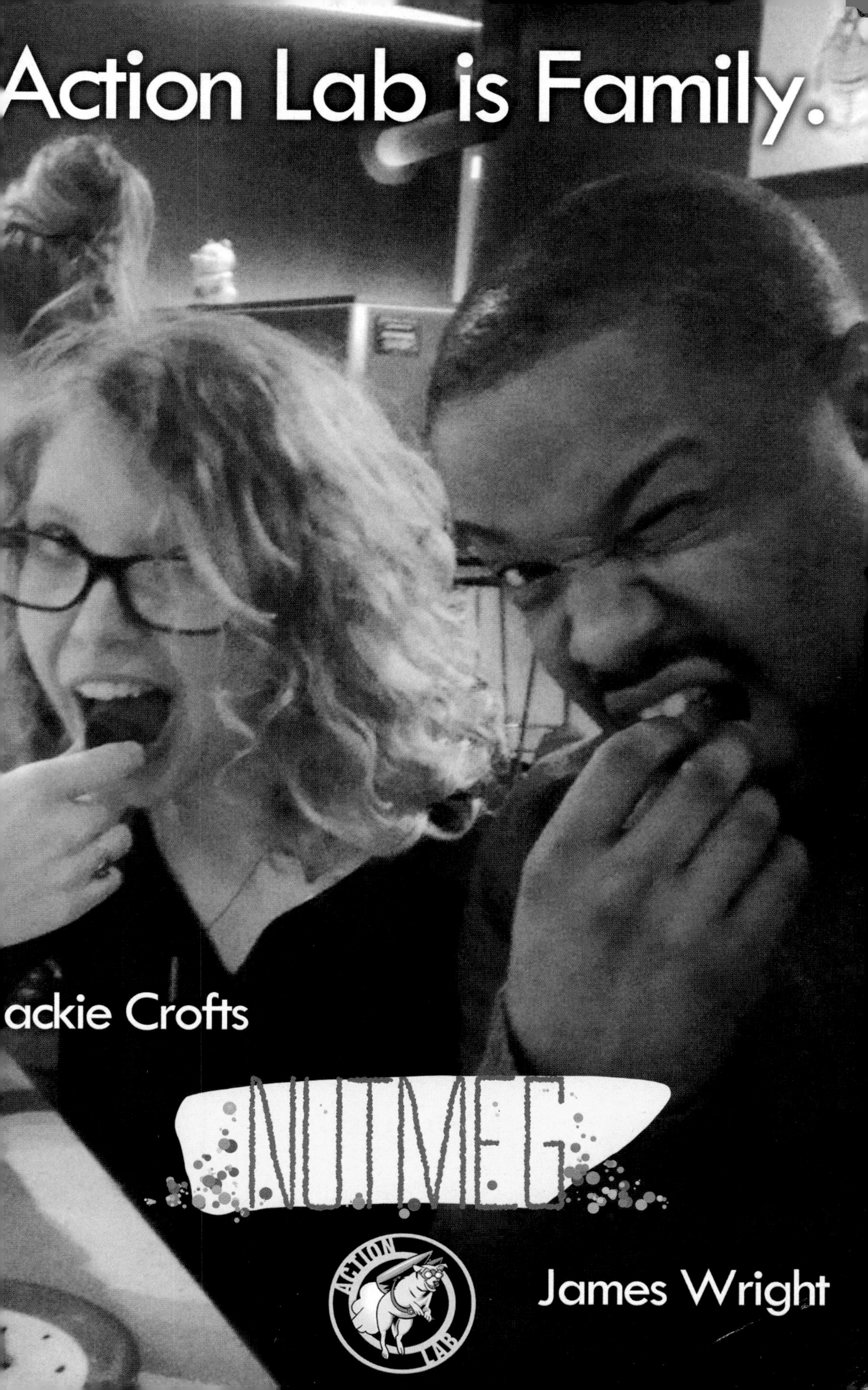
Action Lab is Family.
ackie Crofts
NUTMEG
ACTION LAB
James Wright

ACTION LAB

READ MORE NOW

Hero Cats - Action Lab
www.actionlabcomics.com
00711
7 00465 77241 1

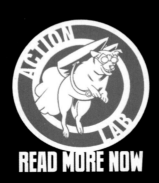

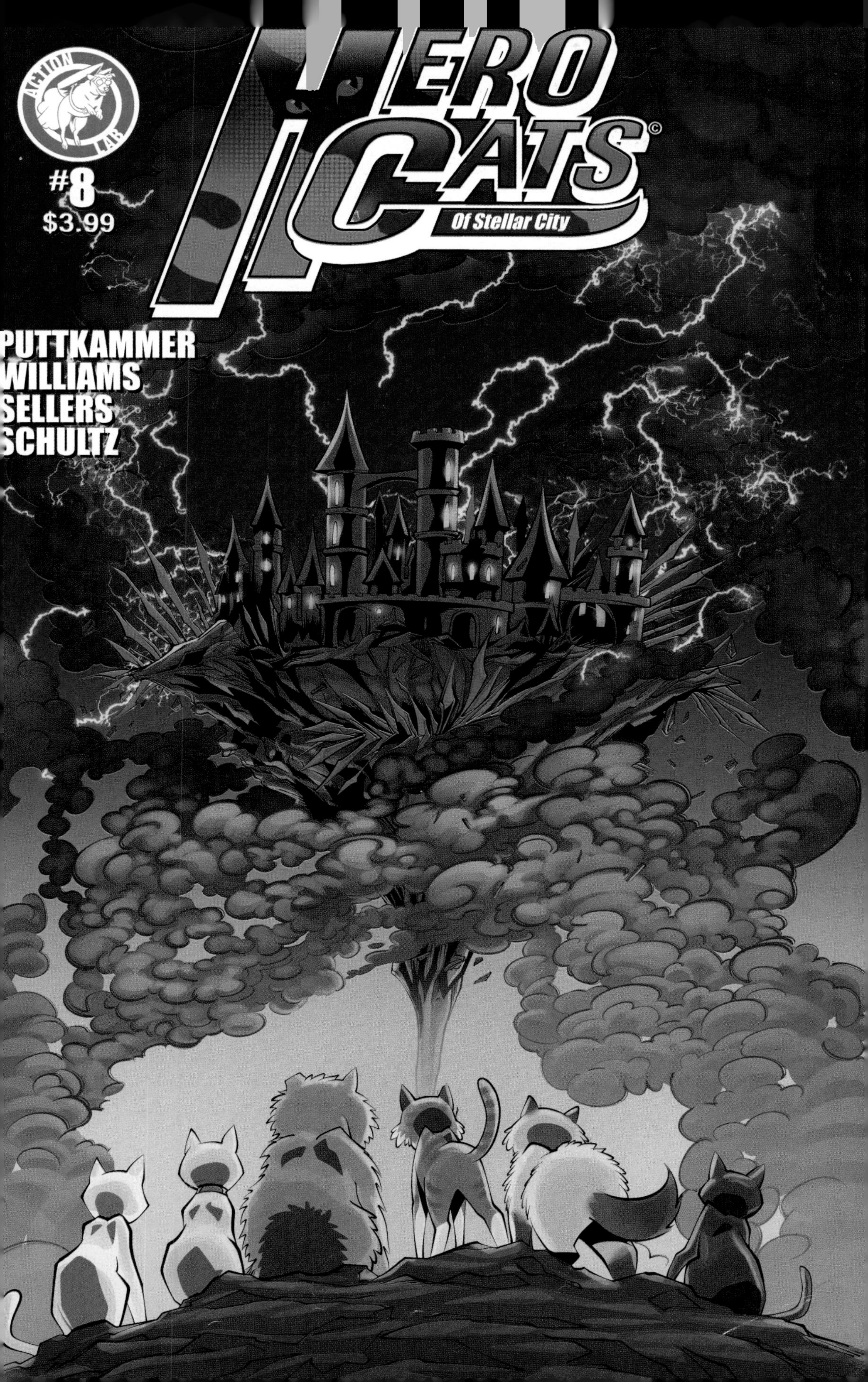

HERO CATS
Of Stellar City
#8
$3.99
PUTTKAMMER
WILLIAMS
SELLERS
SCHULTZ

FROM ALL-AGES TO MATURE READERS ACTION LAB HAS YOU COVERED.

 **Appropriate for everyone.**

 **Appropriate for age 9 and up. Absent of profanity or adult content.**

 **Suggested for 12 and Up. Comics with this rating are comparable to a PG-13 movie rating. Recommended for our teen and young adult readers.**

 **Appropriate for older teens. Similar to Teen, but featuring more mature themes and/or more graphic imagery.**

 **Contains extreme viloence and some nudity. Basically the Rated-R of comics.**

 FIND YOUR NEW FAVORITE COMICS.

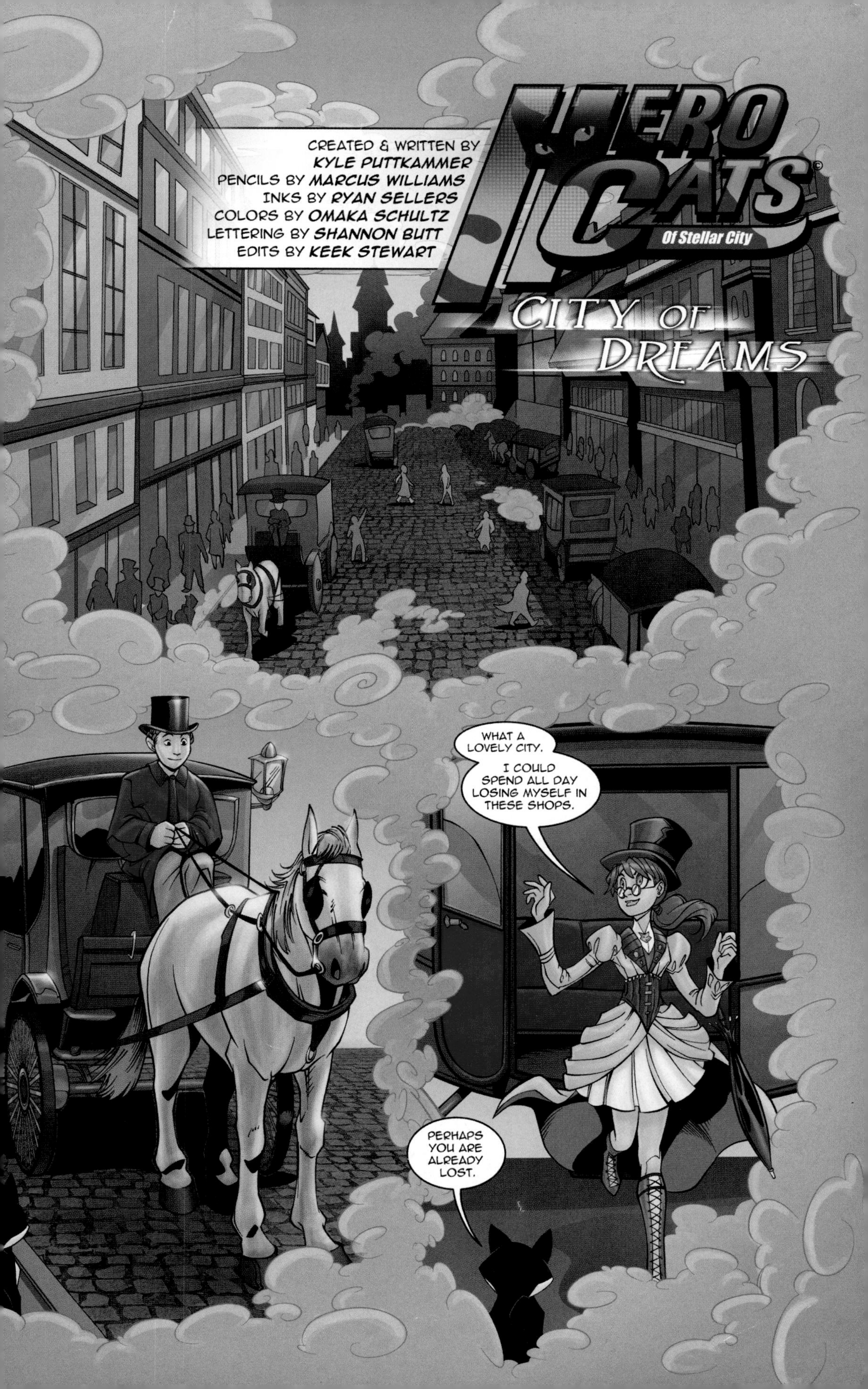
HERO CATS Of Stellar City
CITY OF DREAMS
CREATED & WRITTEN BY KYLE PUTTKAMMER
PENCILS BY MARCUS WILLIAMS
INKS BY RYAN SELLERS
COLORS BY OMAKA SCHULTZ
LETTERING BY SHANNON BUTT
EDITS BY KEEK STEWART
WHAT A LOVELY CITY.
I COULD SPEND ALL DAY LOSING MYSELF IN THESE SHOPS.
PERHAPS YOU ARE ALREADY LOST.

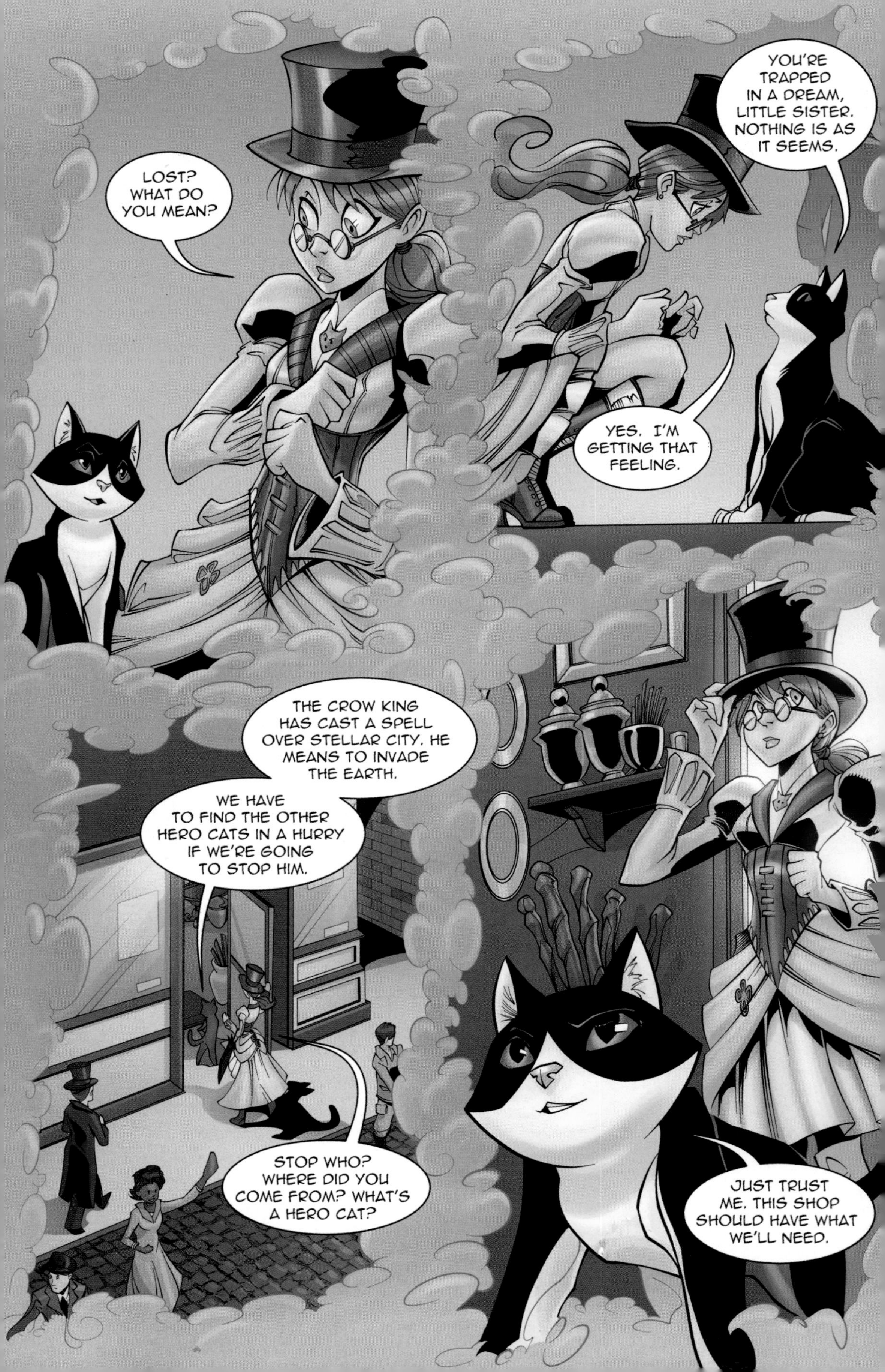
LOST? WHAT DO YOU MEAN?
YOU'RE TRAPPED IN A DREAM, LITTLE SISTER. NOTHING IS AS IT SEEMS.
YES. I'M GETTING THAT FEELING.
THE CROW KING HAS CAST A SPELL OVER STELLAR CITY. HE MEANS TO INVADE THE EARTH.
WE HAVE TO FIND THE OTHER HERO CATS IN A HURRY IF WE'RE GOING TO STOP HIM.
STOP WHO? WHERE DID YOU COME FROM? WHAT'S A HERO CAT?
JUST TRUST ME. THIS SHOP SHOULD HAVE WHAT WE'LL NEED.

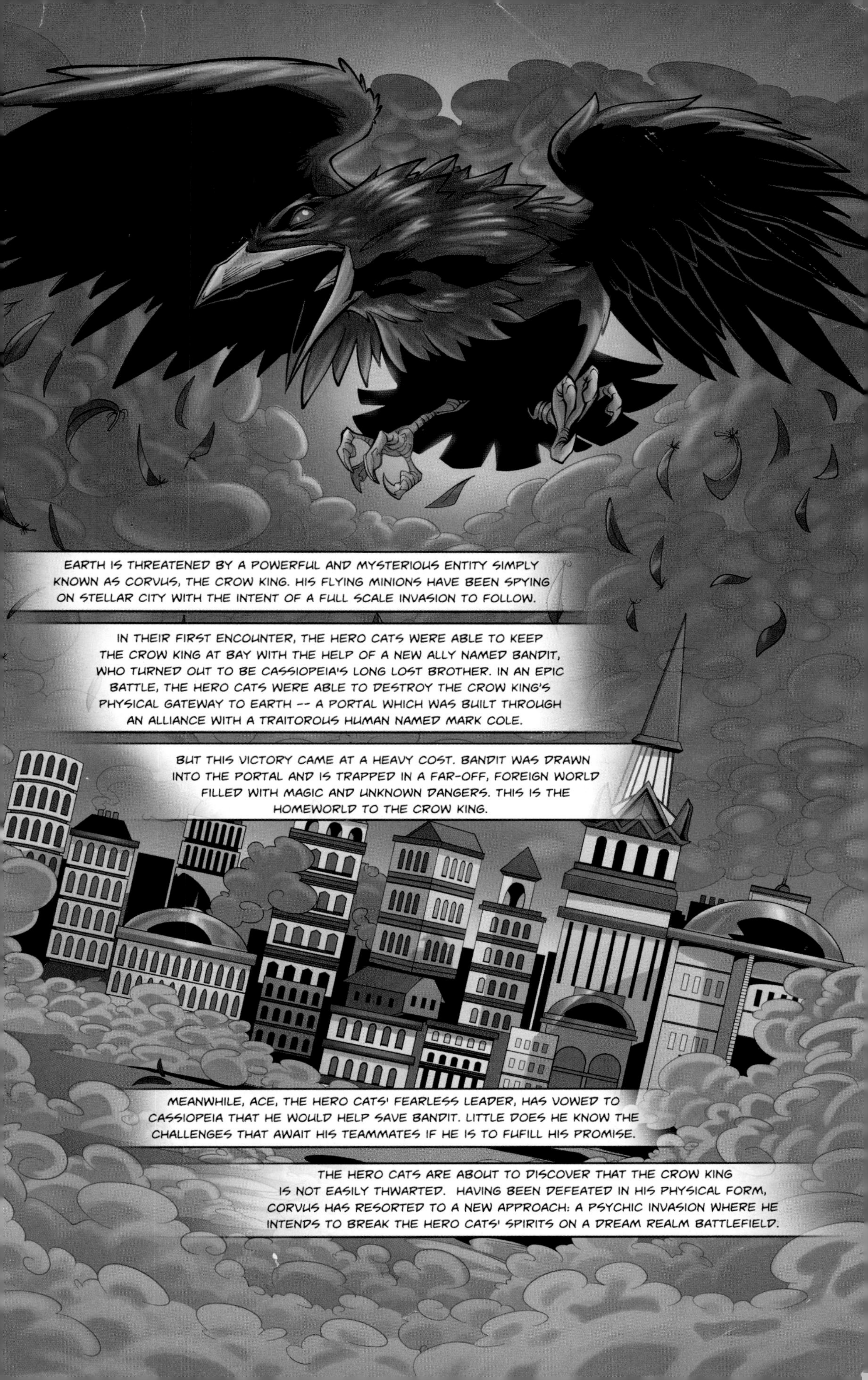
EARTH IS THREATENED BY A POWERFUL AND MYSTERIOUS ENTITY SIMPLY KNOWN AS CORVUS, THE CROW KING. HIS FLYING MINIONS HAVE BEEN SPYING ON STELLAR CITY WITH THE INTENT OF A FULL SCALE INVASION TO FOLLOW.
IN THEIR FIRST ENCOUNTER, THE HERO CATS WERE ABLE TO KEEP THE CROW KING AT BAY WITH THE HELP OF A NEW ALLY NAMED BANDIT, WHO TURNED OUT TO BE CASSIOPEIA'S LONG LOST BROTHER. IN AN EPIC BATTLE, THE HERO CATS WERE ABLE TO DESTROY THE CROW KING'S PHYSICAL GATEWAY TO EARTH -- A PORTAL WHICH WAS BUILT THROUGH AN ALLIANCE WITH A TRAITOROUS HUMAN NAMED MARK COLE.
BUT THIS VICTORY CAME AT A HEAVY COST. BANDIT WAS DRAWN INTO THE PORTAL AND IS TRAPPED IN A FAR-OFF, FOREIGN WORLD FILLED WITH MAGIC AND UNKNOWN DANGERS. THIS IS THE HOMEWORLD TO THE CROW KING.
MEANWHILE, ACE, THE HERO CATS' FEARLESS LEADER, HAS VOWED TO CASSIOPEIA THAT HE WOULD HELP SAVE BANDIT. LITTLE DOES HE KNOW THE CHALLENGES THAT AWAIT HIS TEAMMATES IF HE IS TO FUFILL HIS PROMISE.
THE HERO CATS ARE ABOUT TO DISCOVER THAT THE CROW KING IS NOT EASILY THWARTED. HAVING BEEN DEFEATED IN HIS PHYSICAL FORM, CORVUS HAS RESORTED TO A NEW APPROACH: A PSYCHIC INVASION WHERE HE INTENDS TO BREAK THE HERO CATS' SPIRITS ON A DREAM REALM BATTLEFIELD.

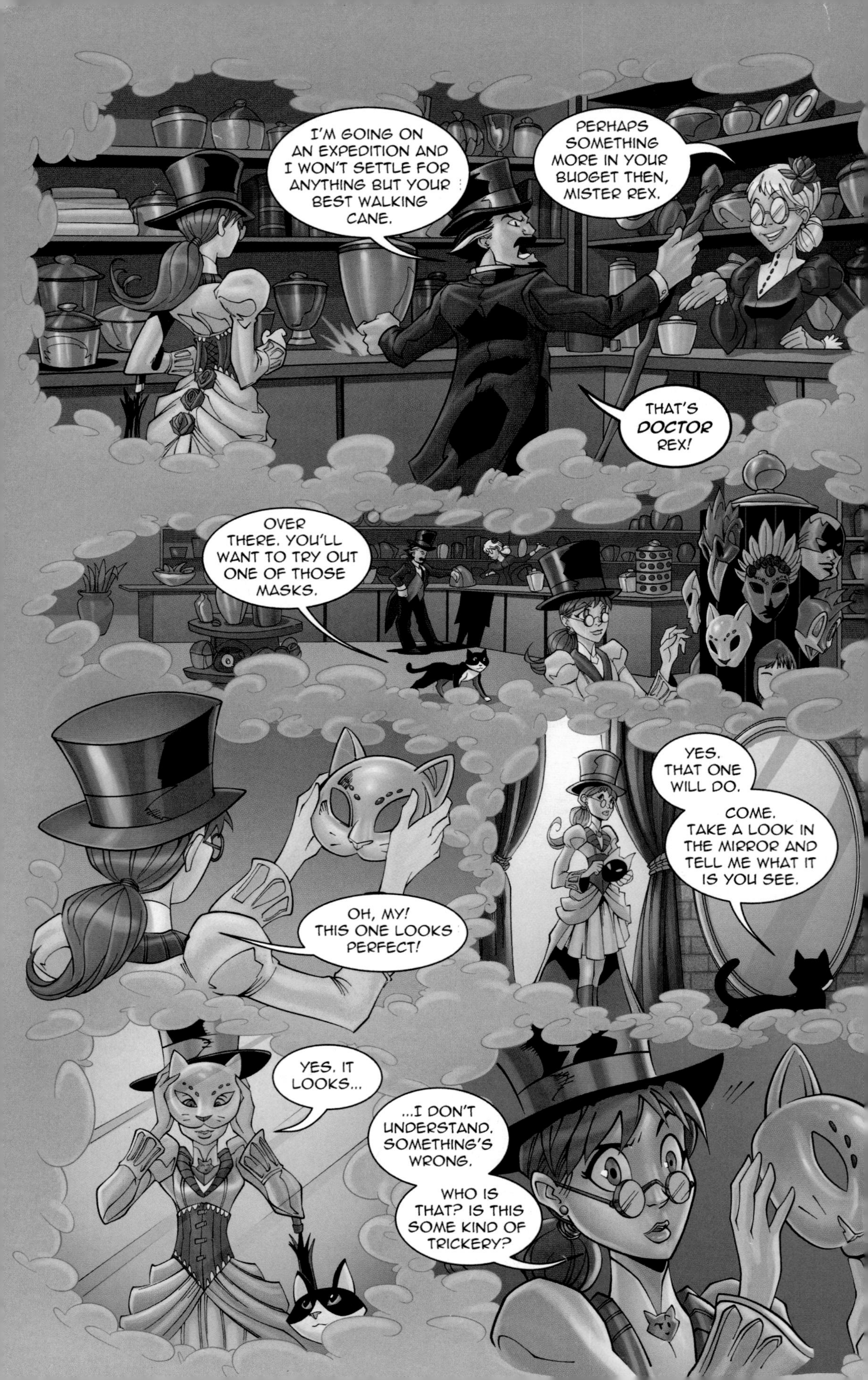
I'M GOING ON AN EXPEDITION AND I WON'T SETTLE FOR ANYTHING BUT YOUR BEST WALKING CANE.
PERHAPS SOMETHING MORE IN YOUR BUDGET THEN, MISTER REX.
THAT'S DOCTOR REX!
OVER THERE. YOU'LL WANT TO TRY OUT ONE OF THOSE MASKS.
OH, MY! THIS ONE LOOKS PERFECT!
YES. THAT ONE WILL DO.
COME. TAKE A LOOK IN THE MIRROR AND TELL ME WHAT IT IS YOU SEE.
YES. IT LOOKS...
...I DON'T UNDERSTAND. SOMETHING'S WRONG.
WHO IS THAT? IS THIS SOME KIND OF TRICKERY?

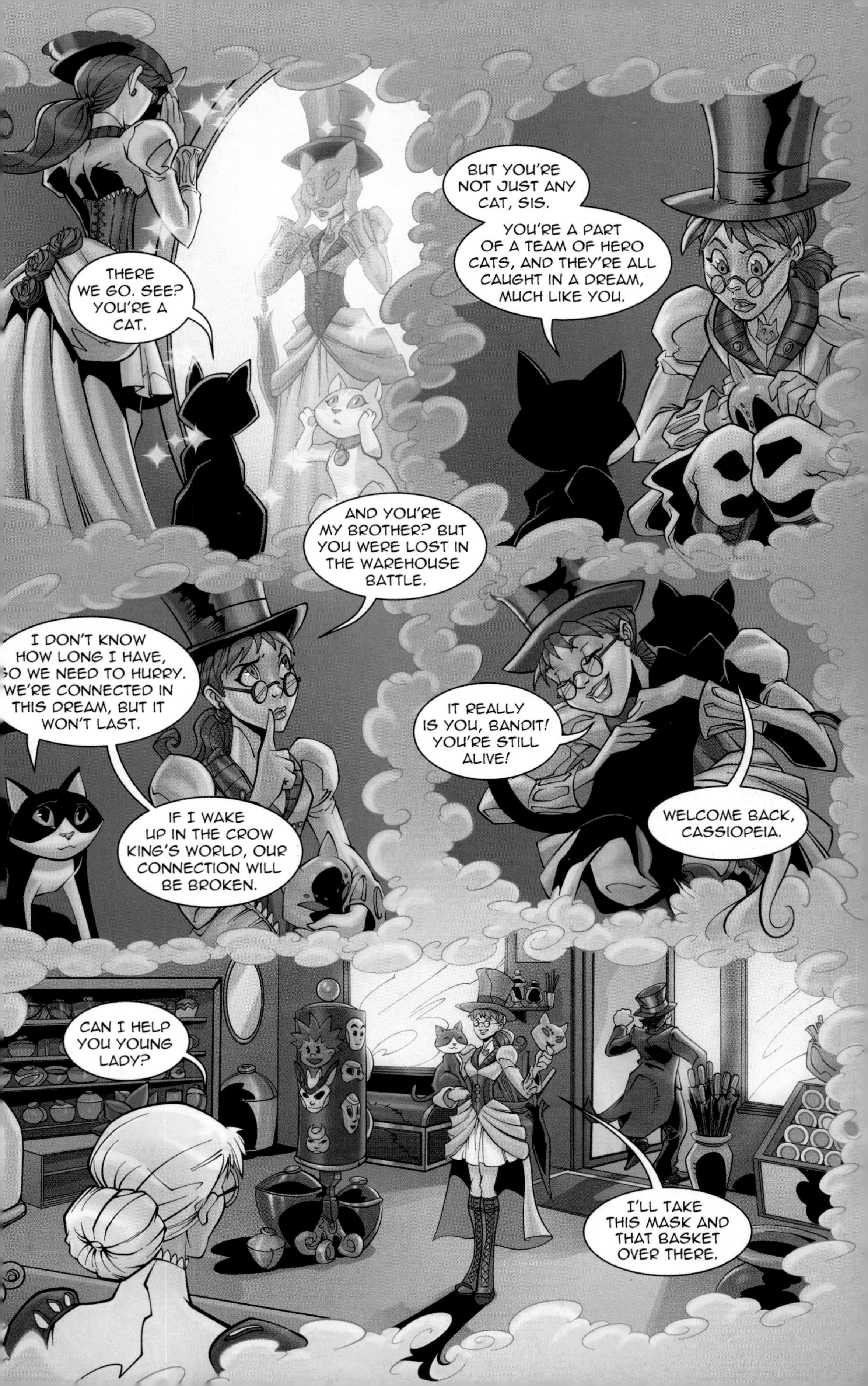
THERE WE GO. SEE? YOU'RE A CAT.
BUT YOU'RE NOT JUST ANY CAT, SIS.
YOU'RE A PART OF A TEAM OF HERO CATS, AND THEY'RE ALL CAUGHT IN A DREAM, MUCH LIKE YOU.
AND YOU'RE MY BROTHER? BUT YOU WERE LOST IN THE WAREHOUSE BATTLE.
I DON'T KNOW HOW LONG I HAVE, SO WE NEED TO HURRY. WE'RE CONNECTED IN THIS DREAM, BUT IT WON'T LAST.
IF I WAKE UP IN THE CROW KING'S WORLD, OUR CONNECTION WILL BE BROKEN.
IT REALLY IS YOU, BANDIT! YOU'RE STILL ALIVE!
WELCOME BACK, CASSIOPEIA.
CAN I HELP YOU YOUNG LADY?
I'LL TAKE THIS MASK AND THAT BASKET OVER THERE.

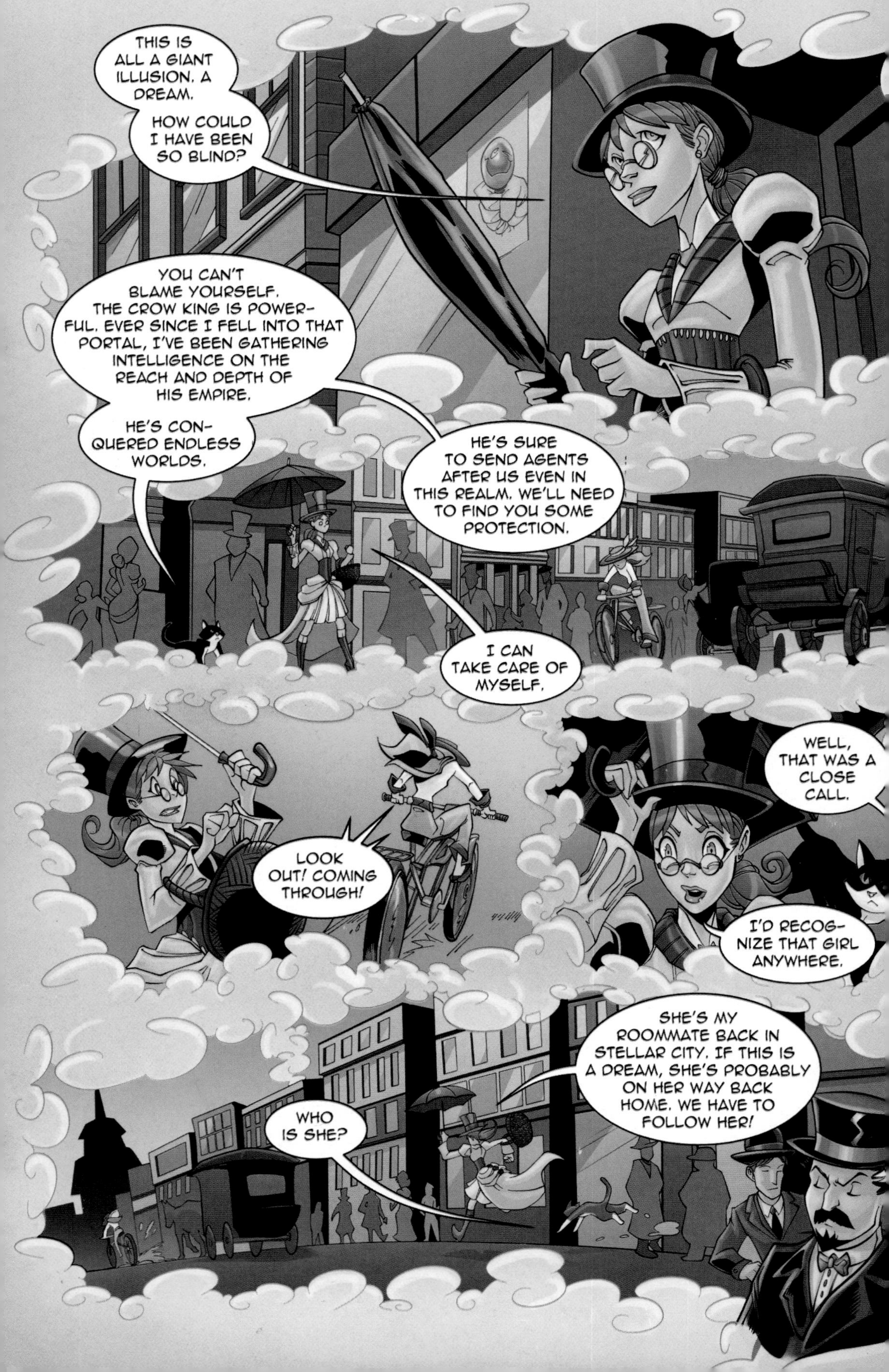
THIS IS ALL A GIANT ILLUSION. A DREAM.
HOW COULD I HAVE BEEN SO BLIND?
YOU CAN'T BLAME YOURSELF. THE CROW KING IS POWER-FUL. EVER SINCE I FELL INTO THAT PORTAL, I'VE BEEN GATHERING INTELLIGENCE ON THE REACH AND DEPTH OF HIS EMPIRE.
HE'S CON-QUERED ENDLESS WORLDS.
HE'S SURE TO SEND AGENTS AFTER US EVEN IN THIS REALM. WE'LL NEED TO FIND YOU SOME PROTECTION.
I CAN TAKE CARE OF MYSELF.
LOOK OUT! COMING THROUGH!
WELL, THAT WAS A CLOSE CALL.
I'D RECOG-NIZE THAT GIRL ANYWHERE.
WHO IS SHE?
SHE'S MY ROOMMATE BACK IN STELLAR CITY. IF THIS IS A DREAM, SHE'S PROBABLY ON HER WAY BACK HOME. WE HAVE TO FOLLOW HER!

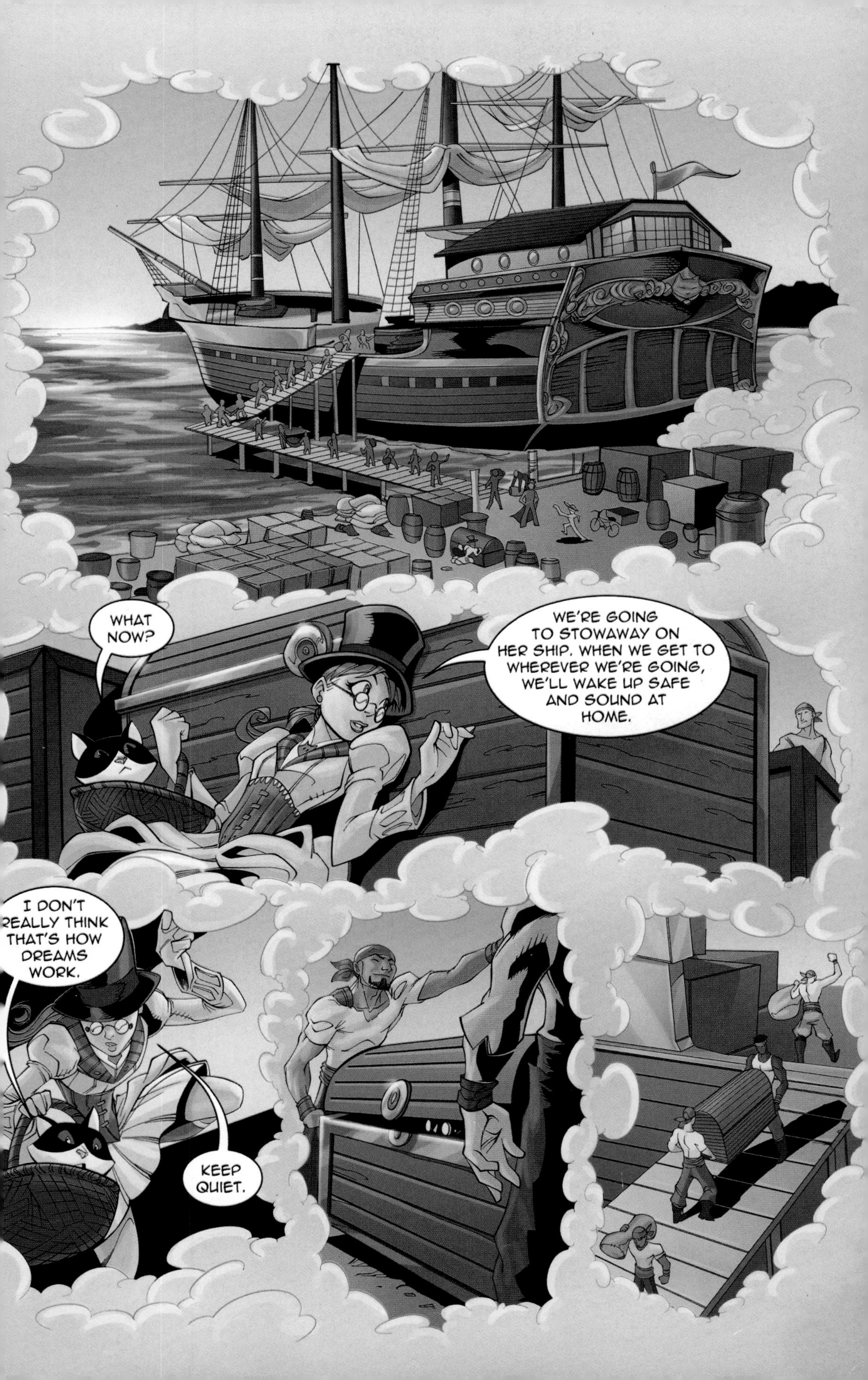
WHAT NOW?
WE'RE GOING TO STOWAWAY ON HER SHIP. WHEN WE GET TO WHEREVER WE'RE GOING, WE'LL WAKE UP SAFE AND SOUND AT HOME.
I DON'T REALLY THINK THAT'S HOW DREAMS WORK.
KEEP QUIET.

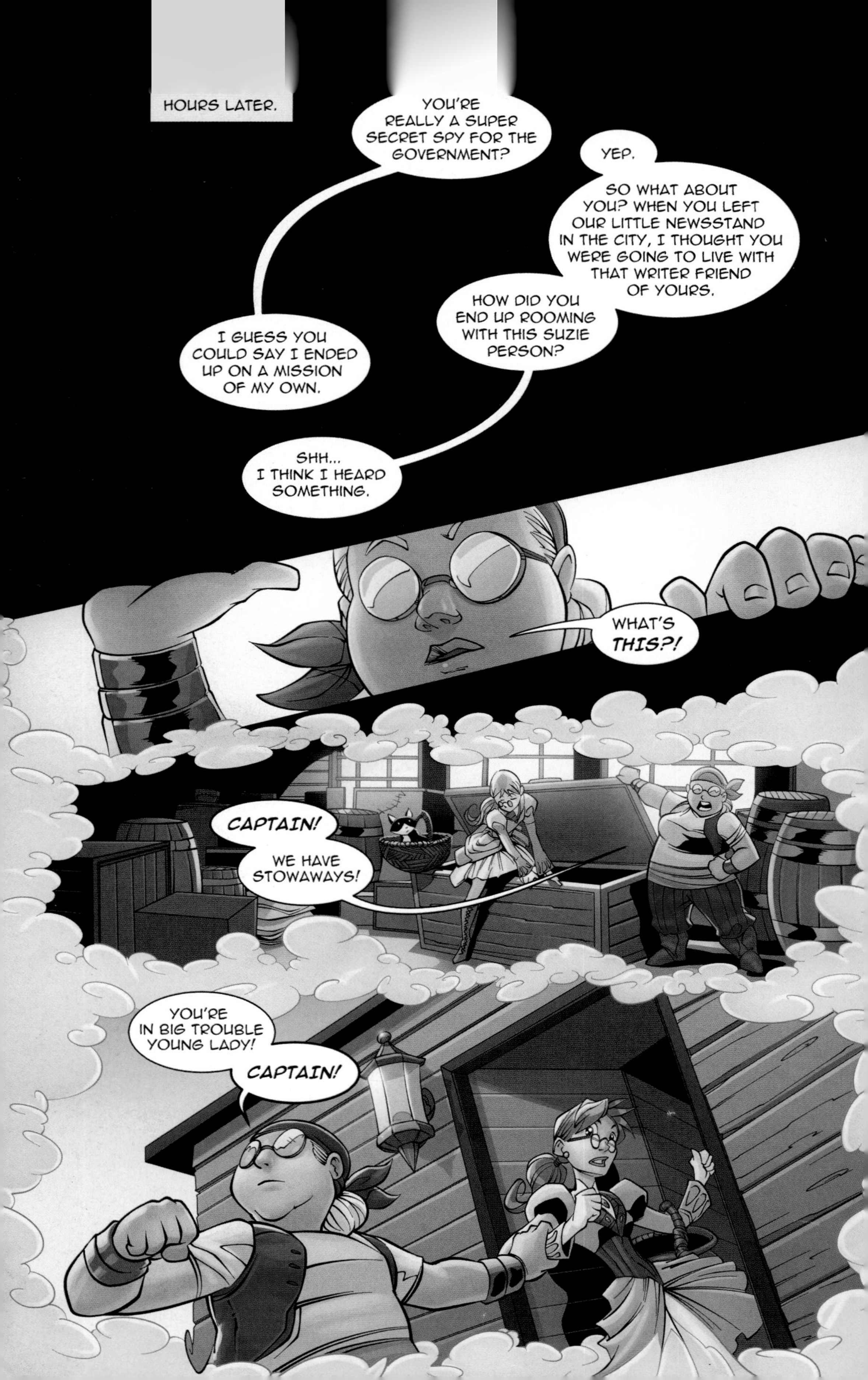
HOURS LATER.
YOU'RE REALLY A SUPER SECRET SPY FOR THE GOVERNMENT?
YEP.
SO WHAT ABOUT YOU? WHEN YOU LEFT OUR LITTLE NEWSSTAND IN THE CITY, I THOUGHT YOU WERE GOING TO LIVE WITH THAT WRITER FRIEND OF YOURS.
HOW DID YOU END UP ROOMING WITH THIS SUZIE PERSON?
I GUESS YOU COULD SAY I ENDED UP ON A MISSION OF MY OWN.
SHH... I THINK I HEARD SOMETHING.
WHAT'S THIS?!
CAPTAIN!
WE HAVE STOWAWAYS!
YOU'RE IN BIG TROUBLE YOUNG LADY!
CAPTAIN!

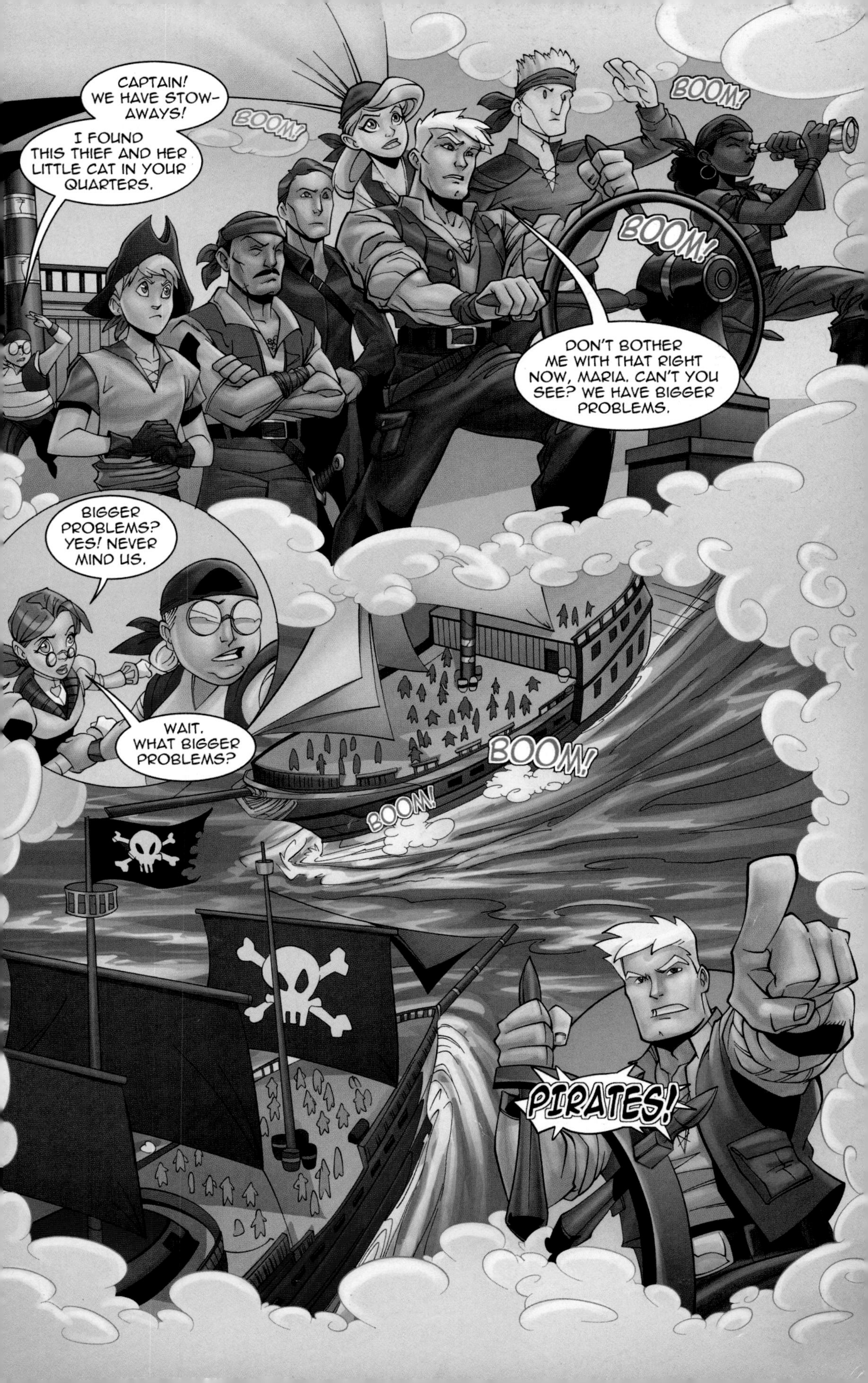
CAPTAIN! WE HAVE STOW-AWAYS!
I FOUND THIS THIEF AND HER LITTLE CAT IN YOUR QUARTERS.
BOOM!
BOOM!
BOOM!
DON'T BOTHER ME WITH THAT RIGHT NOW, MARIA. CAN'T YOU SEE? WE HAVE BIGGER PROBLEMS.
BIGGER PROBLEMS? YES! NEVER MIND US.
WAIT. WHAT BIGGER PROBLEMS?
BOOM!
BOOM!
PIRATES!

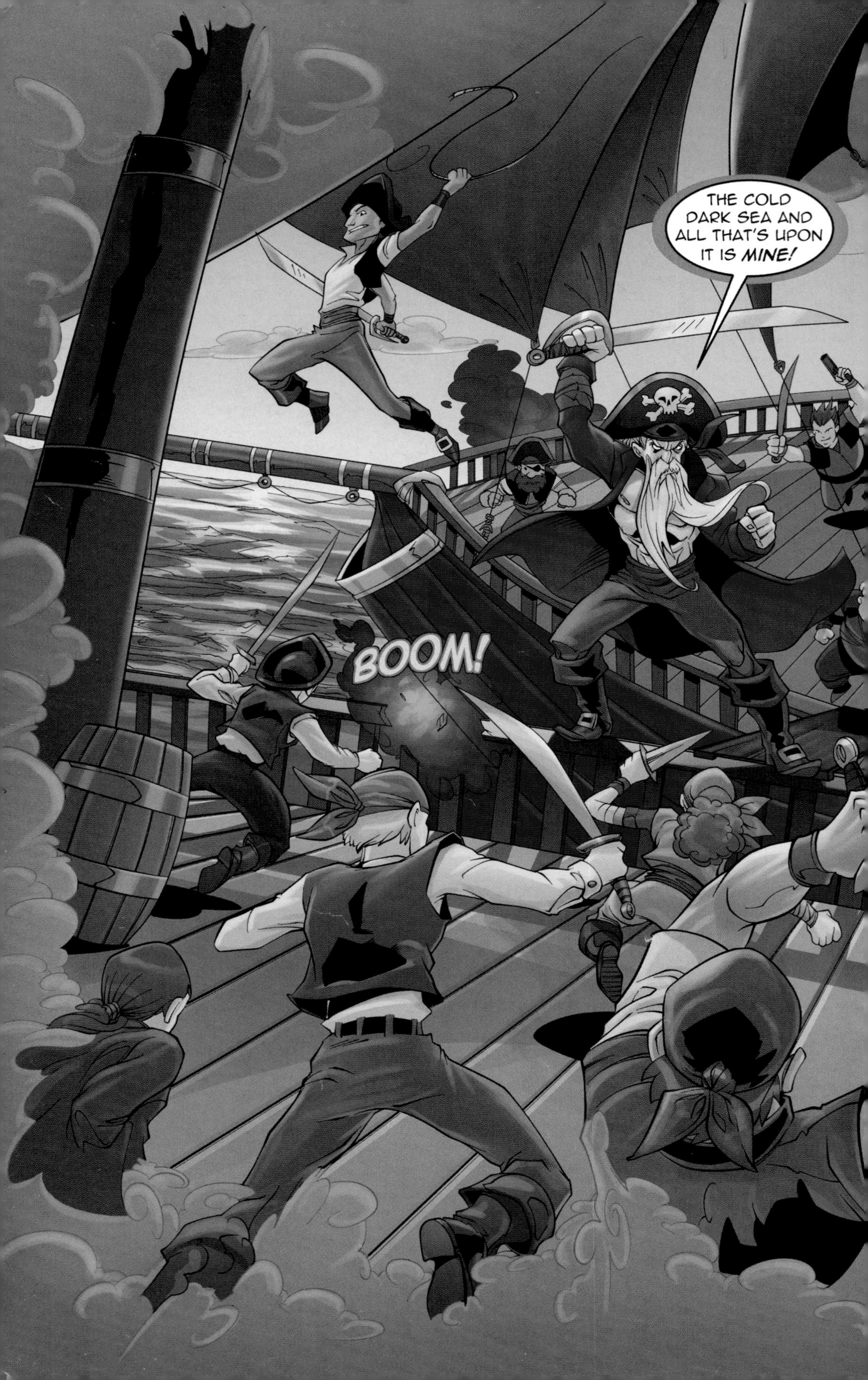
THE COLD DARK SEA AND ALL THAT'S UPON IT IS MINE!
BOOM!

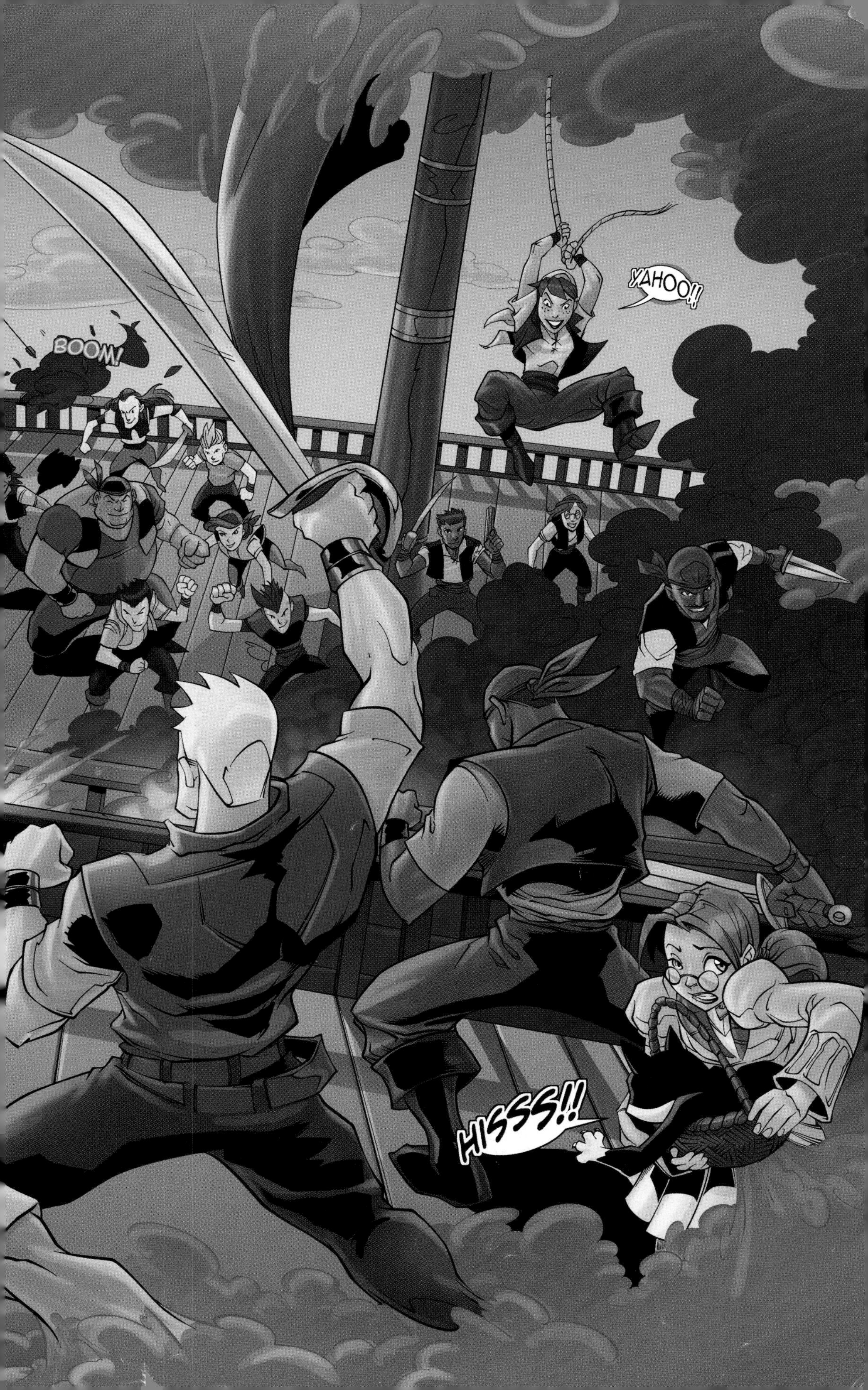
BOOM!
YAHOO!!
HISSS!!

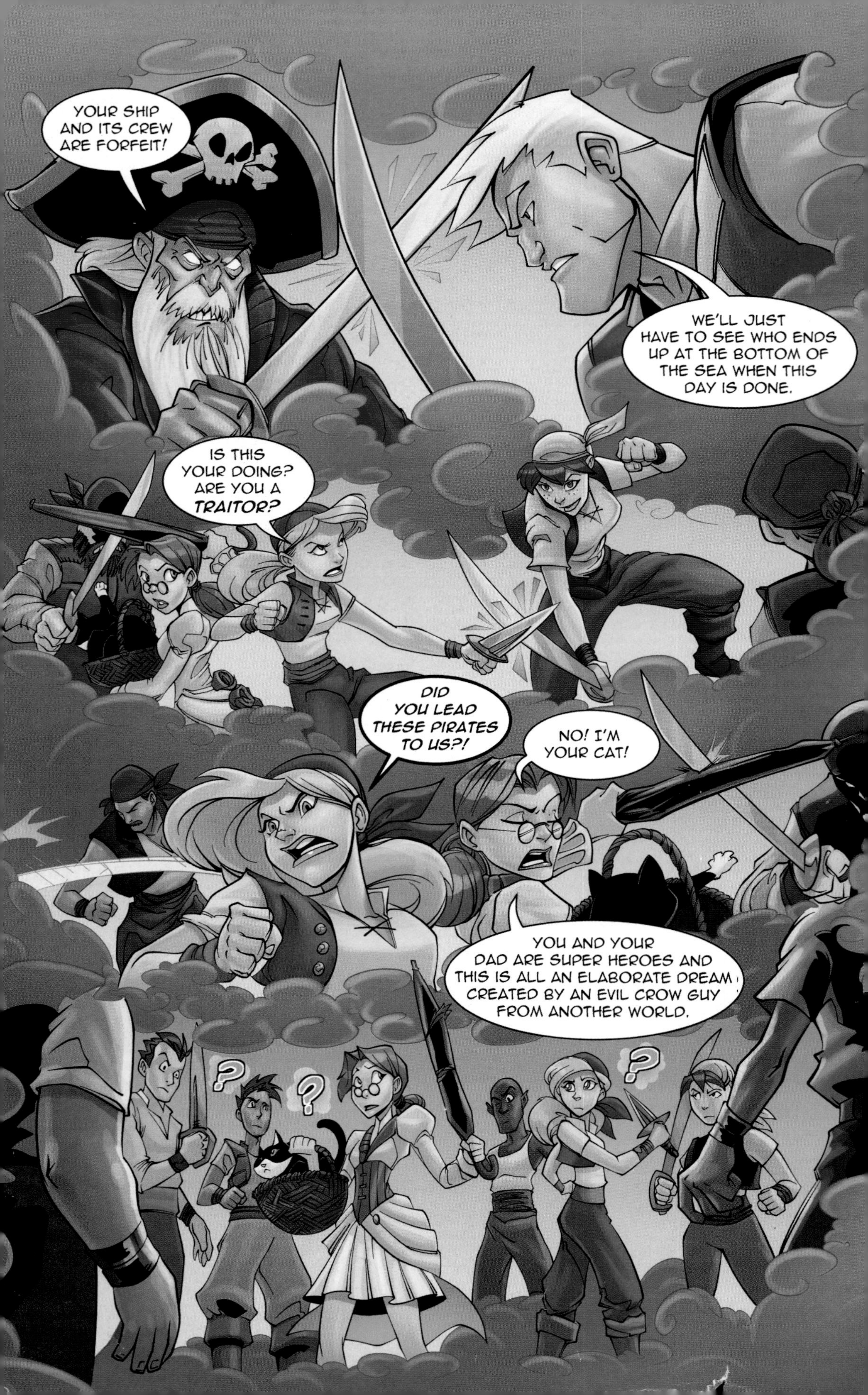
YOUR SHIP AND ITS CREW ARE FORFEIT!
WE'LL JUST HAVE TO SEE WHO ENDS UP AT THE BOTTOM OF THE SEA WHEN THIS DAY IS DONE.
IS THIS YOUR DOING? ARE YOU A *TRAITOR?*
DID YOU LEAD THESE PIRATES TO US?!
NO! I'M YOUR CAT!
YOU AND YOUR DAD ARE SUPER HEROES AND THIS IS ALL AN ELABORATE DREAM CREATED BY AN EVIL CROW GUY FROM ANOTHER WORLD.
?
?
?

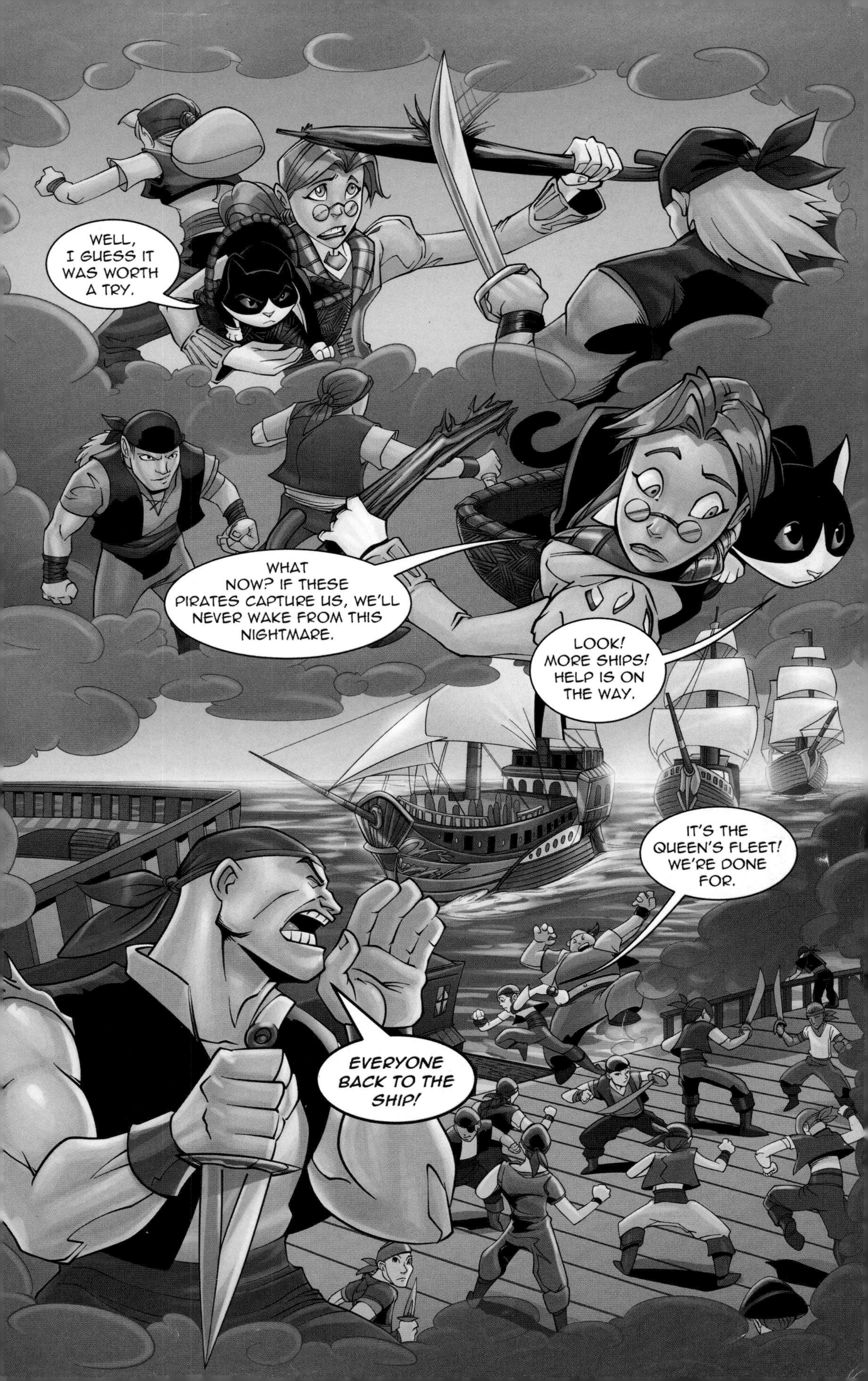
WELL, I GUESS IT WAS WORTH A TRY.
WHAT NOW? IF THESE PIRATES CAPTURE US, WE'LL NEVER WAKE FROM THIS NIGHTMARE.
LOOK! MORE SHIPS! HELP IS ON THE WAY.
IT'S THE QUEEN'S FLEET! WE'RE DONE FOR.
EVERYONE BACK TO THE SHIP!

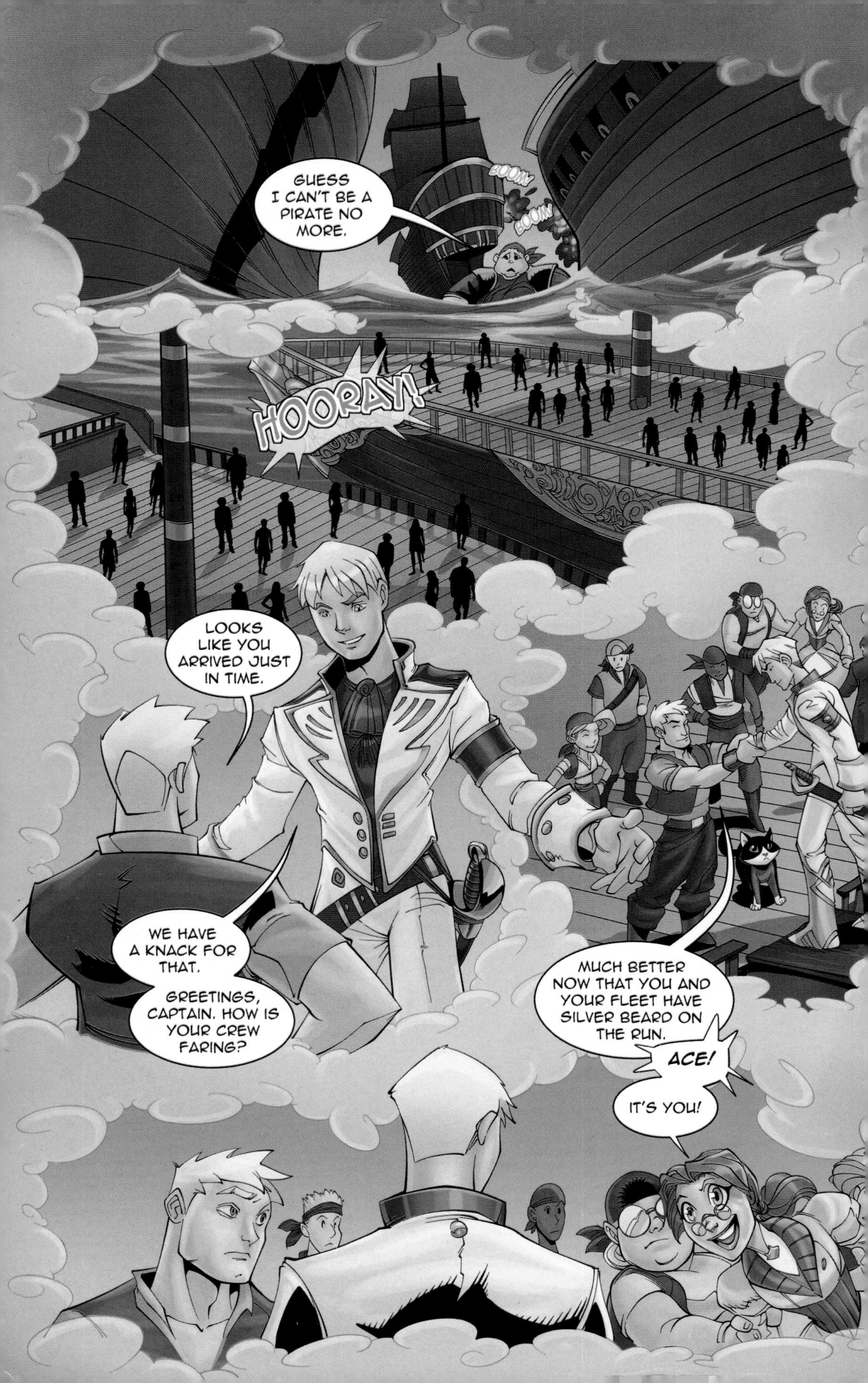
GUESS I CAN'T BE A PIRATE NO MORE.
BOOM!
BOOM!
HOORAY!
LOOKS LIKE YOU ARRIVED JUST IN TIME.
WE HAVE A KNACK FOR THAT.
GREETINGS, CAPTAIN. HOW IS YOUR CREW FARING?
MUCH BETTER NOW THAT YOU AND YOUR FLEET HAVE SILVER BEARD ON THE RUN.
ACE!
IT'S YOU!

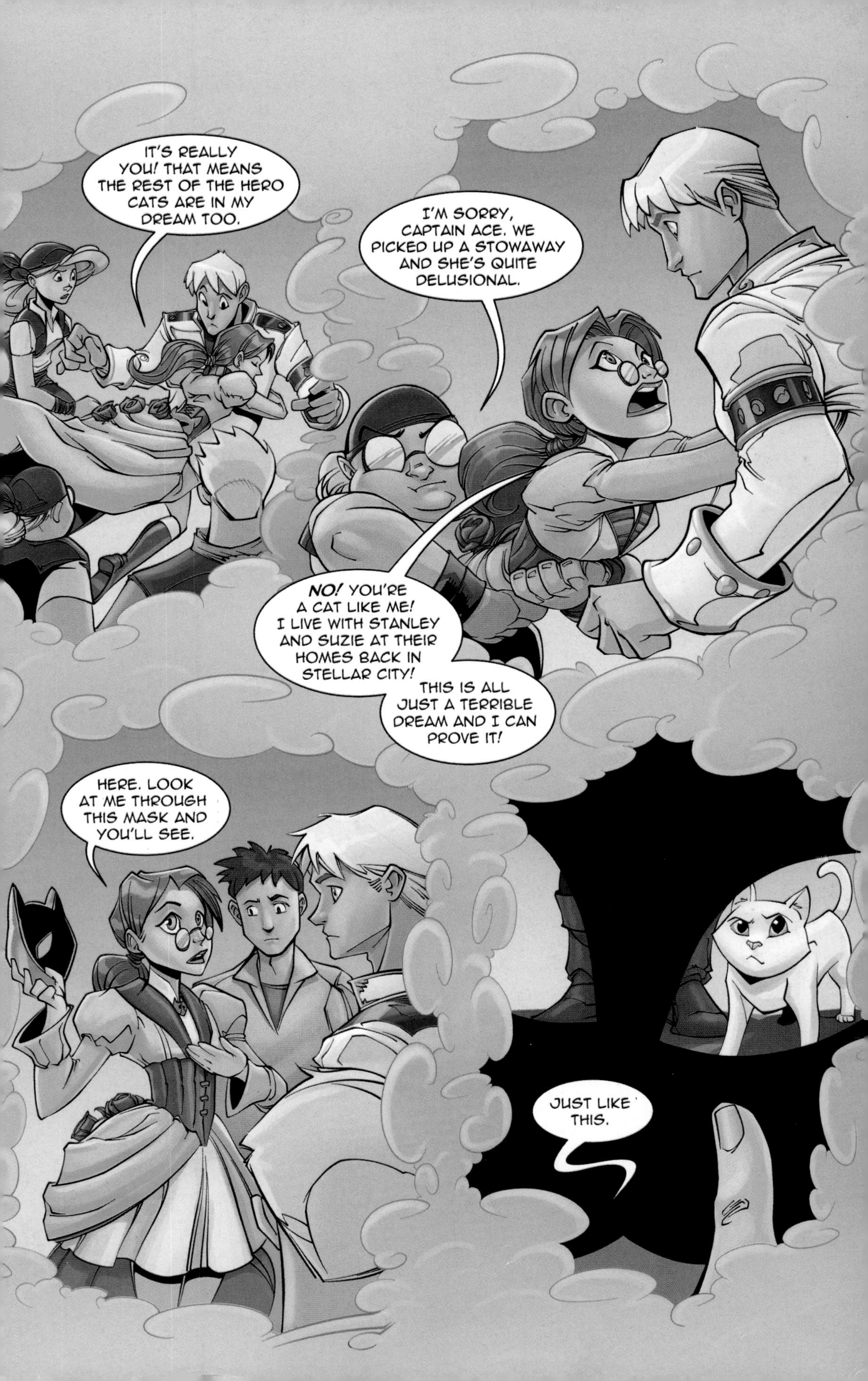
IT'S REALLY YOU! THAT MEANS THE REST OF THE HERO CATS ARE IN MY DREAM TOO.
I'M SORRY, CAPTAIN ACE. WE PICKED UP A STOWAWAY AND SHE'S QUITE DELUSIONAL.
NO! YOU'RE A CAT LIKE ME! I LIVE WITH STANLEY AND SUZIE AT THEIR HOMES BACK IN STELLAR CITY!
THIS IS ALL JUST A TERRIBLE DREAM AND I CAN PROVE IT!
HERE. LOOK AT ME THROUGH THIS MASK AND YOU'LL SEE.
JUST LIKE THIS.

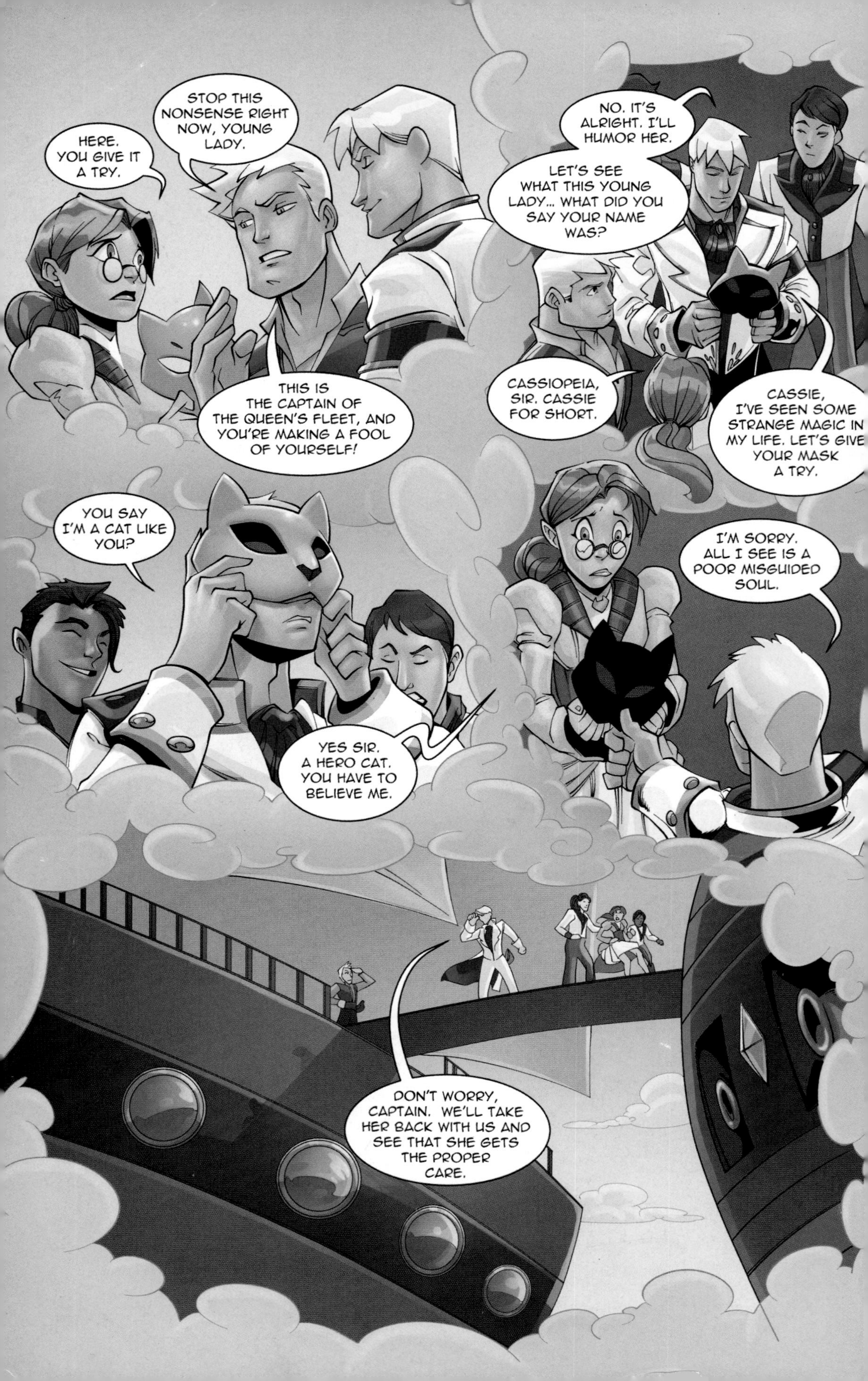
HERE. YOU GIVE IT A TRY.
STOP THIS NONSENSE RIGHT NOW, YOUNG LADY.
THIS IS THE CAPTAIN OF THE QUEEN'S FLEET, AND YOU'RE MAKING A FOOL OF YOURSELF!
NO. IT'S ALRIGHT. I'LL HUMOR HER.
LET'S SEE WHAT THIS YOUNG LADY... WHAT DID YOU SAY YOUR NAME WAS?
CASSIOPEIA, SIR. CASSIE FOR SHORT.
CASSIE, I'VE SEEN SOME STRANGE MAGIC IN MY LIFE. LET'S GIVE YOUR MASK A TRY.
YOU SAY I'M A CAT LIKE YOU?
YES SIR. A HERO CAT. YOU HAVE TO BELIEVE ME.
I'M SORRY. ALL I SEE IS A POOR MISGUIDED SOUL.
DON'T WORRY, CAPTAIN. WE'LL TAKE HER BACK WITH US AND SEE THAT SHE GETS THE PROPER CARE.

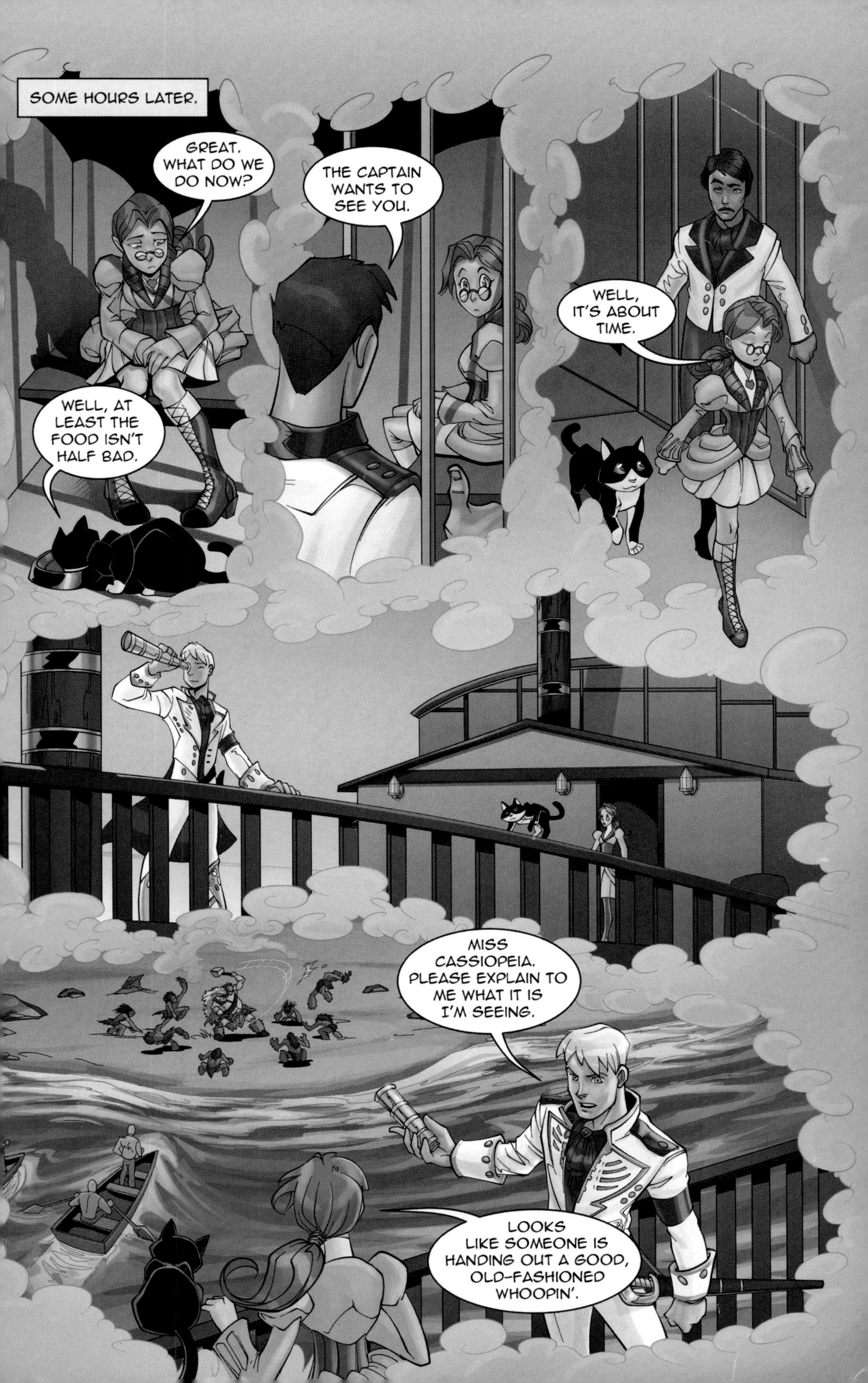
SOME HOURS LATER.
GREAT. WHAT DO WE DO NOW?
WELL, AT LEAST THE FOOD ISN'T HALF BAD.
THE CAPTAIN WANTS TO SEE YOU.
WELL, IT'S ABOUT TIME.
MISS CASSIOPEIA. PLEASE EXPLAIN TO ME WHAT IT IS I'M SEEING.
LOOKS LIKE SOMEONE IS HANDING OUT A GOOD, OLD-FASHIONED WHOOPIN'.

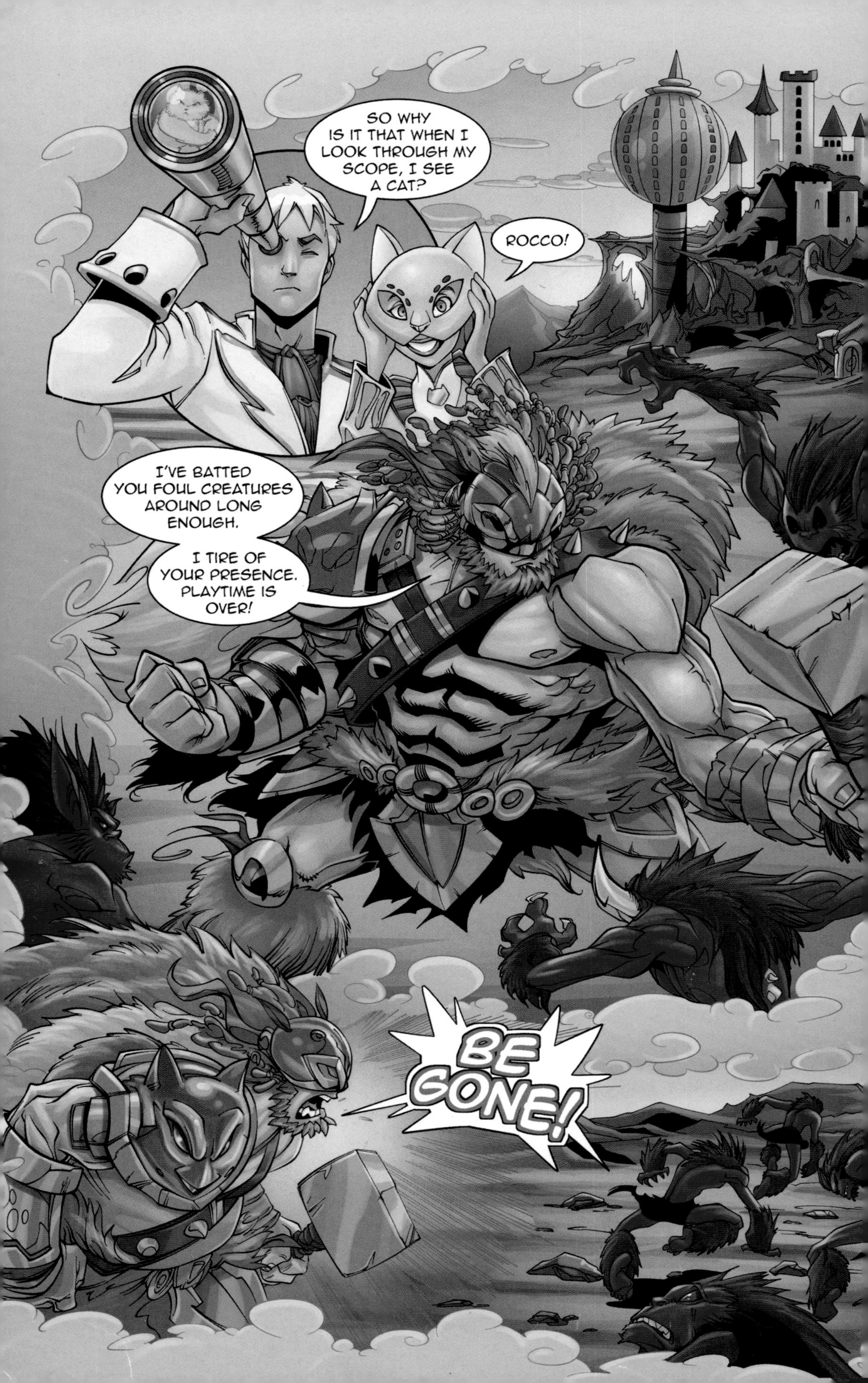
SO WHY IS IT THAT WHEN I LOOK THROUGH MY SCOPE, I SEE A CAT?
ROCCO!
I'VE BATTED YOU FOUL CREATURES AROUND LONG ENOUGH.
I TIRE OF YOUR PRESENCE. PLAYTIME IS OVER!
BE GONE!

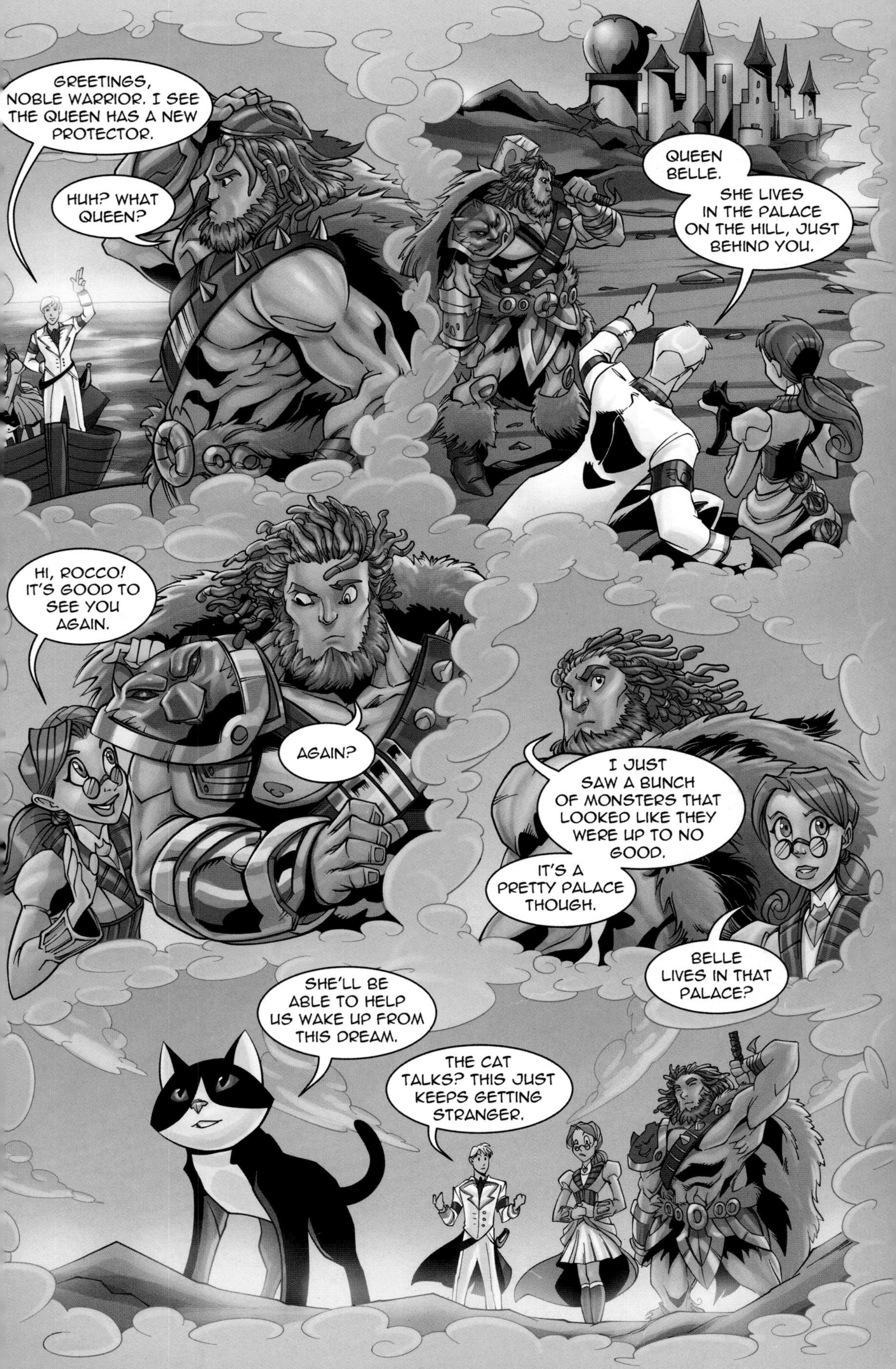
GREETINGS, NOBLE WARRIOR. I SEE THE QUEEN HAS A NEW PROTECTOR.
HUH? WHAT QUEEN?
QUEEN BELLE.
SHE LIVES IN THE PALACE ON THE HILL, JUST BEHIND YOU.
HI, ROCCO! IT'S GOOD TO SEE YOU AGAIN.
AGAIN?
I JUST SAW A BUNCH OF MONSTERS THAT LOOKED LIKE THEY WERE UP TO NO GOOD.
IT'S A PRETTY PALACE THOUGH.
BELLE LIVES IN THAT PALACE?
SHE'LL BE ABLE TO HELP US WAKE UP FROM THIS DREAM.
THE CAT TALKS? THIS JUST KEEPS GETTING STRANGER.

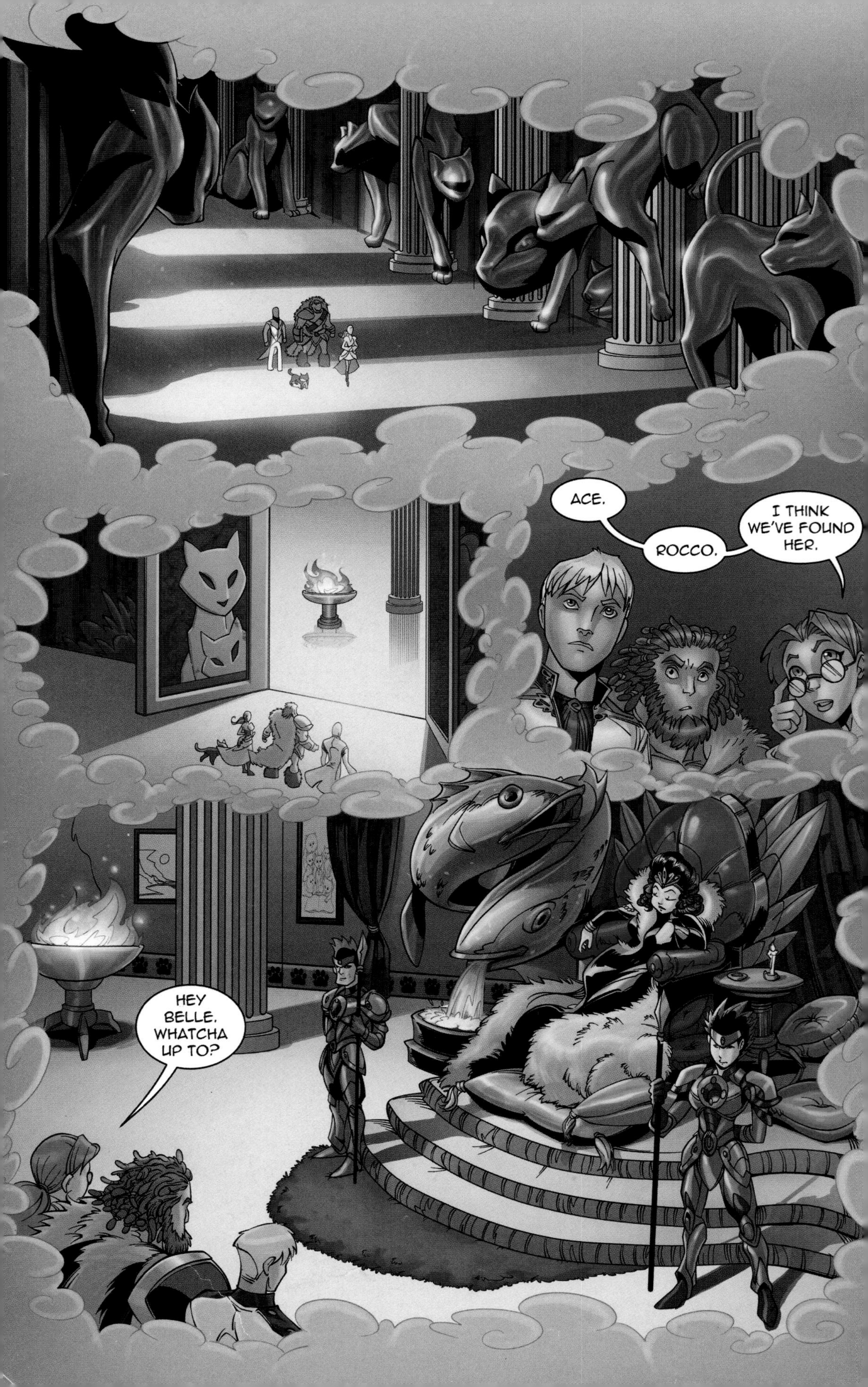
ACE.
ROCCO.
I THINK WE'VE FOUND HER.
HEY BELLE. WHATCHA UP TO?

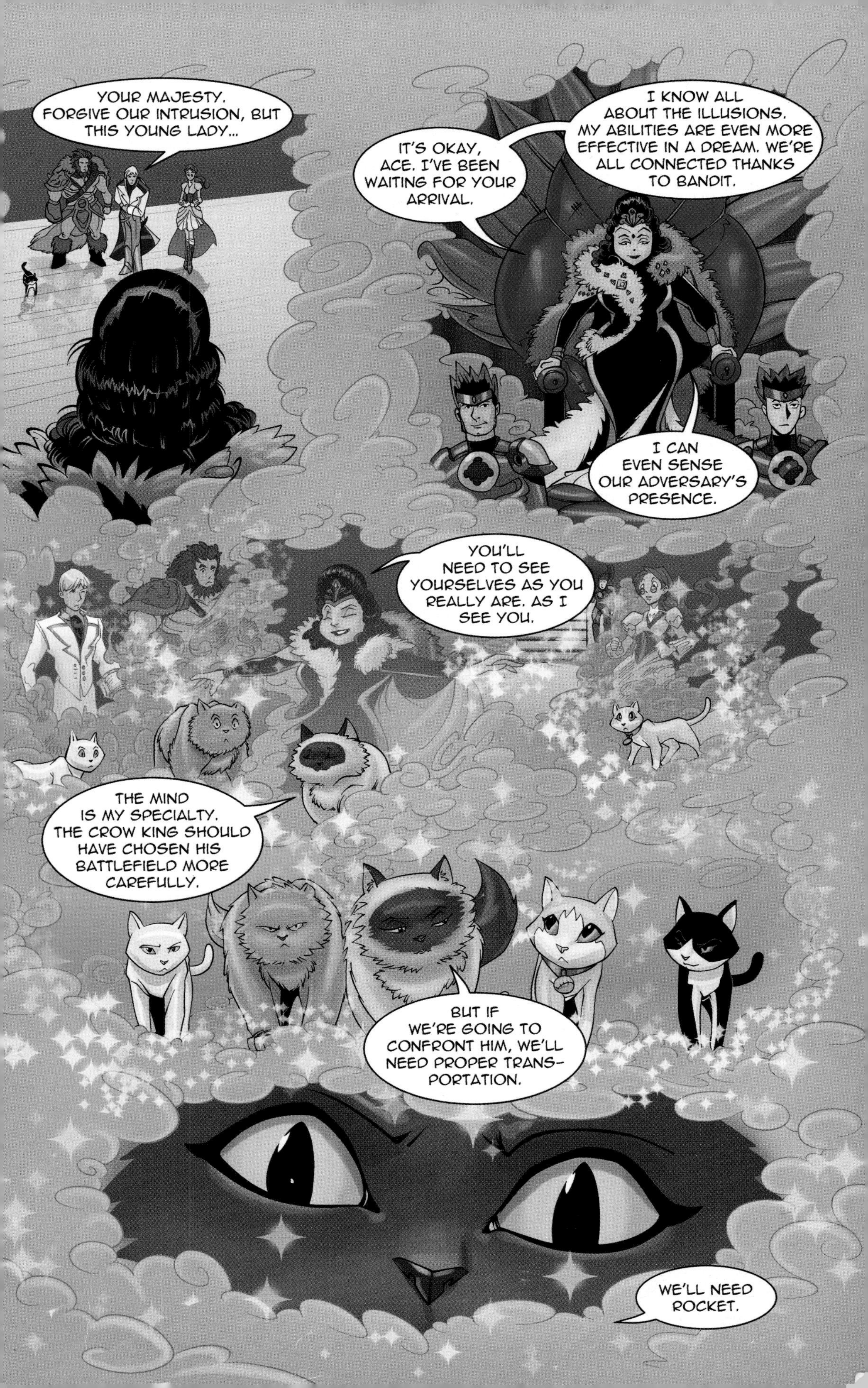
YOUR MAJESTY. FORGIVE OUR INTRUSION, BUT THIS YOUNG LADY...
IT'S OKAY, ACE. I'VE BEEN WAITING FOR YOUR ARRIVAL.
I KNOW ALL ABOUT THE ILLUSIONS. MY ABILITIES ARE EVEN MORE EFFECTIVE IN A DREAM. WE'RE ALL CONNECTED THANKS TO BANDIT.
I CAN EVEN SENSE OUR ADVERSARY'S PRESENCE.
YOU'LL NEED TO SEE YOURSELVES AS YOU REALLY ARE. AS I SEE YOU.
THE MIND IS MY SPECIALTY. THE CROW KING SHOULD HAVE CHOSEN HIS BATTLEFIELD MORE CAREFULLY.
BUT IF WE'RE GOING TO CONFRONT HIM, WE'LL NEED PROPER TRANS-PORTATION.
WE'LL NEED ROCKET.

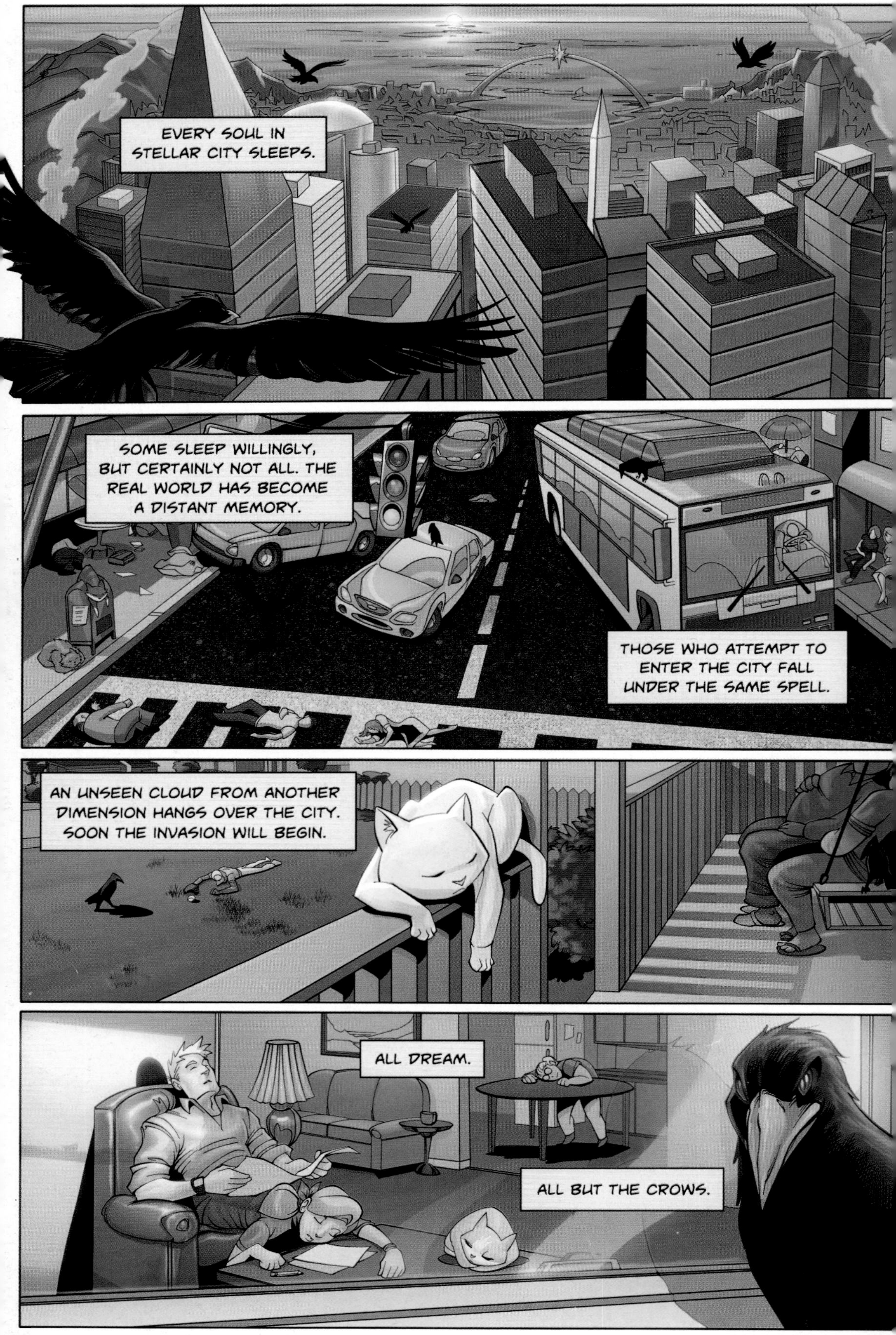
EVERY SOUL IN STELLAR CITY SLEEPS.
SOME SLEEP WILLINGLY, BUT CERTAINLY NOT ALL. THE REAL WORLD HAS BECOME A DISTANT MEMORY.
THOSE WHO ATTEMPT TO ENTER THE CITY FALL UNDER THE SAME SPELL.
AN UNSEEN CLOUD FROM ANOTHER DIMENSION HANGS OVER THE CITY. SOON THE INVASION WILL BEGIN.
ALL DREAM.
ALL BUT THE CROWS.

HERO CHAT

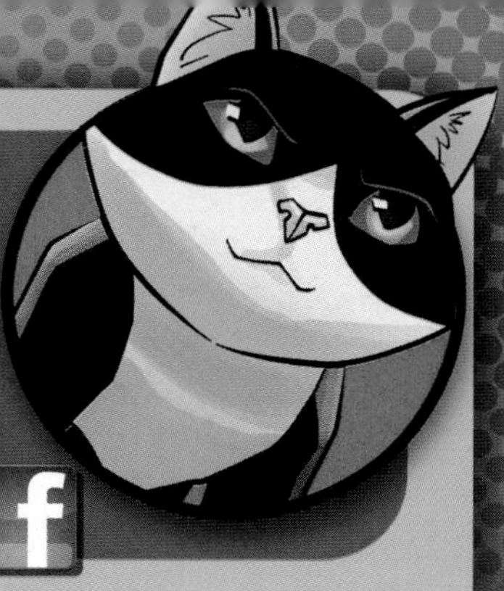

HEY CATS & KIDS! OUR TEAM HAS BEEN TORN APART AND CAST INTO ALL THE CORNERS OF A DREAM. HOPEFULLY I CAN REUNITE THEM. IT'S THE ONLY WAY WE CAN DEFEAT THE CROW KING.

DRESS UP AS YOUR FAVORITE CAT AND WE'LL SEE YOU AT THE COMIC CONS! POST PICS TO HEROCATS FACEBOOK:

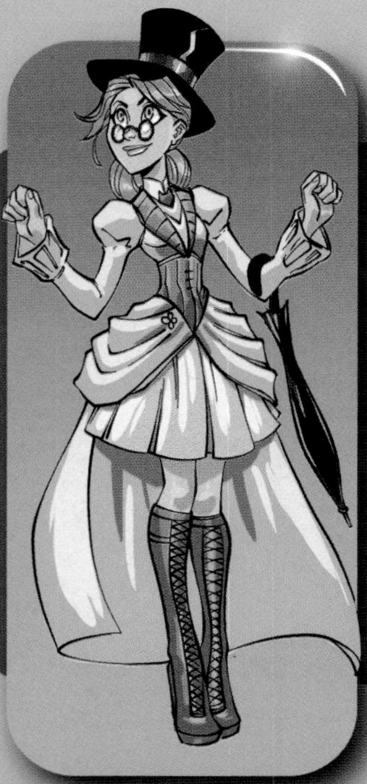

LADY CASSIOPEIA

LIVING THE GOOD LIFE AND ON A SPENDING SPREE. CASSIE HAS ALL SHE COULD ASK FOR. SHE WASTES HER DAYS LEISURELY SHOPPING IN THE DOWNTOWN DISTRICT.

CATS DON'T WORRY ABOUT MONEY, THEY JUST SEE SHINY THINGS. THE PERFECT DISTRACTION TO KEEP HER SEPARATED FROM HER FROM HER FRIENDS.
THE CROW KING'S TRAP IS SET.

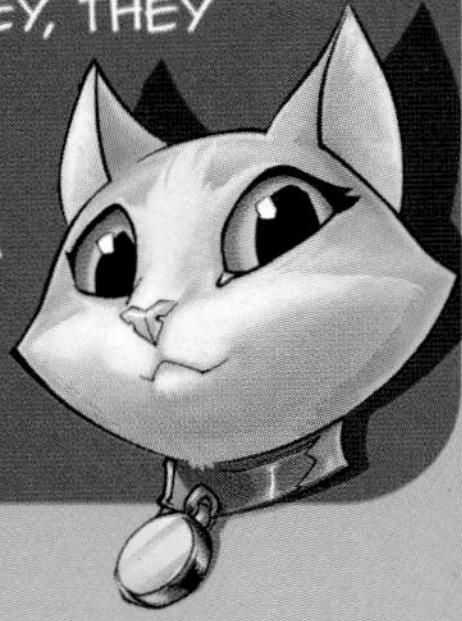

CAPTAIN ACE

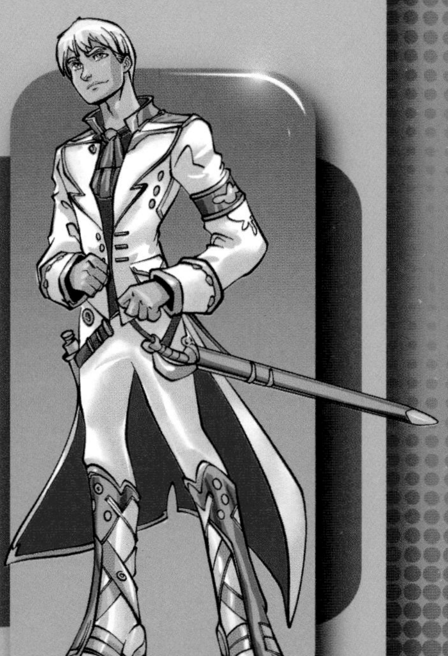

ALL ACE EVER WANTED WAS TO LIVE A LIFE OF MEANING. HE HAS RISEN UP THE RANKS AND IS CAPTAIN OF THE QUEEN'S FLEET. ACE IS A NATURAL LEADER AND HAS ASSEMBLED THE FINEST CREW. THEY ARE HIS BROTHERS IN ARMS.
HE HAS ALL HE COULD ASK FOR.
WHY LOOK FOR MORE?

THE CROW KING'S TRAP IS STRONG.

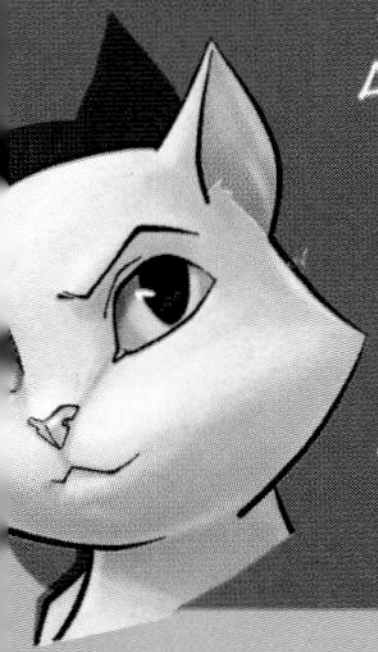

QUEEN BELLE

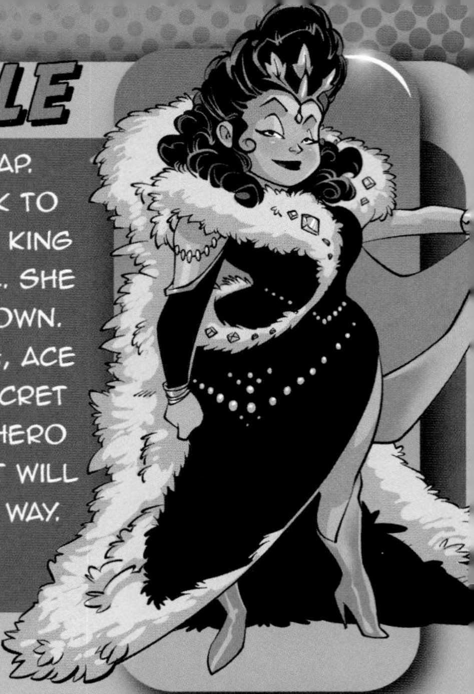

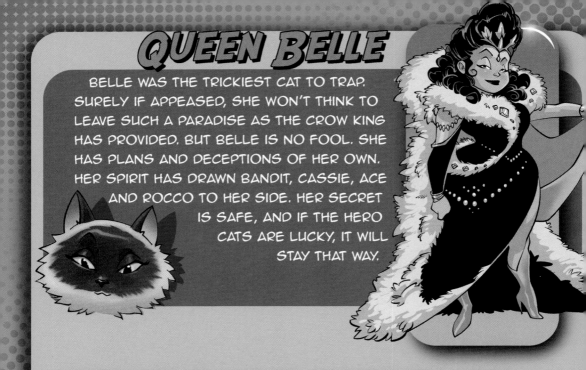

BELLE WAS THE TRICKIEST CAT TO TRAP. SURELY IF APPEASED, SHE WON'T THINK TO LEAVE SUCH A PARADISE AS THE CROW KING HAS PROVIDED. BUT BELLE IS NO FOOL. SHE HAS PLANS AND DECEPTIONS OF HER OWN. HER SPIRIT HAS DRAWN BANDIT, CASSIE, ACE AND ROCCO TO HER SIDE. HER SECRET IS SAFE, AND IF THE HERO CATS ARE LUCKY, IT WILL STAY THAT WAY.

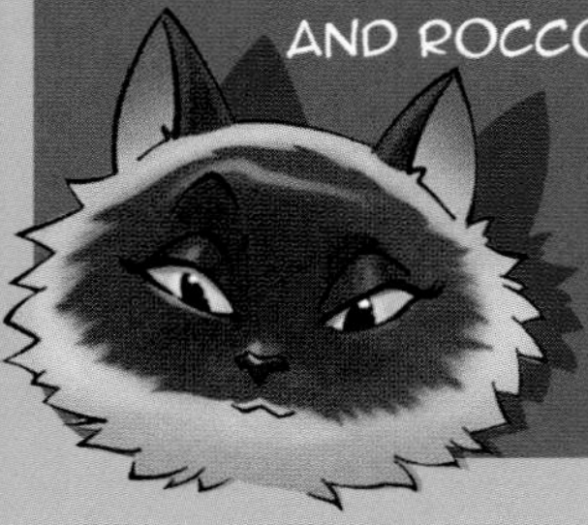

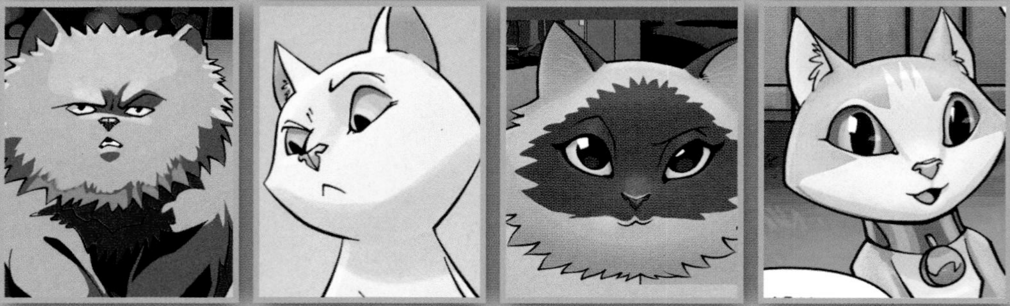

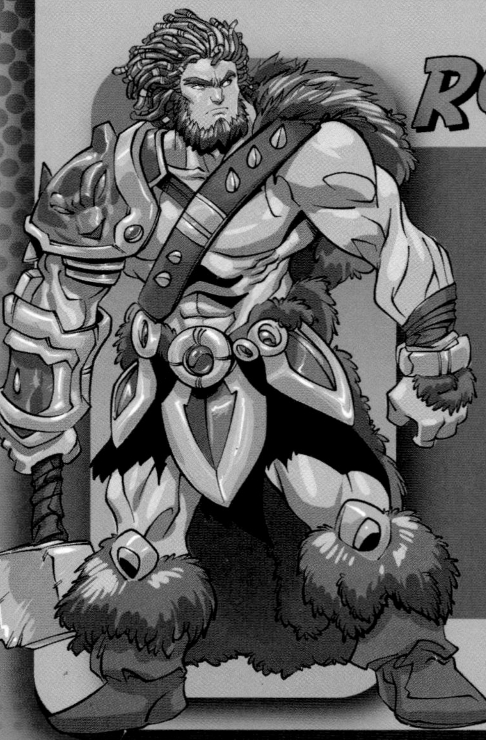

ROCCO THE MASSIVE

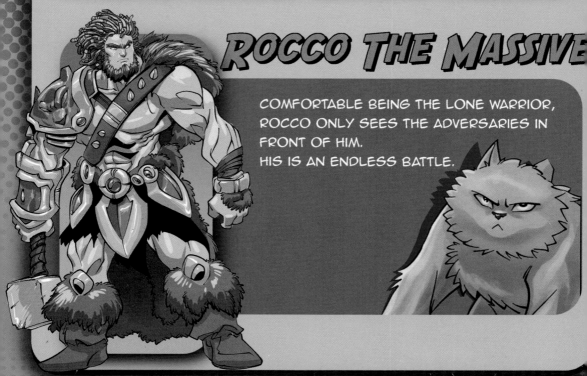

COMFORTABLE BEING THE LONE WARRIOR, ROCCO ONLY SEES THE ADVERSARIES IN FRONT OF HIM.
HIS IS AN ENDLESS BATTLE.

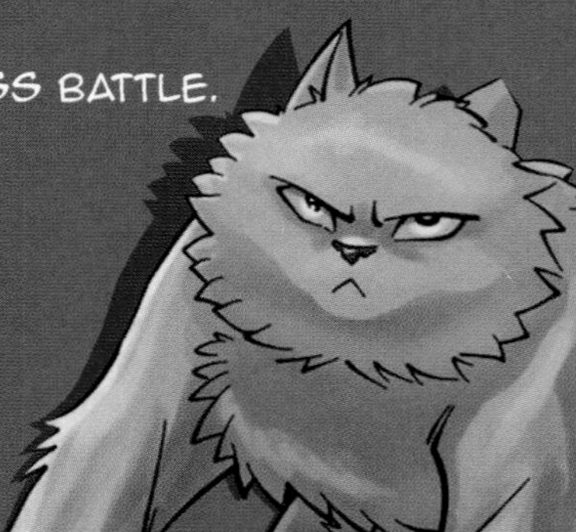

GOLDEN CAT MASK

A CHARMING GOLD PLATED CAT MASK THAT WAS MADE WITH CARE AND ATTENTION TO DETAIL. IT WAS OWNED BY A YOUNG CHILD OF ROYAL DESCENT AT ONE TIME BUT WAS TOSSED OUT WHEN THE CHILD GREW BORED WITH IT.

CAPTAINS' LOOKING GLASS

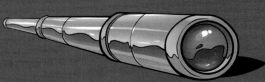

A GIFT FROM THE QUEEN HERSELF TO EACH OF HER HANDPICKED NAVAL CAPTAINS, THIS GOLD PLATED TELESCOPE IS NOTHING SHORT OF HANDHELD STATUS SYMBLE.

MONSTER CLAN MASK

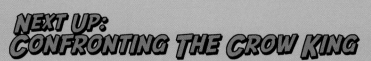

A GIFT BESTOWED BY THE OCEAN ISLAND CLAN TO WHOMEVER CAN DEFEAT THE LARGEST WATER BEAST AND RETURN WITH PROOF. THE FEATHERS ARE ADDITIONAL TOKENS THAT VALIDATE THE ACHIEVEMENT.

FOLLOW MIDNIGHT'S MISSION

A NEW BOOK!
STORY BY
KYLE PUTTKAMMER
ART BY
ALEX OGLE

NEXT UP: CONFRONTING THE CROW KING

write to us @ Kyle@galacticquest.com

Bryan Seaton - Publisher
Kevin Freeman - President
Dave Dwench - Creative Director
Shawn Gabborin - Editor in Chief
Jamal Igle & Vito Delsante -
Co-Directors of Marketing
Jim Dietz - Social Media Director
Jeremy Whitley - Education Outreach Director
Chad Cicconi & Colleen Boyd
- Associate Editors

HERO CATS #8, October 2015

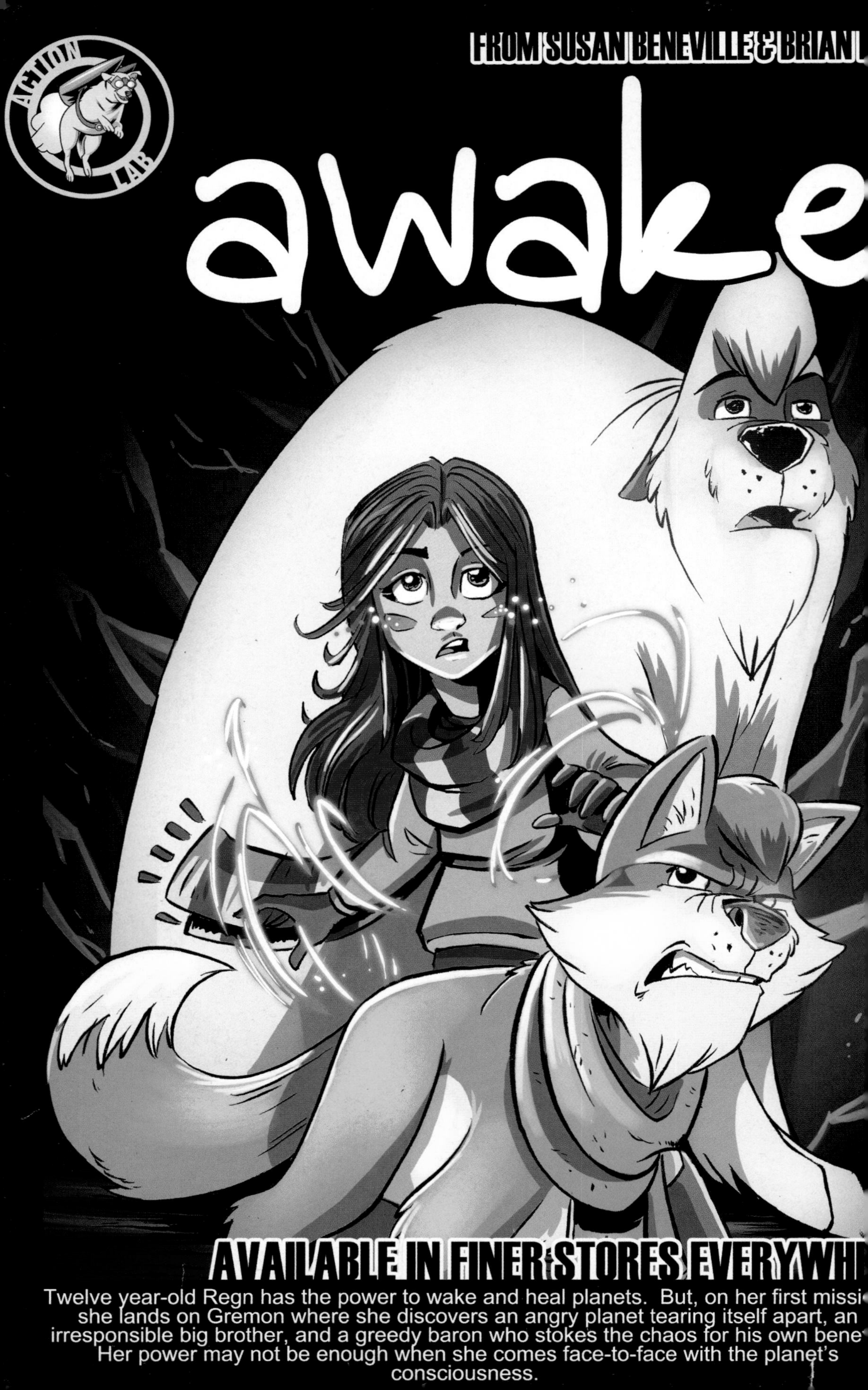
ACTION LAB
FROM SUSAN BENEVILLE & BRIAN L
awake
AVAILABLE IN FINER STORES EVERYWH
Twelve year-old Regn has the power to wake and heal planets. But, on her first missi
she lands on Gremon where she discovers an angry planet tearing itself apart, an
irresponsible big brother, and a greedy baron who stokes the chaos for his own bene
Her power may not be enough when she comes face-to-face with the planet's
consciousness.

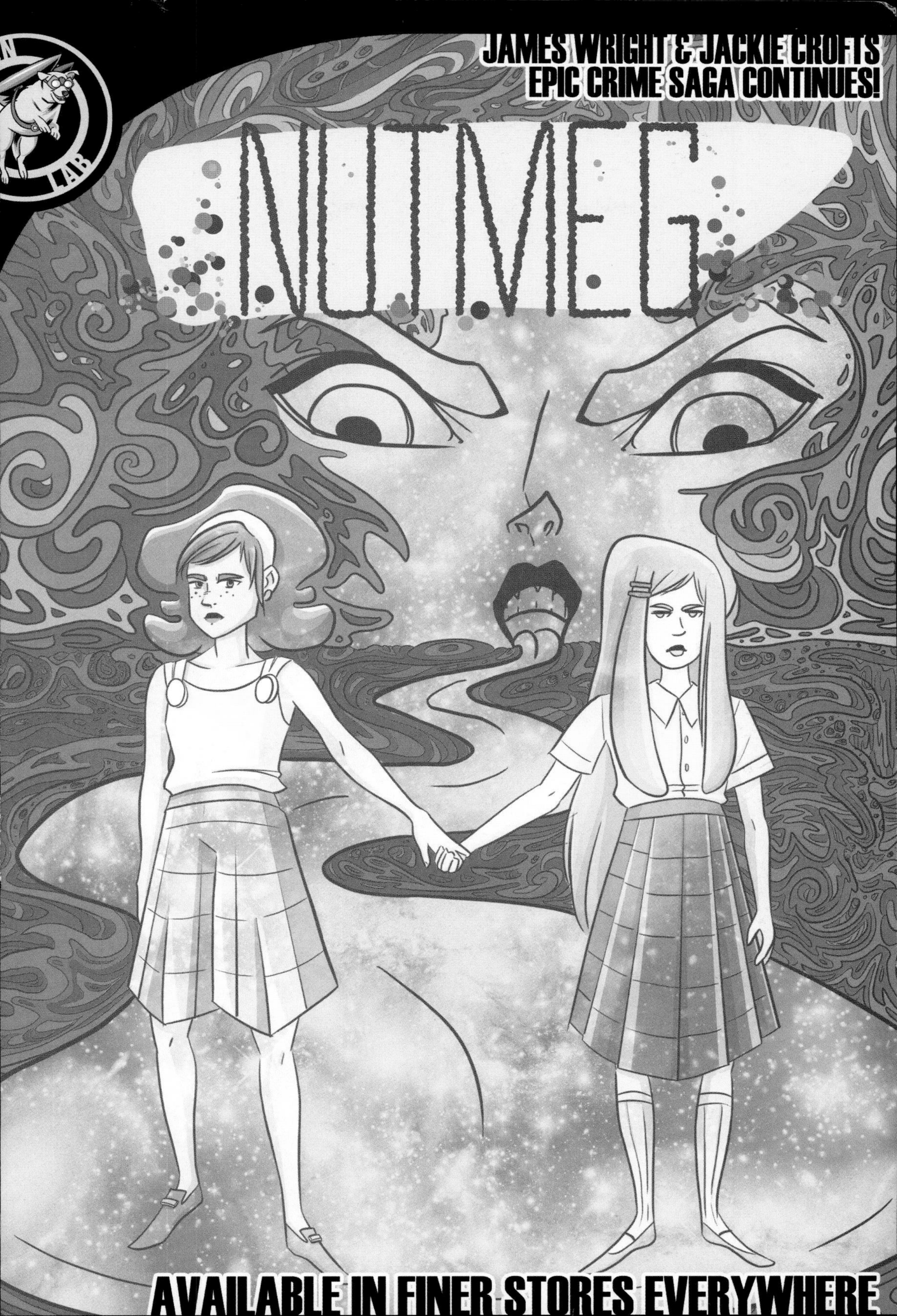

JAMES WRIGHT & JACKIE CROFTS
EPIC CRIME SAGA CONTINUES!
NUTMEG
AVAILABLE IN FINER STORES EVERYWHERE

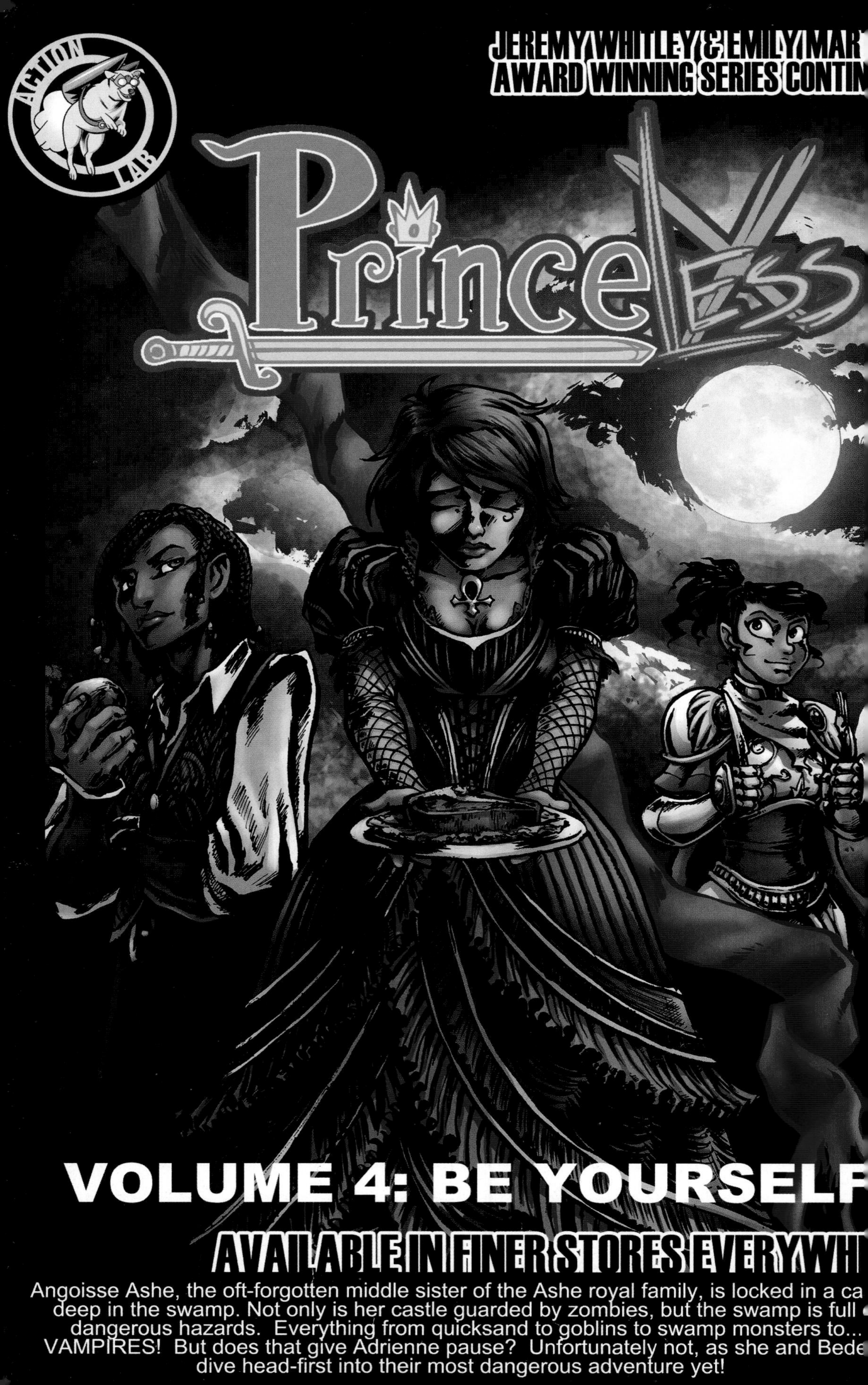
ACTION LAB
JEREMY WHITLEY & EMILY MART
AWARD WINNING SERIES CONTIN
Princeless
VOLUME 4: BE YOURSELF
AVAILABLE IN FINER STORES EVERYWH
Angoisse Ashe, the oft-forgotten middle sister of the Ashe royal family, is locked in a ca
deep in the swamp. Not only is her castle guarded by zombies, but the swamp is full
dangerous hazards. Everything from quicksand to goblins to swamp monsters to...
VAMPIRES! But does that give Adrienne pause? Unfortunately not, as she and Bede
dive head-first into their most dangerous adventure yet!

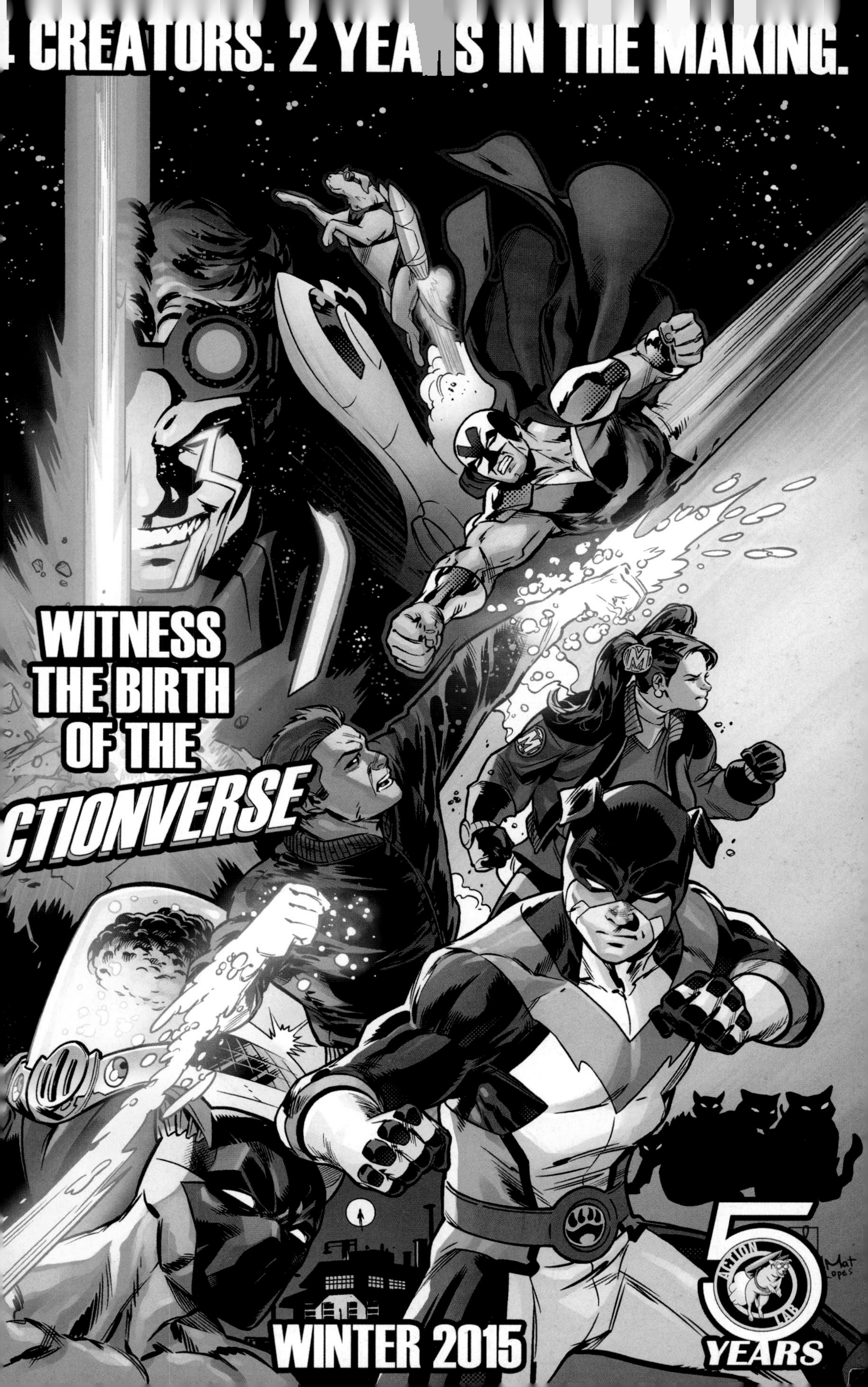
CREATORS. 2 YEA S IN THE MAKING.
WITNESS
THE BIRTH
OF THE
CTIONVERSE
Mat Lopes
ACTION LAB
5
YEARS
WINTER 2015

READ MORE NOW

ACTIONLABCOMICS.COM

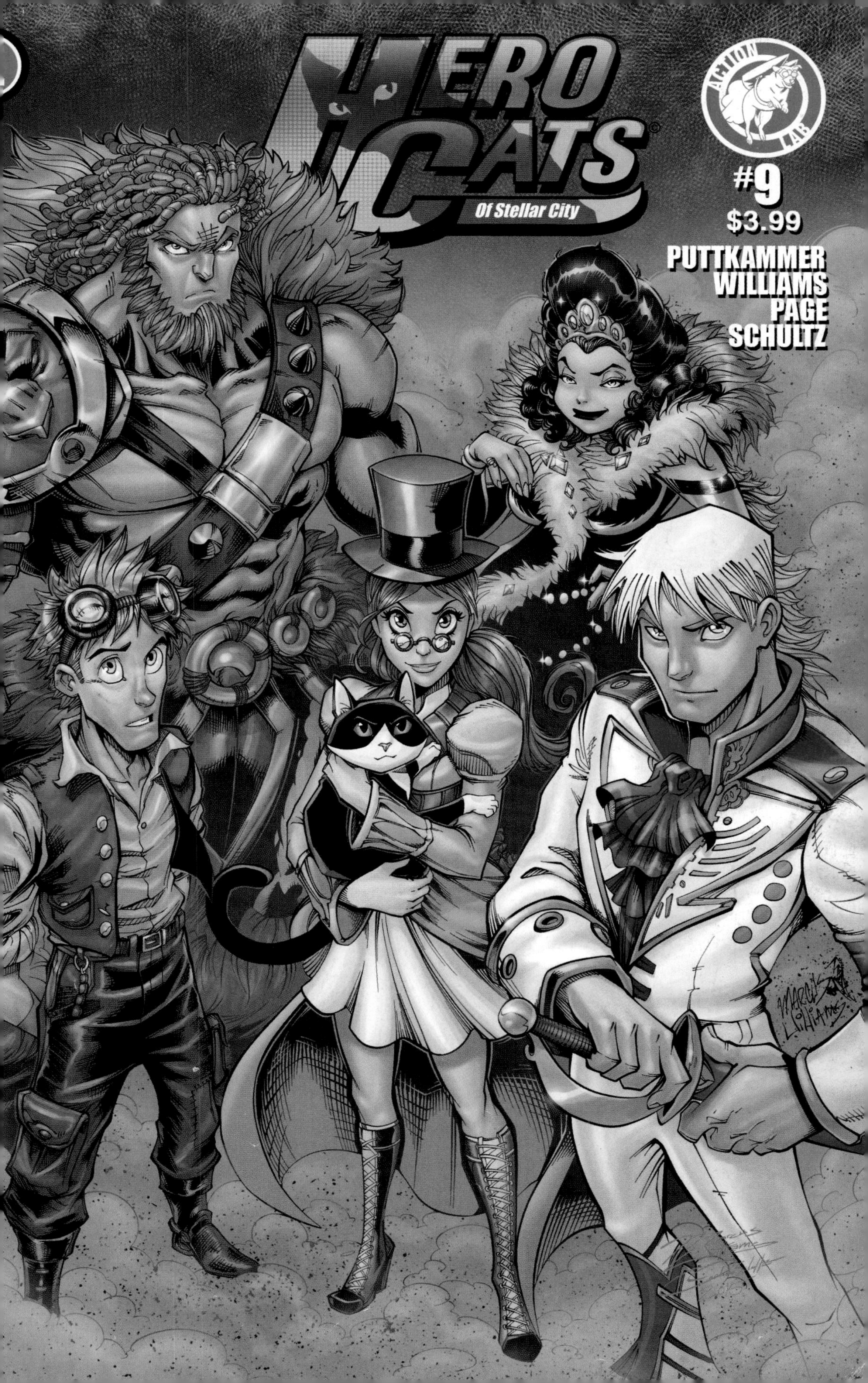
HERO CATS
Of Stellar City
ACTION LAB
#9
$3.99
PUTTKAMMER
WILLIAMS
PAGE
SCHULTZ

FROM ALL-AGES TO MATURE READERS ACTION LAB HAS YOU COVERED.

 **Appropriate for everyone.**

 **Appropriate for age 9 and up. Absent of profanity or adult content.**

 **Suggested for 12 and Up. Comics with this rating are comparable to a PG-13 movie rating. Recommended for our teen and young adult readers.**

 **Appropriate for older teens. Similar to Teen, but featuring more mature themes and/or more graphic imagery.**

 **Contains extreme viloence and some nudity. Basically the Rated-R of comics.**

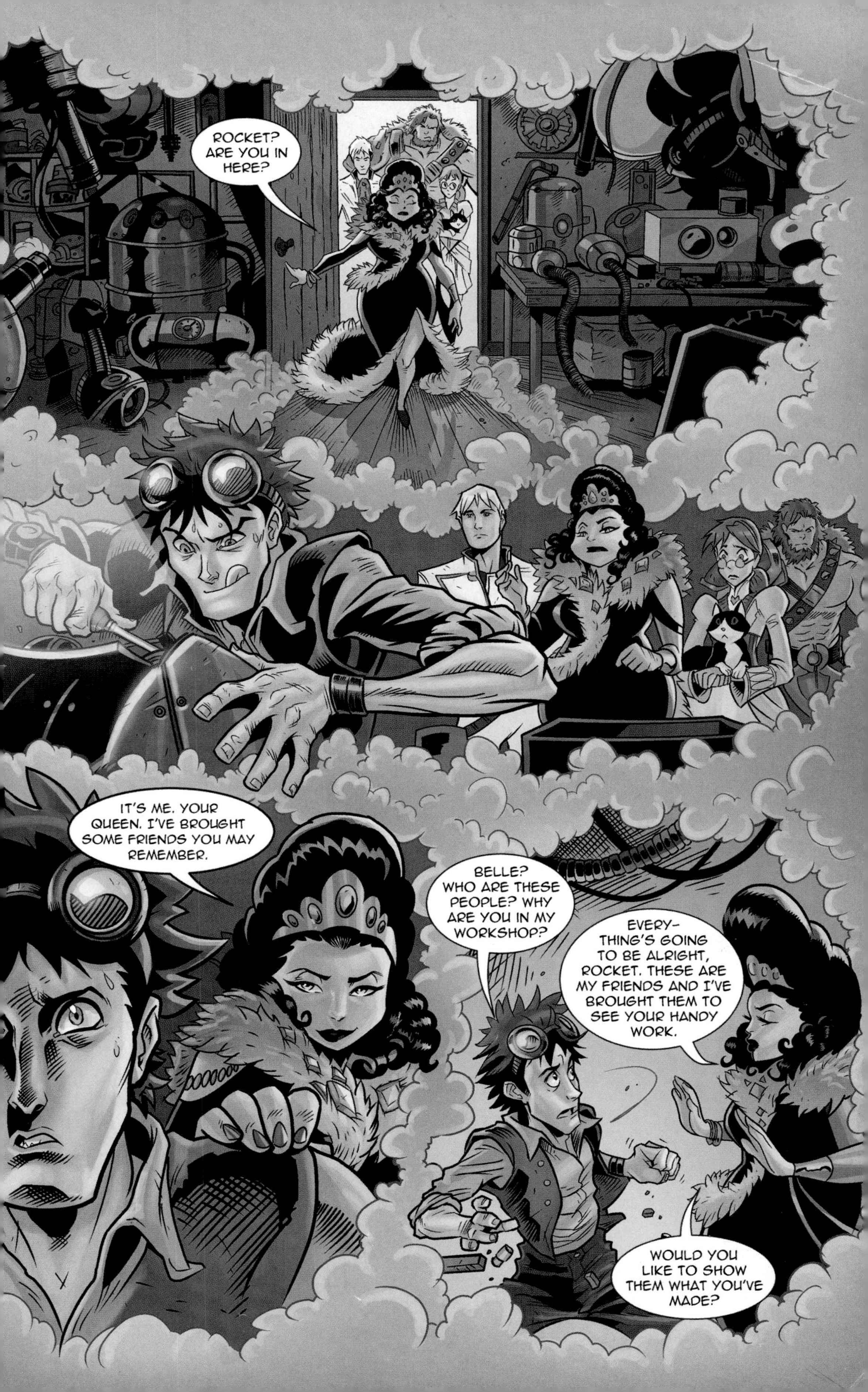

ROCKET? ARE YOU IN HERE?
IT'S ME. YOUR QUEEN. I'VE BROUGHT SOME FRIENDS YOU MAY REMEMBER.
BELLE? WHO ARE THESE PEOPLE? WHY ARE YOU IN MY WORKSHOP?
EVERY-THING'S GOING TO BE ALRIGHT, ROCKET. THESE ARE MY FRIENDS AND I'VE BROUGHT THEM TO SEE YOUR HANDY WORK.
WOULD YOU LIKE TO SHOW THEM WHAT YOU'VE MADE?

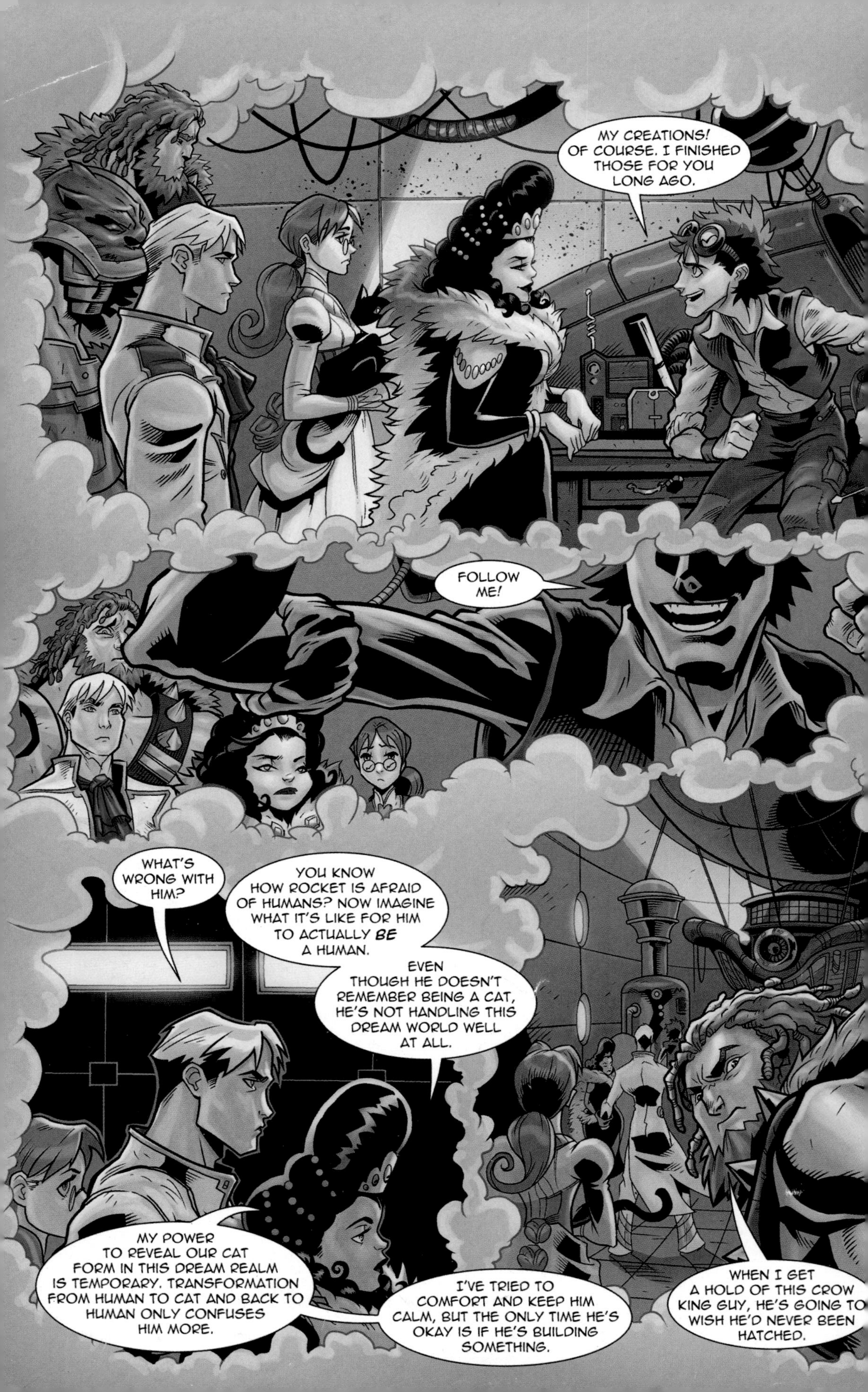
MY CREATIONS! OF COURSE. I FINISHED THOSE FOR YOU LONG AGO.
FOLLOW ME!
WHAT'S WRONG WITH HIM?
YOU KNOW HOW ROCKET IS AFRAID OF HUMANS? NOW IMAGINE WHAT IT'S LIKE FOR HIM TO ACTUALLY *BE* A HUMAN.
EVEN THOUGH HE DOESN'T REMEMBER BEING A CAT, HE'S NOT HANDLING THIS DREAM WORLD WELL AT ALL.
MY POWER TO REVEAL OUR CAT FORM IN THIS DREAM REALM IS TEMPORARY. TRANSFORMATION FROM HUMAN TO CAT AND BACK TO HUMAN ONLY CONFUSES HIM MORE.
I'VE TRIED TO COMFORT AND KEEP HIM CALM, BUT THE ONLY TIME HE'S OKAY IS IF HE'S BUILDING SOMETHING.
WHEN I GET A HOLD OF THIS CROW KING GUY, HE'S GOING TO WISH HE'D NEVER BEEN HATCHED.

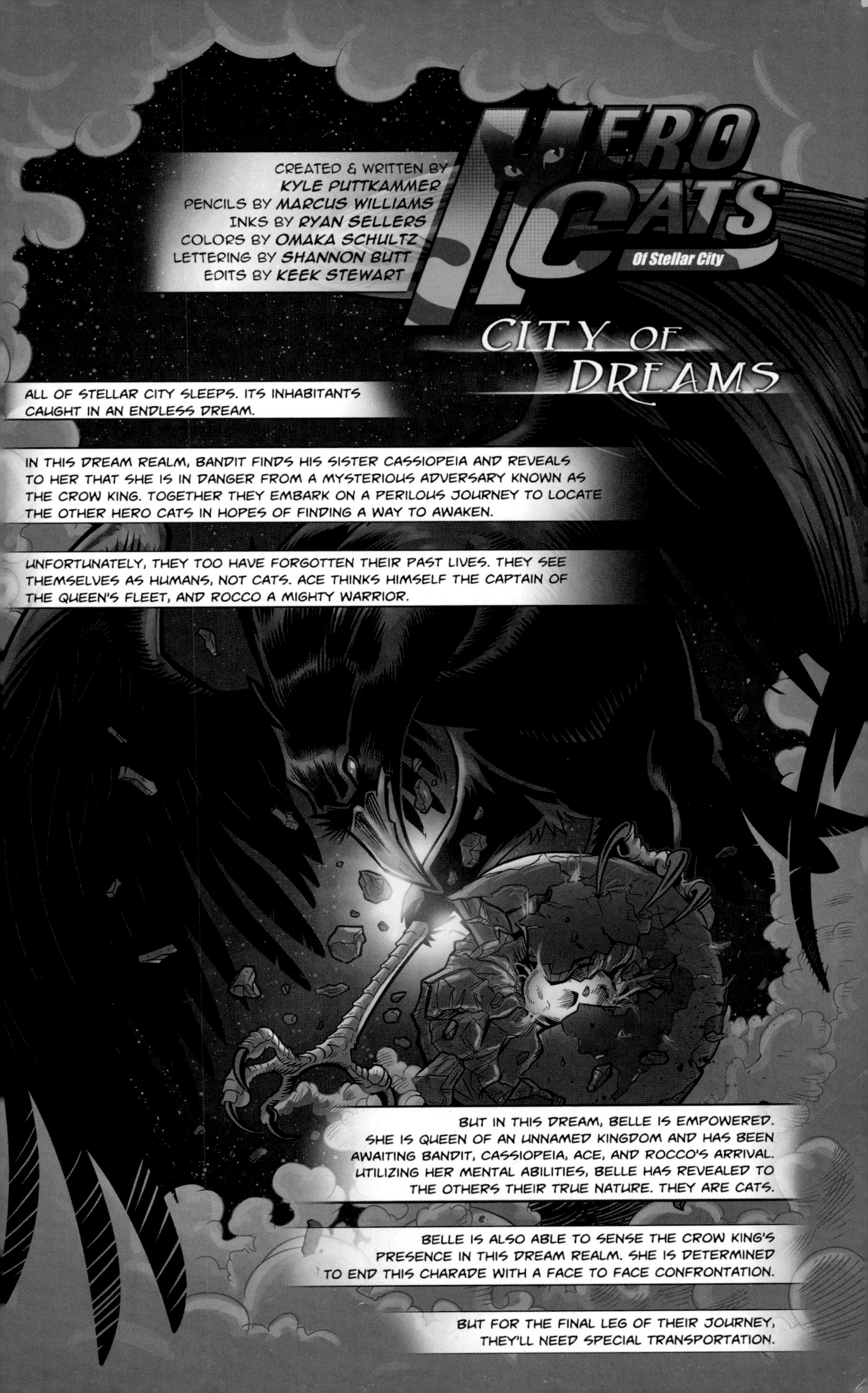
HERO CATS
Of Stellar City
CREATED & WRITTEN BY KYLE PUTTKAMMER
PENCILS BY MARCUS WILLIAMS
INKS BY RYAN SELLERS
COLORS BY OMAKA SCHULTZ
LETTERING BY SHANNON BUTT
EDITS BY KEEK STEWART
CITY OF DREAMS
ALL OF STELLAR CITY SLEEPS. ITS INHABITANTS CAUGHT IN AN ENDLESS DREAM.
IN THIS DREAM REALM, BANDIT FINDS HIS SISTER CASSIOPEIA AND REVEALS TO HER THAT SHE IS IN DANGER FROM A MYSTERIOUS ADVERSARY KNOWN AS THE CROW KING. TOGETHER THEY EMBARK ON A PERILOUS JOURNEY TO LOCATE THE OTHER HERO CATS IN HOPES OF FINDING A WAY TO AWAKEN.
UNFORTUNATELY, THEY TOO HAVE FORGOTTEN THEIR PAST LIVES. THEY SEE THEMSELVES AS HUMANS, NOT CATS. ACE THINKS HIMSELF THE CAPTAIN OF THE QUEEN'S FLEET, AND ROCCO A MIGHTY WARRIOR.
BUT IN THIS DREAM, BELLE IS EMPOWERED. SHE IS QUEEN OF AN UNNAMED KINGDOM AND HAS BEEN AWAITING BANDIT, CASSIOPEIA, ACE, AND ROCCO'S ARRIVAL. UTILIZING HER MENTAL ABILITIES, BELLE HAS REVEALED TO THE OTHERS THEIR TRUE NATURE. THEY ARE CATS.
BELLE IS ALSO ABLE TO SENSE THE CROW KING'S PRESENCE IN THIS DREAM REALM. SHE IS DETERMINED TO END THIS CHARADE WITH A FACE TO FACE CONFRONTATION.
BUT FOR THE FINAL LEG OF THEIR JOURNEY, THEY'LL NEED SPECIAL TRANSPORTATION.

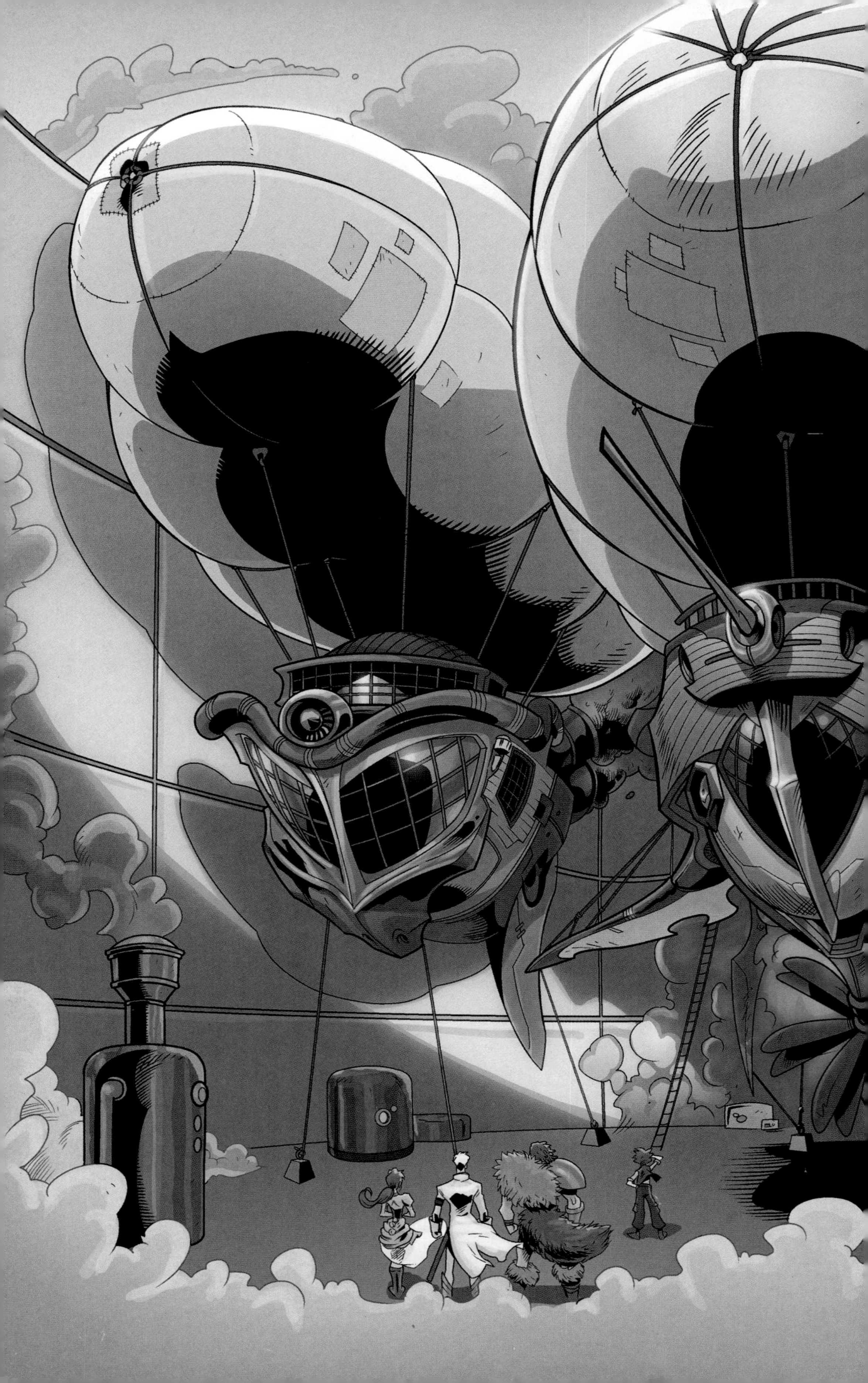

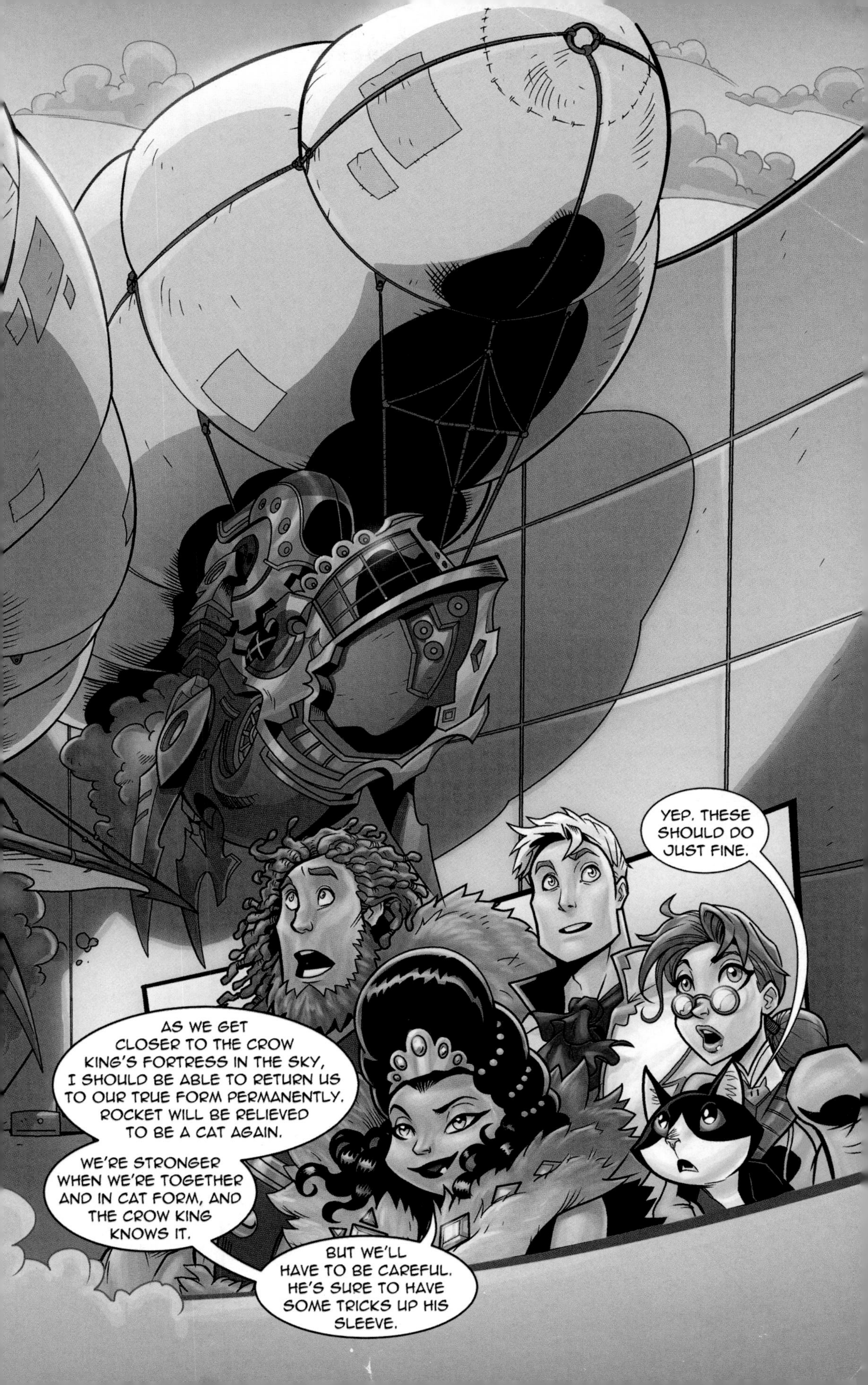
YEP. THESE SHOULD DO JUST FINE.
AS WE GET CLOSER TO THE CROW KING'S FORTRESS IN THE SKY, I SHOULD BE ABLE TO RETURN US TO OUR TRUE FORM PERMANENTLY. ROCKET WILL BE RELIEVED TO BE A CAT AGAIN.
WE'RE STRONGER WHEN WE'RE TOGETHER AND IN CAT FORM, AND THE CROW KING KNOWS IT.
BUT WE'LL HAVE TO BE CAREFUL. HE'S SURE TO HAVE SOME TRICKS UP HIS SLEEVE.

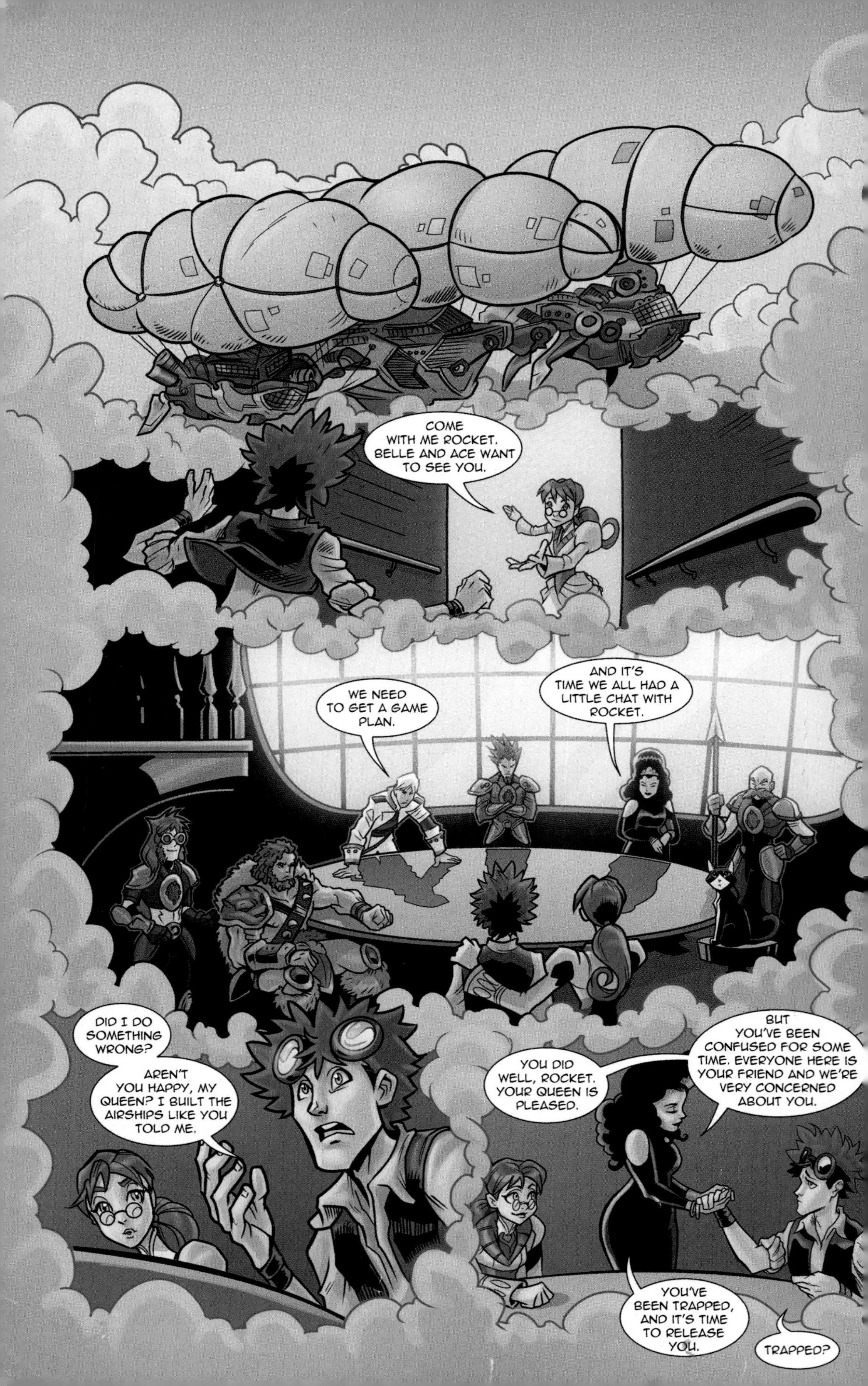
COME WITH ME ROCKET. BELLE AND ACE WANT TO SEE YOU.
WE NEED TO GET A GAME PLAN.
AND IT'S TIME WE ALL HAD A LITTLE CHAT WITH ROCKET.
DID I DO SOMETHING WRONG?
AREN'T YOU HAPPY, MY QUEEN? I BUILT THE AIRSHIPS LIKE YOU TOLD ME.
YOU DID WELL, ROCKET. YOUR QUEEN IS PLEASED.
BUT YOU'VE BEEN CONFUSED FOR SOME TIME. EVERYONE HERE IS YOUR FRIEND AND WE'RE VERY CONCERNED ABOUT YOU.
YOU'VE BEEN TRAPPED, AND IT'S TIME TO RELEASE YOU.
TRAPPED?

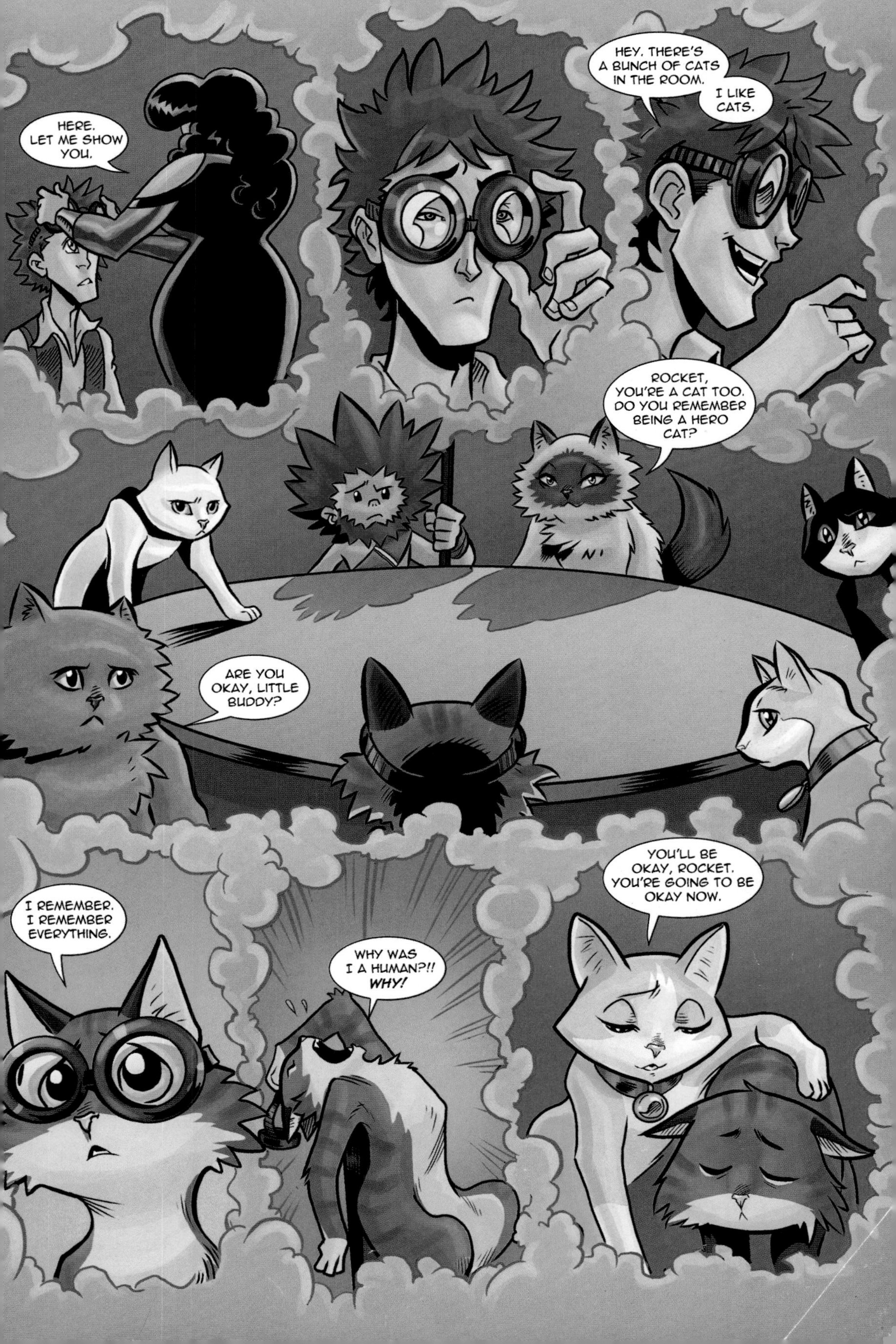
HERE. LET ME SHOW YOU.
HEY. THERE'S A BUNCH OF CATS IN THE ROOM.
I LIKE CATS.
ROCKET, YOU'RE A CAT TOO. DO YOU REMEMBER BEING A HERO CAT?
ARE YOU OKAY, LITTLE BUDDY?
I REMEMBER. I REMEMBER EVERYTHING.
WHY WAS I A HUMAN?!! *WHY!*
YOU'LL BE OKAY, ROCKET. YOU'RE GOING TO BE OKAY NOW.

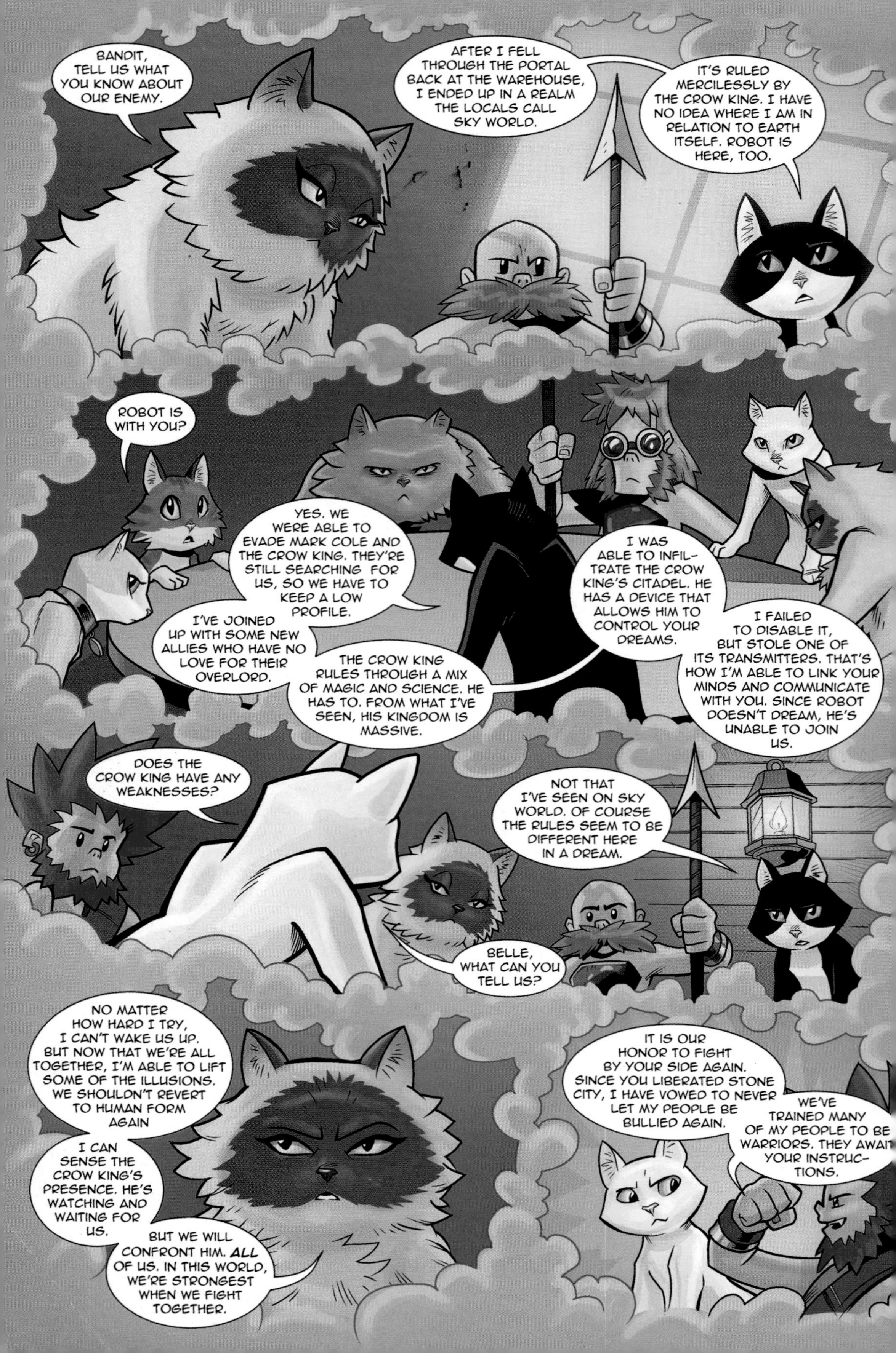
BANDIT, TELL US WHAT YOU KNOW ABOUT OUR ENEMY.
AFTER I FELL THROUGH THE PORTAL BACK AT THE WAREHOUSE, I ENDED UP IN A REALM THE LOCALS CALL SKY WORLD.
IT'S RULED MERCILESSLY BY THE CROW KING. I HAVE NO IDEA WHERE I AM IN RELATION TO EARTH ITSELF. ROBOT IS HERE, TOO.
ROBOT IS WITH YOU?
YES. WE WERE ABLE TO EVADE MARK COLE AND THE CROW KING. THEY'RE STILL SEARCHING FOR US, SO WE HAVE TO KEEP A LOW PROFILE.
I'VE JOINED UP WITH SOME NEW ALLIES WHO HAVE NO LOVE FOR THEIR OVERLORD.
THE CROW KING RULES THROUGH A MIX OF MAGIC AND SCIENCE. HE HAS TO. FROM WHAT I'VE SEEN, HIS KINGDOM IS MASSIVE.
I WAS ABLE TO INFILTRATE THE CROW KING'S CITADEL. HE HAS A DEVICE THAT ALLOWS HIM TO CONTROL YOUR DREAMS.
I FAILED TO DISABLE IT, BUT STOLE ONE OF ITS TRANSMITTERS. THAT'S HOW I'M ABLE TO LINK YOUR MINDS AND COMMUNICATE WITH YOU. SINCE ROBOT DOESN'T DREAM, HE'S UNABLE TO JOIN US.
DOES THE CROW KING HAVE ANY WEAKNESSES?
NOT THAT I'VE SEEN ON SKY WORLD. OF COURSE THE RULES SEEM TO BE DIFFERENT HERE IN A DREAM.
BELLE, WHAT CAN YOU TELL US?
NO MATTER HOW HARD I TRY, I CAN'T WAKE US UP. BUT NOW THAT WE'RE ALL TOGETHER, I'M ABLE TO LIFT SOME OF THE ILLUSIONS. WE SHOULDN'T REVERT TO HUMAN FORM AGAIN
I CAN SENSE THE CROW KING'S PRESENCE. HE'S WATCHING AND WAITING FOR US.
BUT WE WILL CONFRONT HIM. ***ALL*** OF US. IN THIS WORLD, WE'RE STRONGEST WHEN WE FIGHT TOGETHER.
IT IS OUR HONOR TO FIGHT BY YOUR SIDE AGAIN. SINCE YOU LIBERATED STONE CITY, I HAVE VOWED TO NEVER LET MY PEOPLE BE BULLIED AGAIN.
WE'VE TRAINED MANY OF MY PEOPLE TO BE WARRIORS. THEY AWAIT YOUR INSTRUCTIONS.

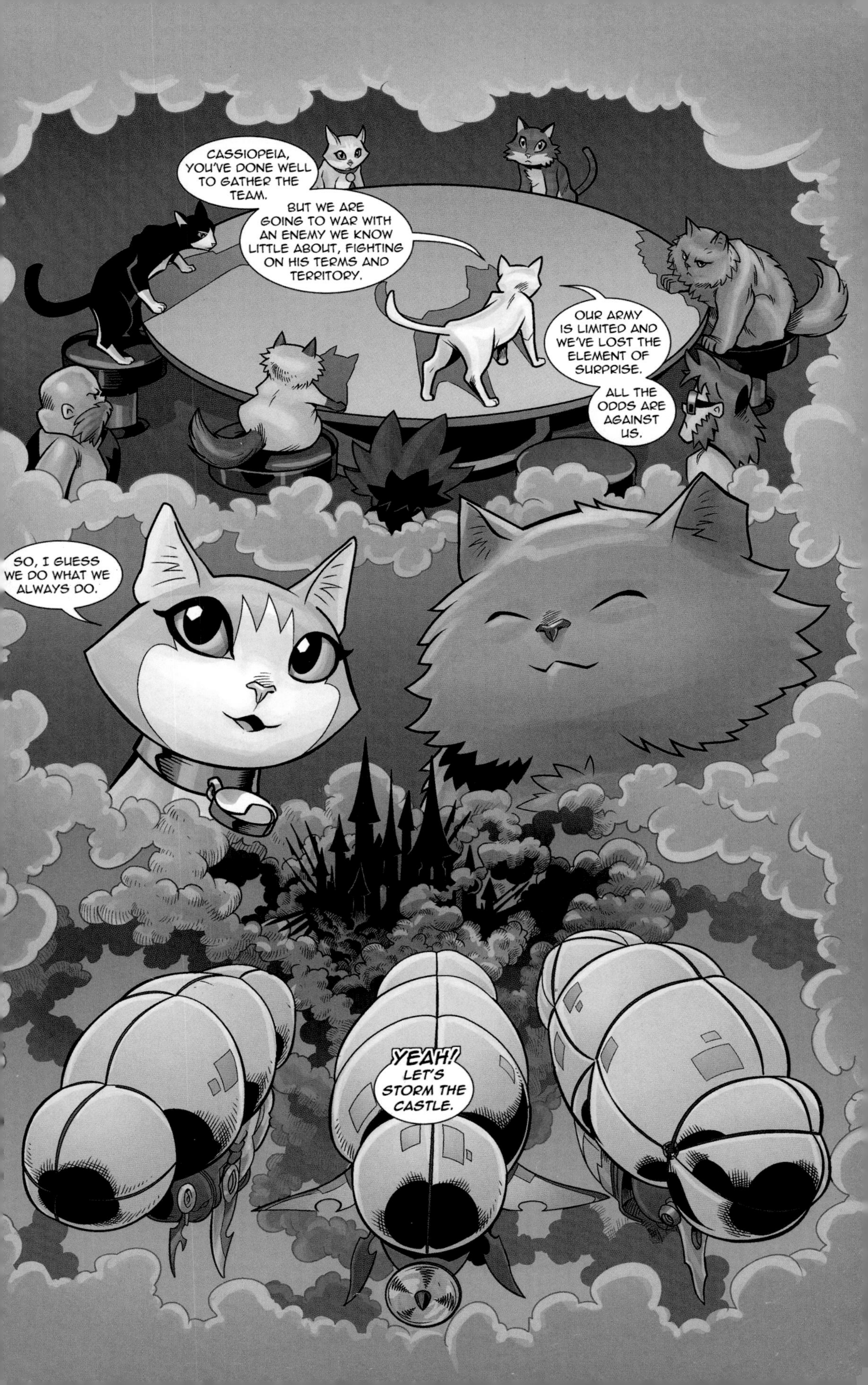
CASSIOPEIA, YOU'VE DONE WELL TO GATHER THE TEAM.
BUT WE ARE GOING TO WAR WITH AN ENEMY WE KNOW LITTLE ABOUT, FIGHTING ON HIS TERMS AND TERRITORY.
OUR ARMY IS LIMITED AND WE'VE LOST THE ELEMENT OF SURPRISE.
ALL THE ODDS ARE AGAINST US.
SO, I GUESS WE DO WHAT WE ALWAYS DO.
YEAH! LET'S STORM THE CASTLE.

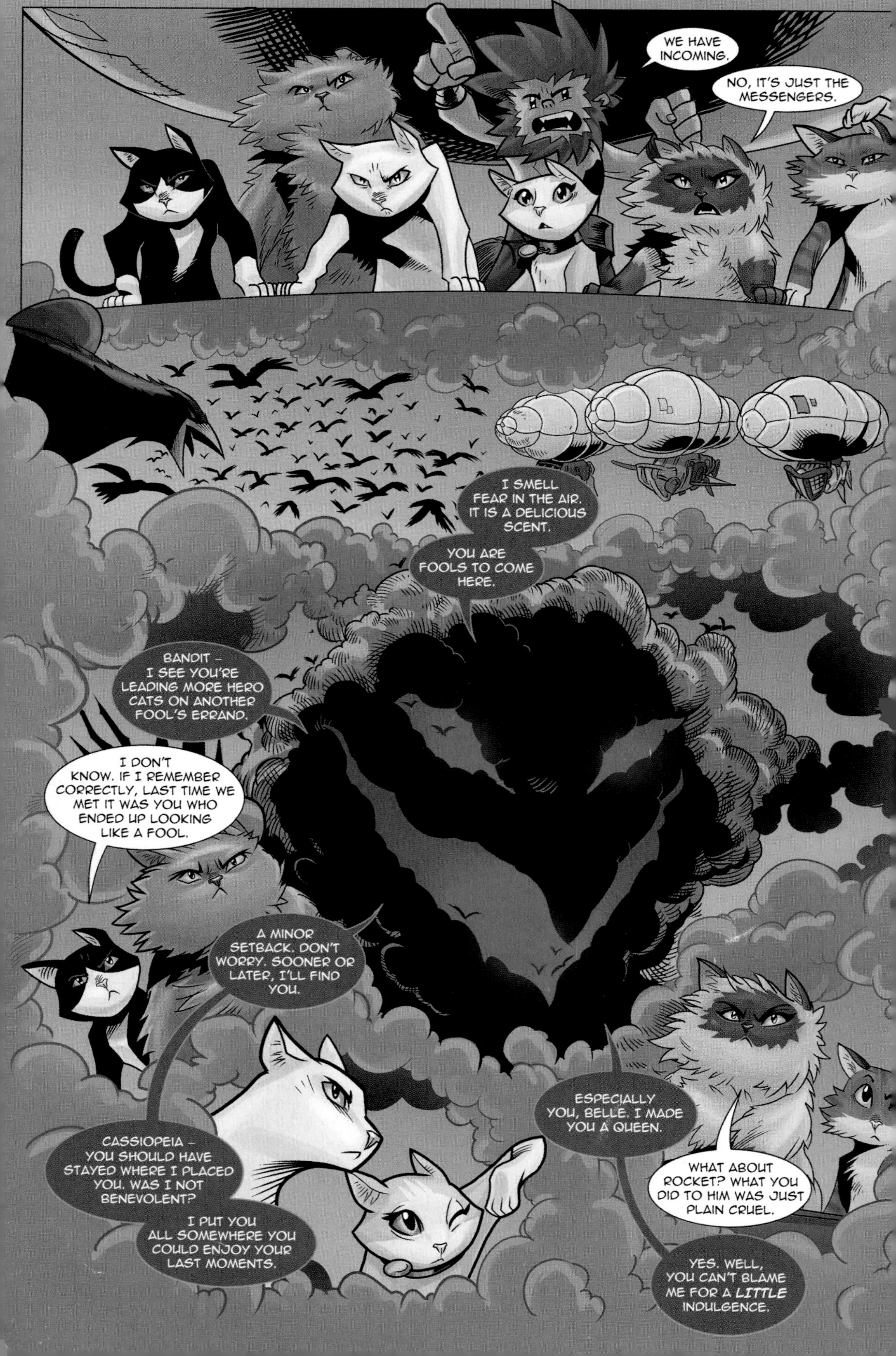
WE HAVE INCOMING.
NO, IT'S JUST THE MESSENGERS.
I SMELL FEAR IN THE AIR. IT IS A DELICIOUS SCENT.
YOU ARE FOOLS TO COME HERE.
BANDIT – I SEE YOU'RE LEADING MORE HERO CATS ON ANOTHER FOOL'S ERRAND.
I DON'T KNOW. IF I REMEMBER CORRECTLY, LAST TIME WE MET IT WAS YOU WHO ENDED UP LOOKING LIKE A FOOL.
A MINOR SETBACK. DON'T WORRY. SOONER OR LATER, I'LL FIND YOU.
CASSIOPEIA – YOU SHOULD HAVE STAYED WHERE I PLACED YOU. WAS I NOT BENEVOLENT?
I PUT YOU ALL SOMEWHERE YOU COULD ENJOY YOUR LAST MOMENTS.
ESPECIALLY YOU, BELLE. I MADE YOU A QUEEN.
WHAT ABOUT ROCKET? WHAT YOU DID TO HIM WAS JUST PLAIN CRUEL.
YES. WELL, YOU CAN'T BLAME ME FOR A *LITTLE* INDULGENCE.

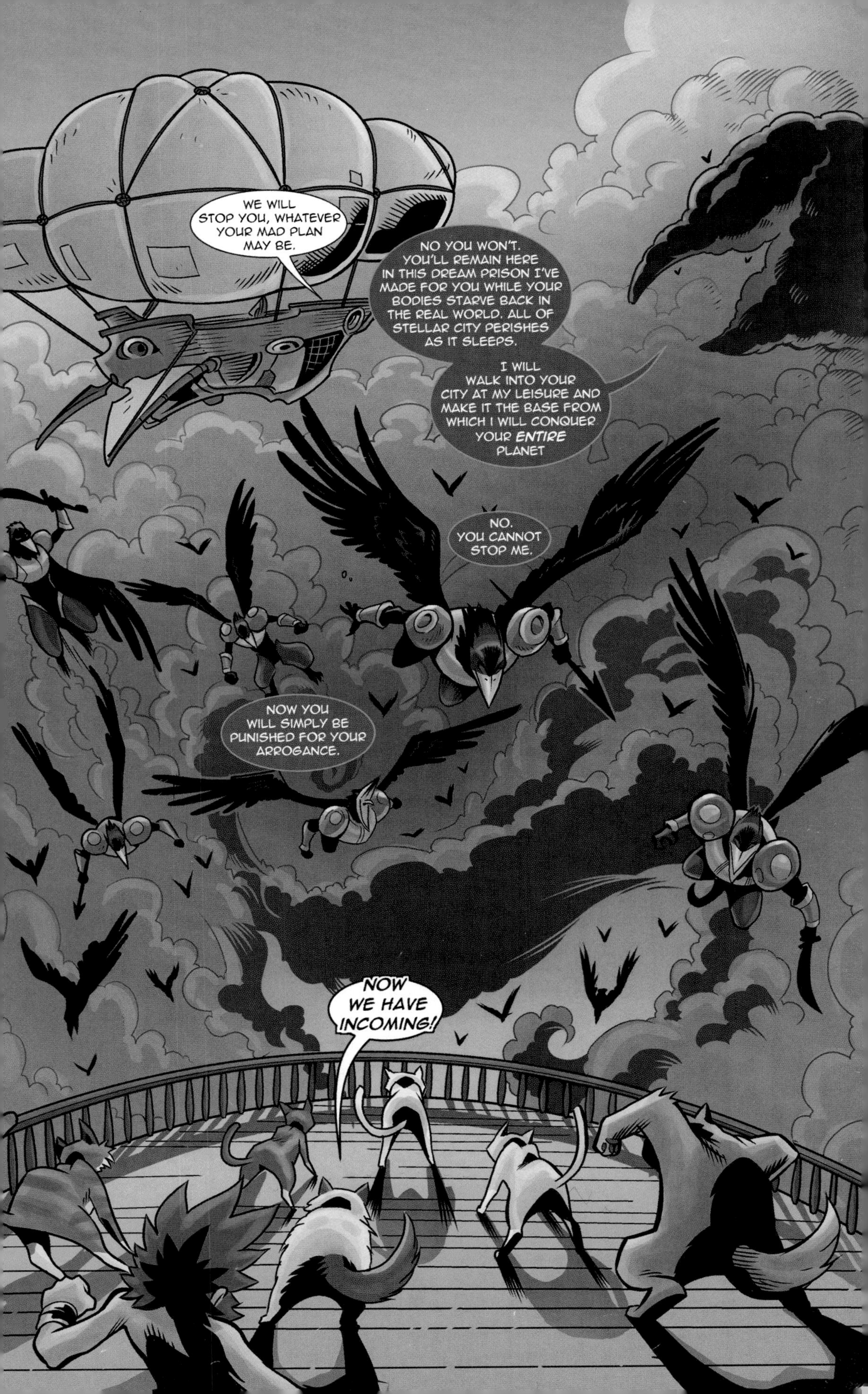

WE WILL STOP YOU, WHATEVER YOUR MAD PLAN MAY BE.
NO YOU WON'T. YOU'LL REMAIN HERE IN THIS DREAM PRISON I'VE MADE FOR YOU WHILE YOUR BODIES STARVE BACK IN THE REAL WORLD. ALL OF STELLAR CITY PERISHES AS IT SLEEPS.
I WILL WALK INTO YOUR CITY AT MY LEISURE AND MAKE IT THE BASE FROM WHICH I WILL CONQUER YOUR ENTIRE PLANET
NO. YOU CANNOT STOP ME.
NOW YOU WILL SIMPLY BE PUNISHED FOR YOUR ARROGANCE.
NOW WE HAVE INCOMING!

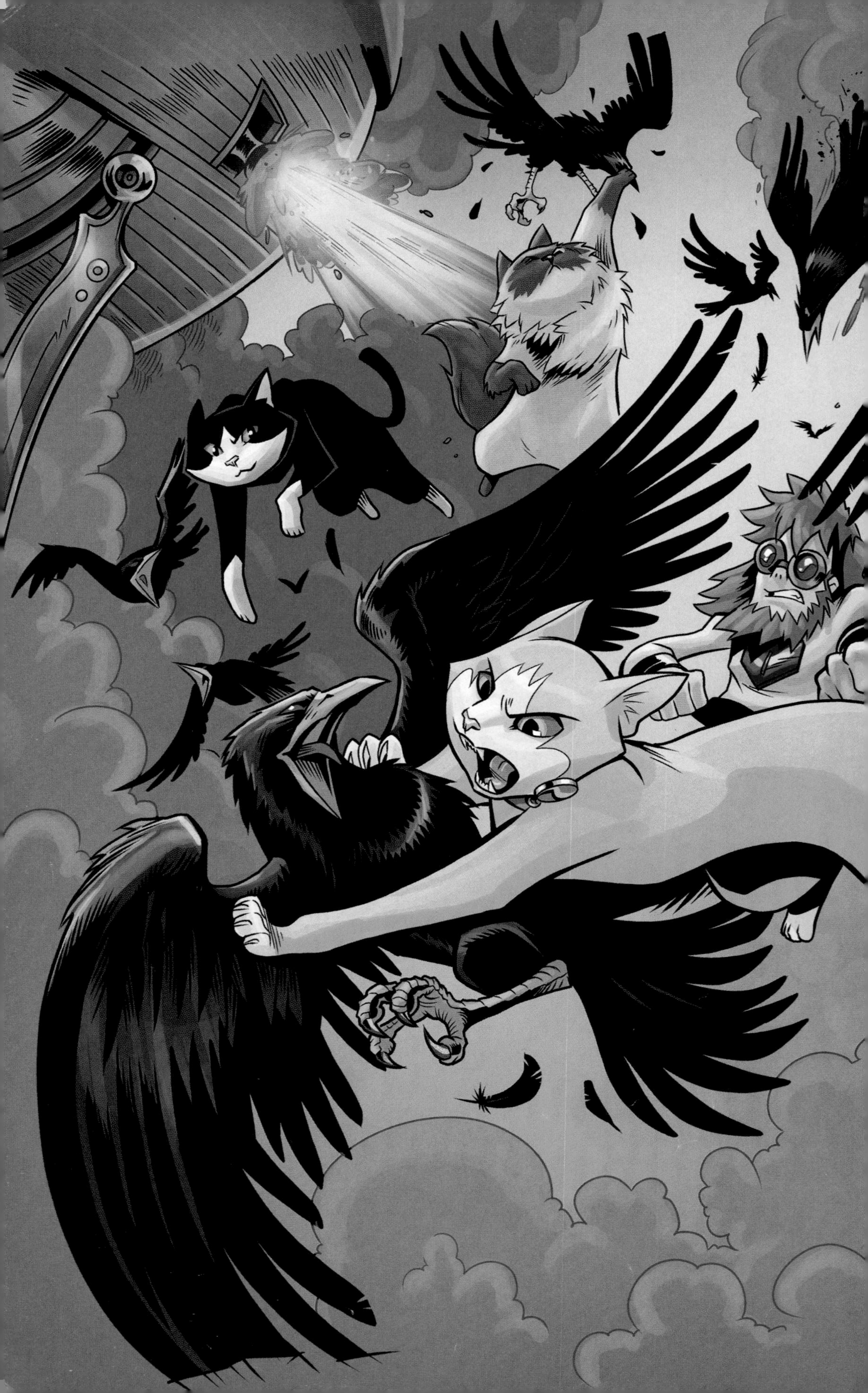

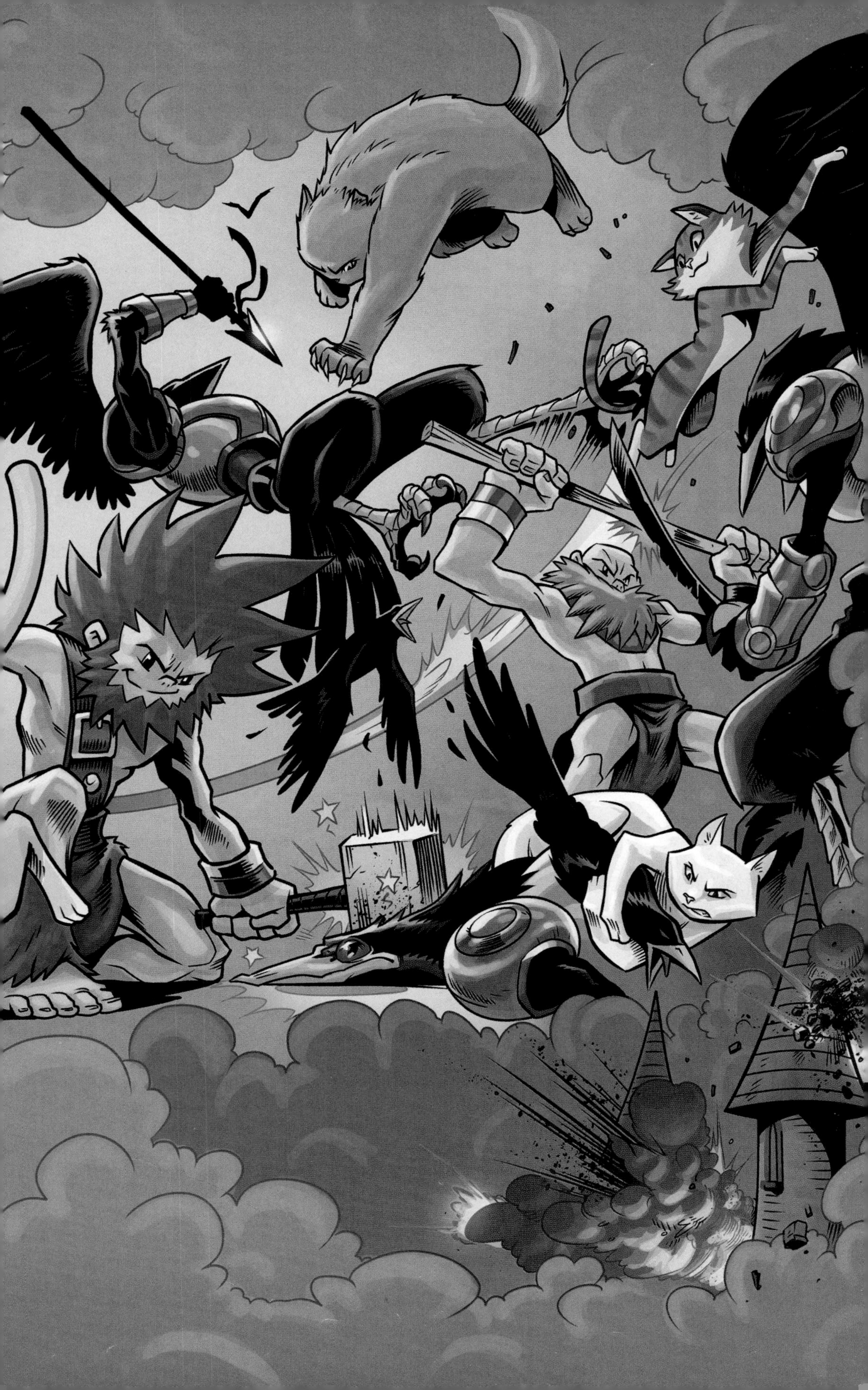

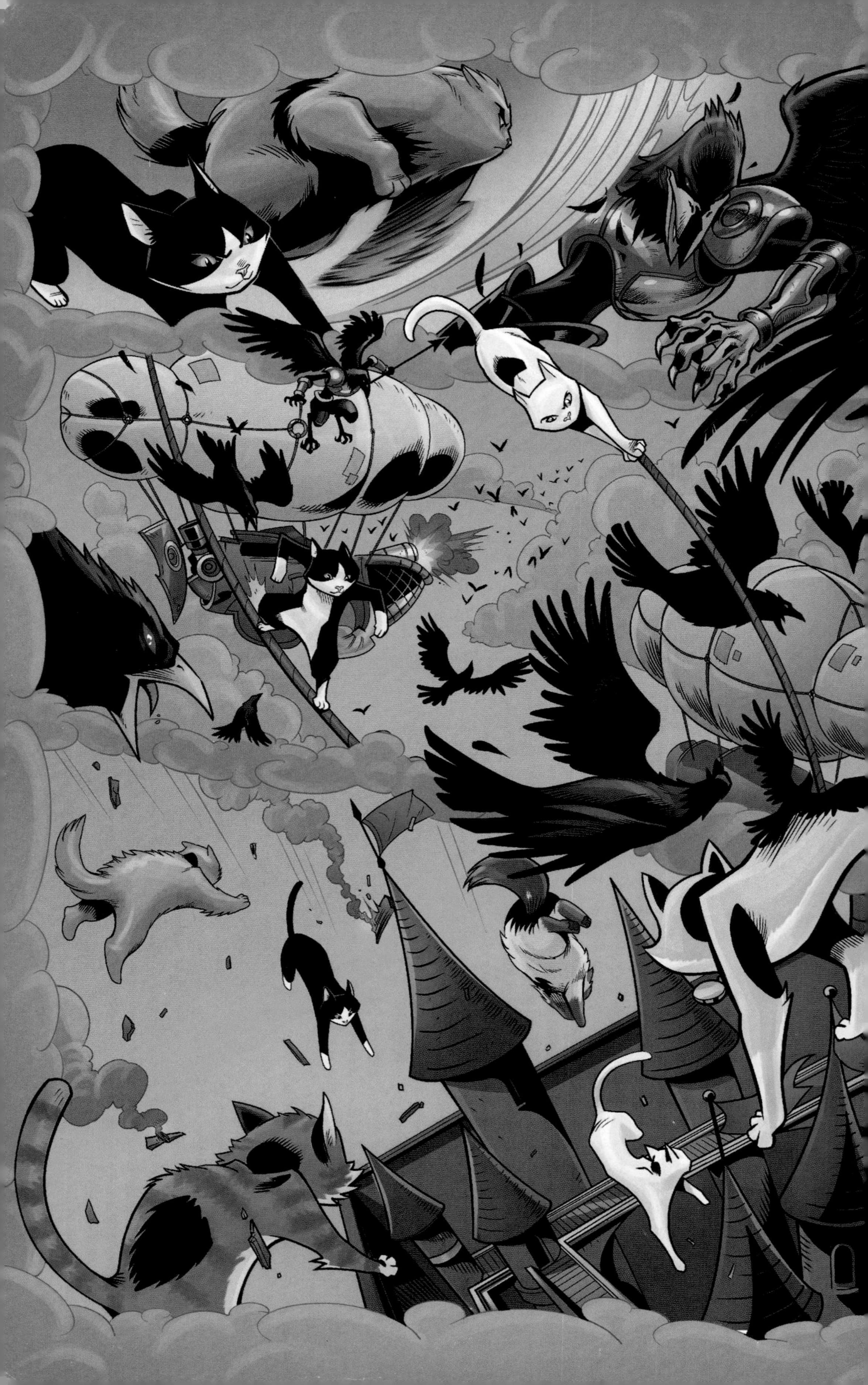

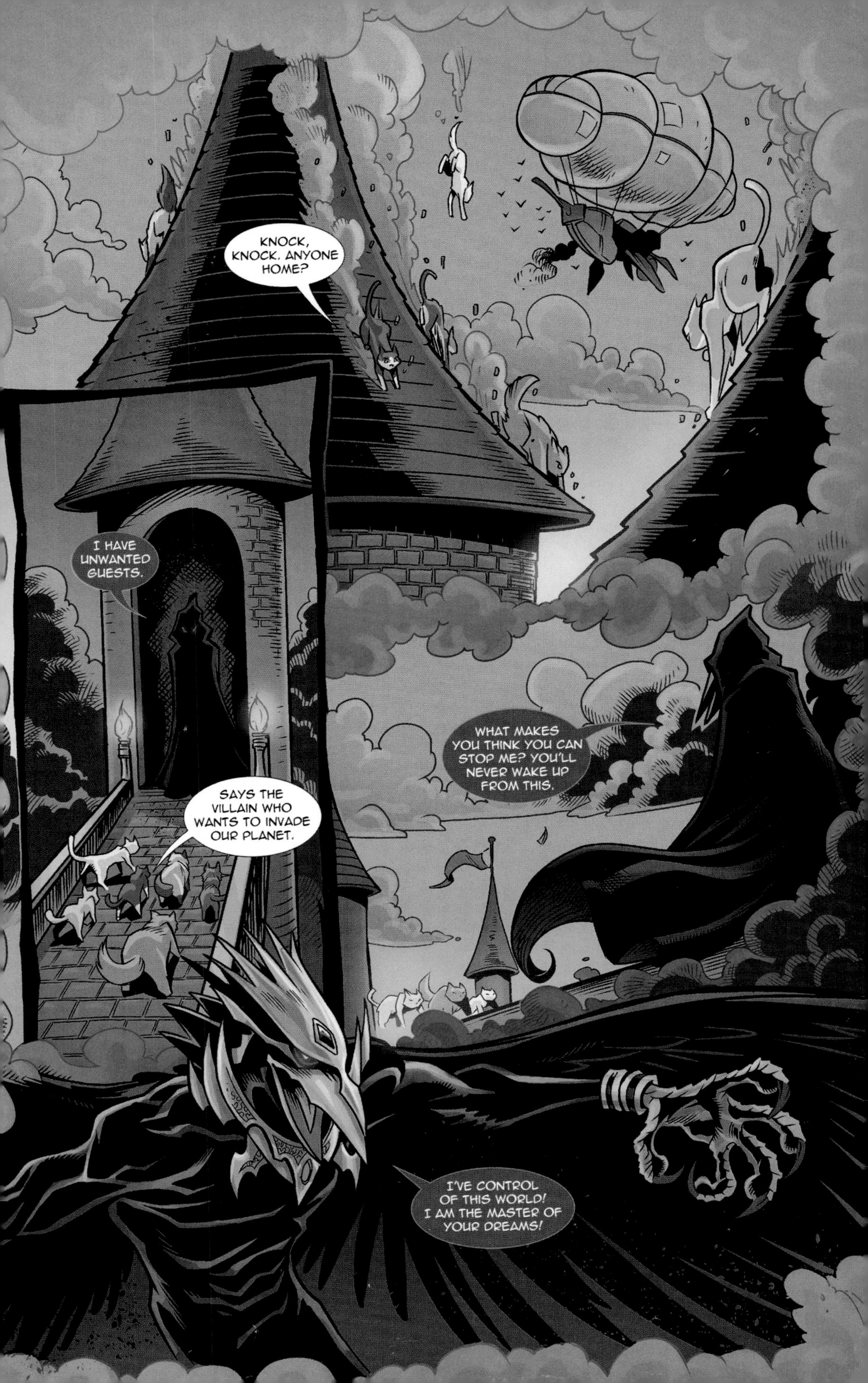
KNOCK, KNOCK. ANYONE HOME?
I HAVE UNWANTED GUESTS.
WHAT MAKES YOU THINK YOU CAN STOP ME? YOU'LL NEVER WAKE UP FROM THIS.
SAYS THE VILLAIN WHO WANTS TO INVADE OUR PLANET.
I'VE CONTROL OF THIS WORLD! I AM THE MASTER OF YOUR DREAMS!

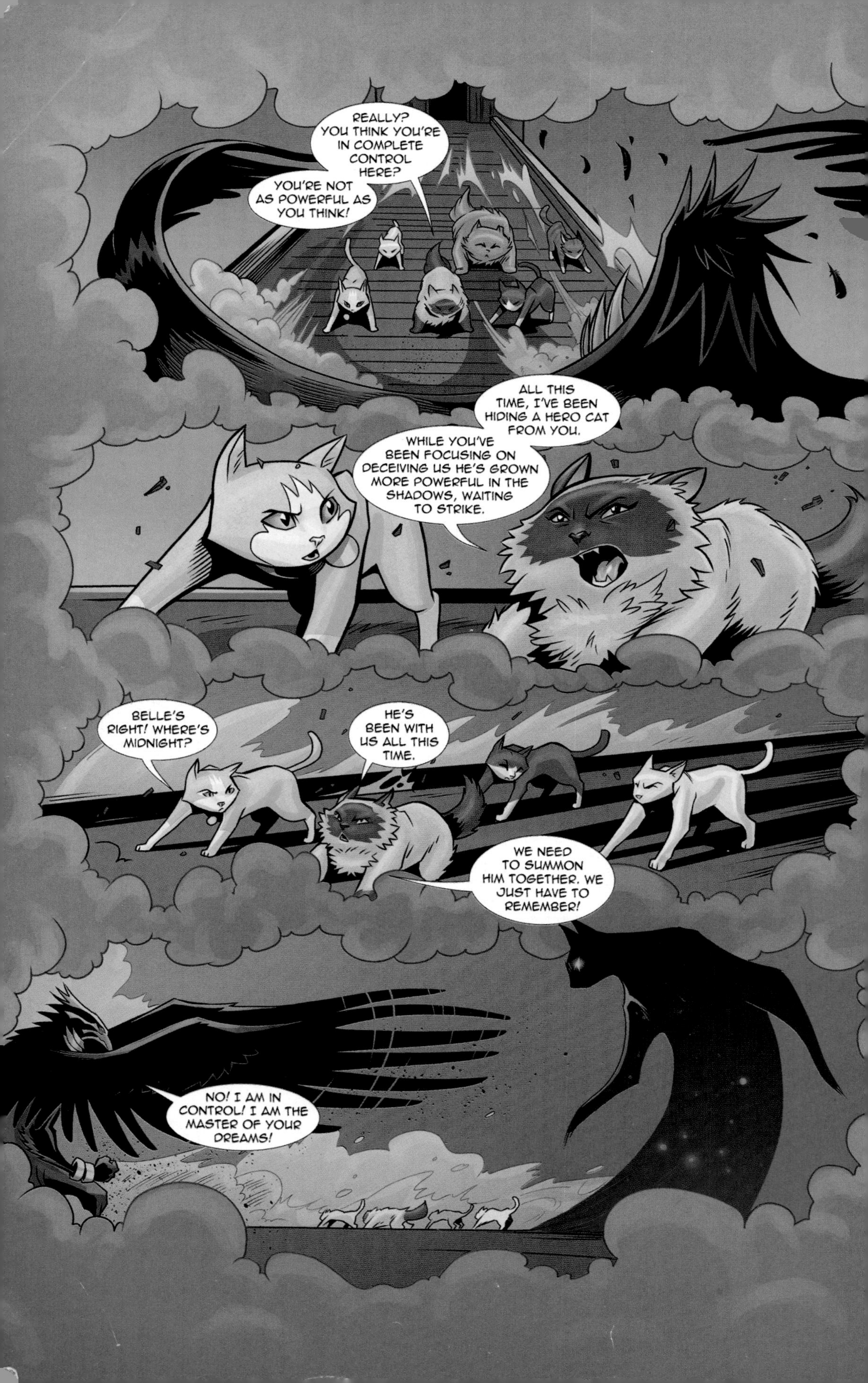
REALLY? YOU THINK YOU'RE IN COMPLETE CONTROL HERE?
YOU'RE NOT AS POWERFUL AS YOU THINK!
ALL THIS TIME, I'VE BEEN HIDING A HERO CAT FROM YOU.
WHILE YOU'VE BEEN FOCUSING ON DECEIVING US HE'S GROWN MORE POWERFUL IN THE SHADOWS, WAITING TO STRIKE.
BELLE'S RIGHT! WHERE'S MIDNIGHT?
HE'S BEEN WITH US ALL THIS TIME.
WE NEED TO SUMMON HIM TOGETHER. WE JUST HAVE TO REMEMBER!
NO! I AM IN CONTROL! I AM THE MASTER OF YOUR DREAMS!

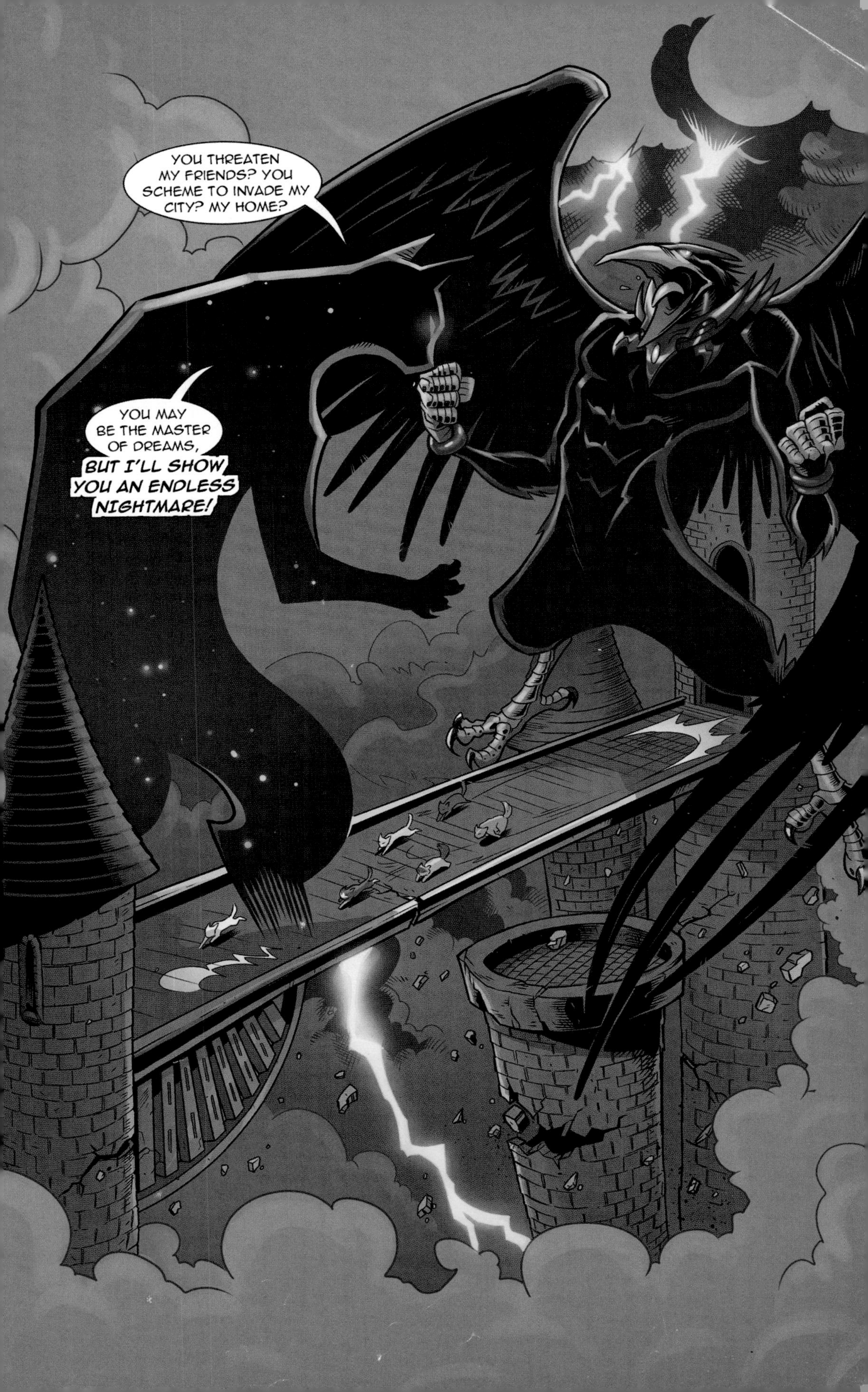
YOU THREATEN MY FRIENDS? YOU SCHEME TO INVADE MY CITY? MY HOME?
YOU MAY BE THE MASTER OF DREAMS, **BUT I'LL SHOW YOU AN ENDLESS NIGHTMARE!**

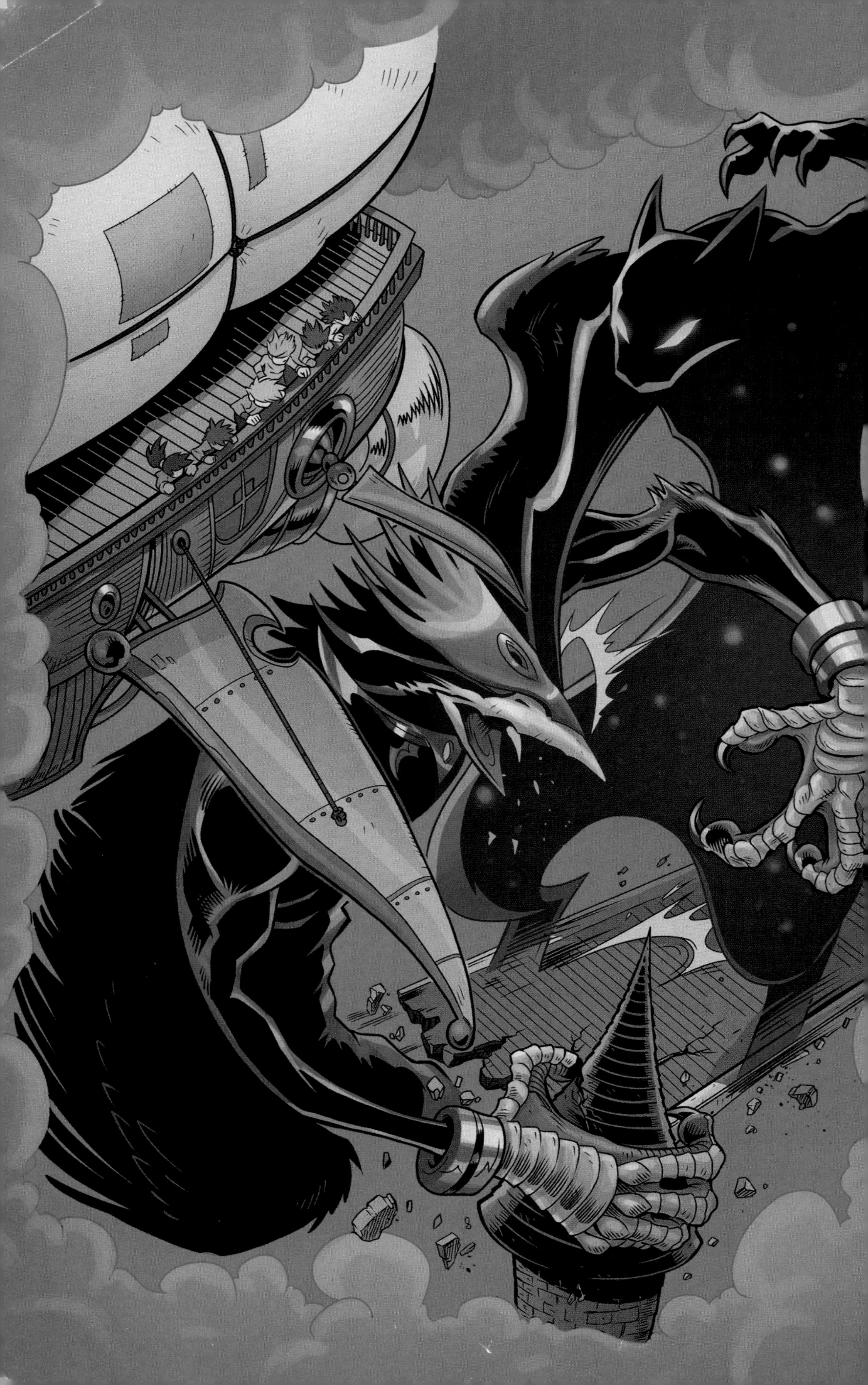

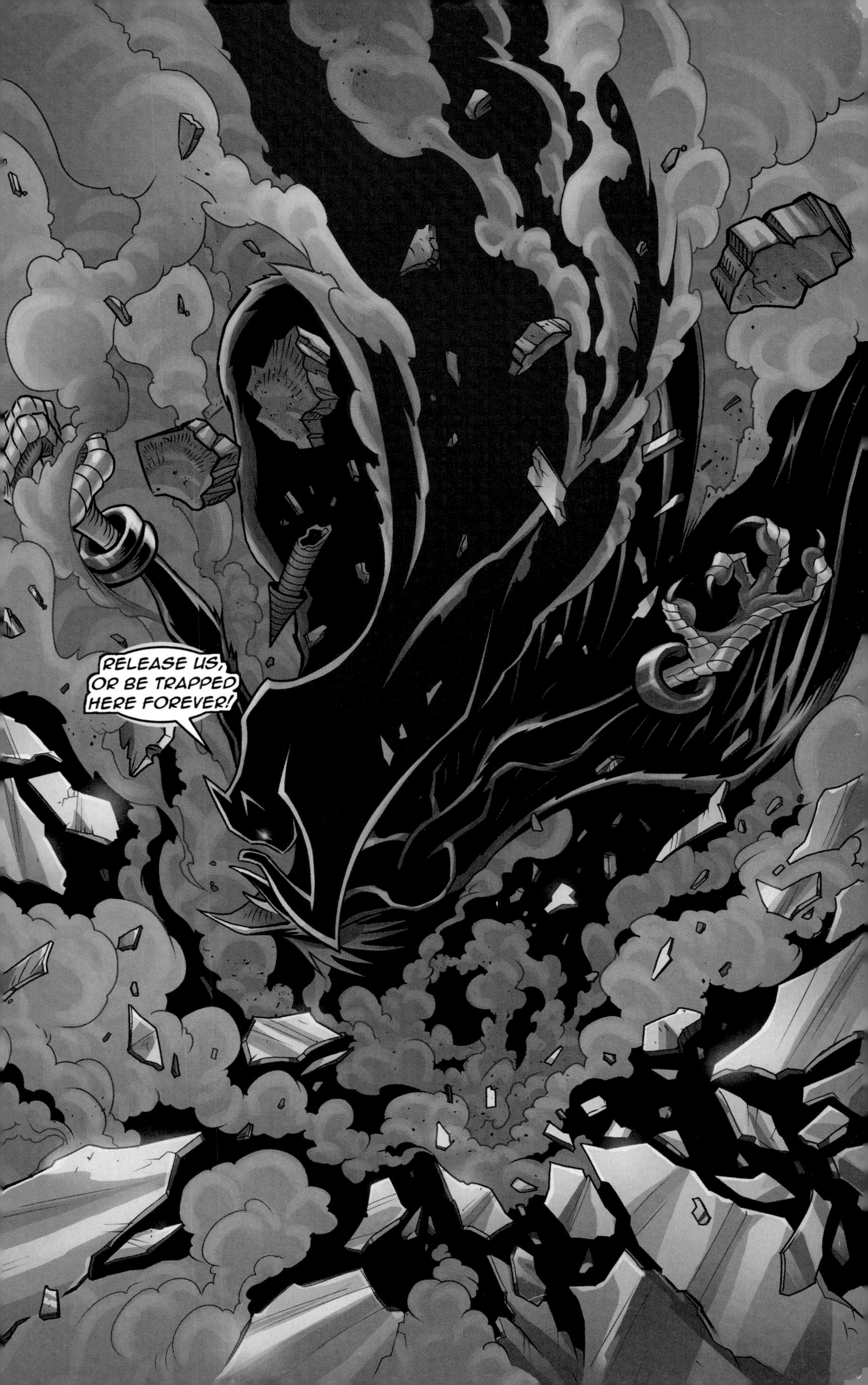
RELEASE US, OR BE TRAPPED HERE FOREVER!

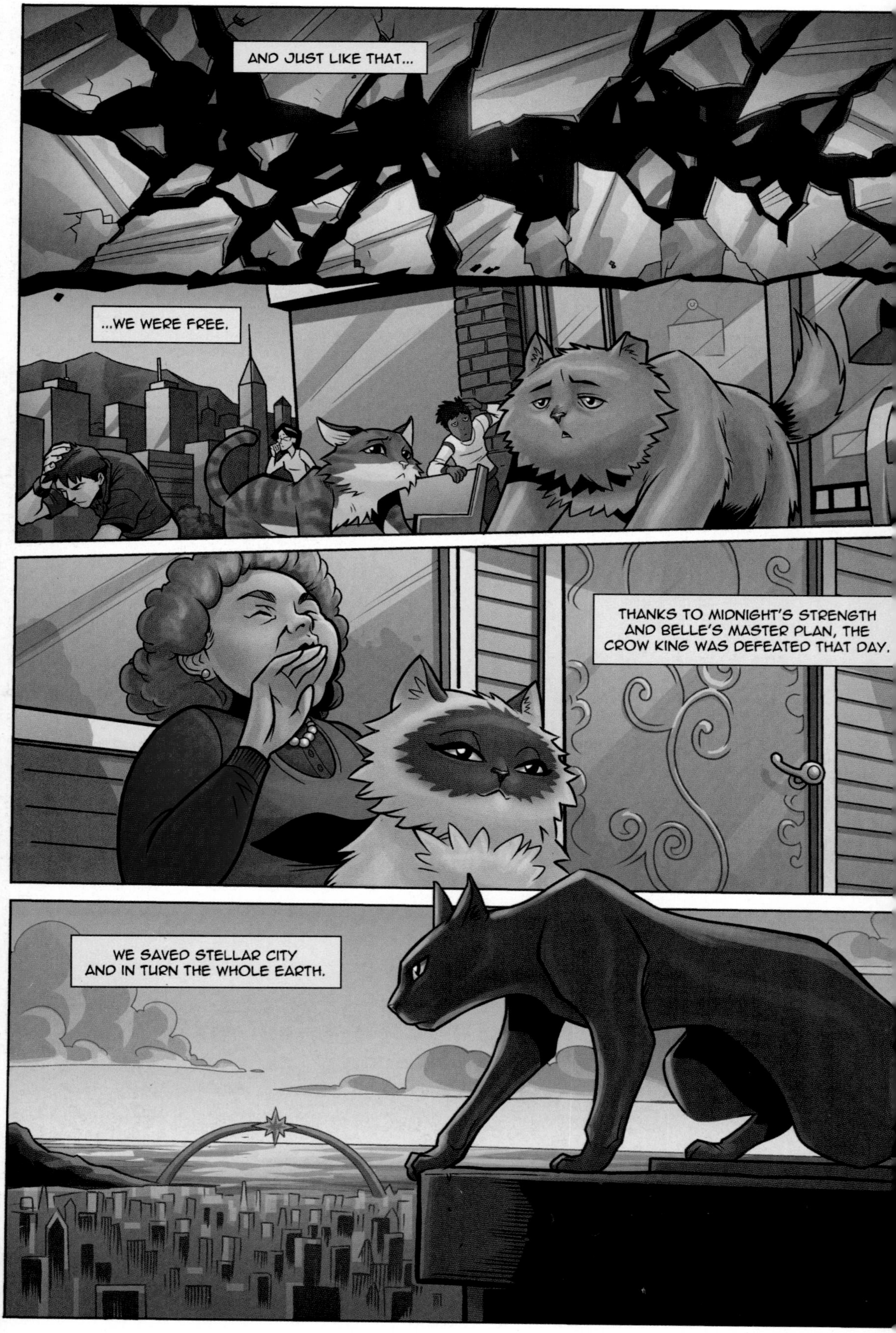
AND JUST LIKE THAT...
...WE WERE FREE.
THANKS TO MIDNIGHT'S STRENGTH AND BELLE'S MASTER PLAN, THE CROW KING WAS DEFEATED THAT DAY.
WE SAVED STELLAR CITY AND IN TURN THE WHOLE EARTH.

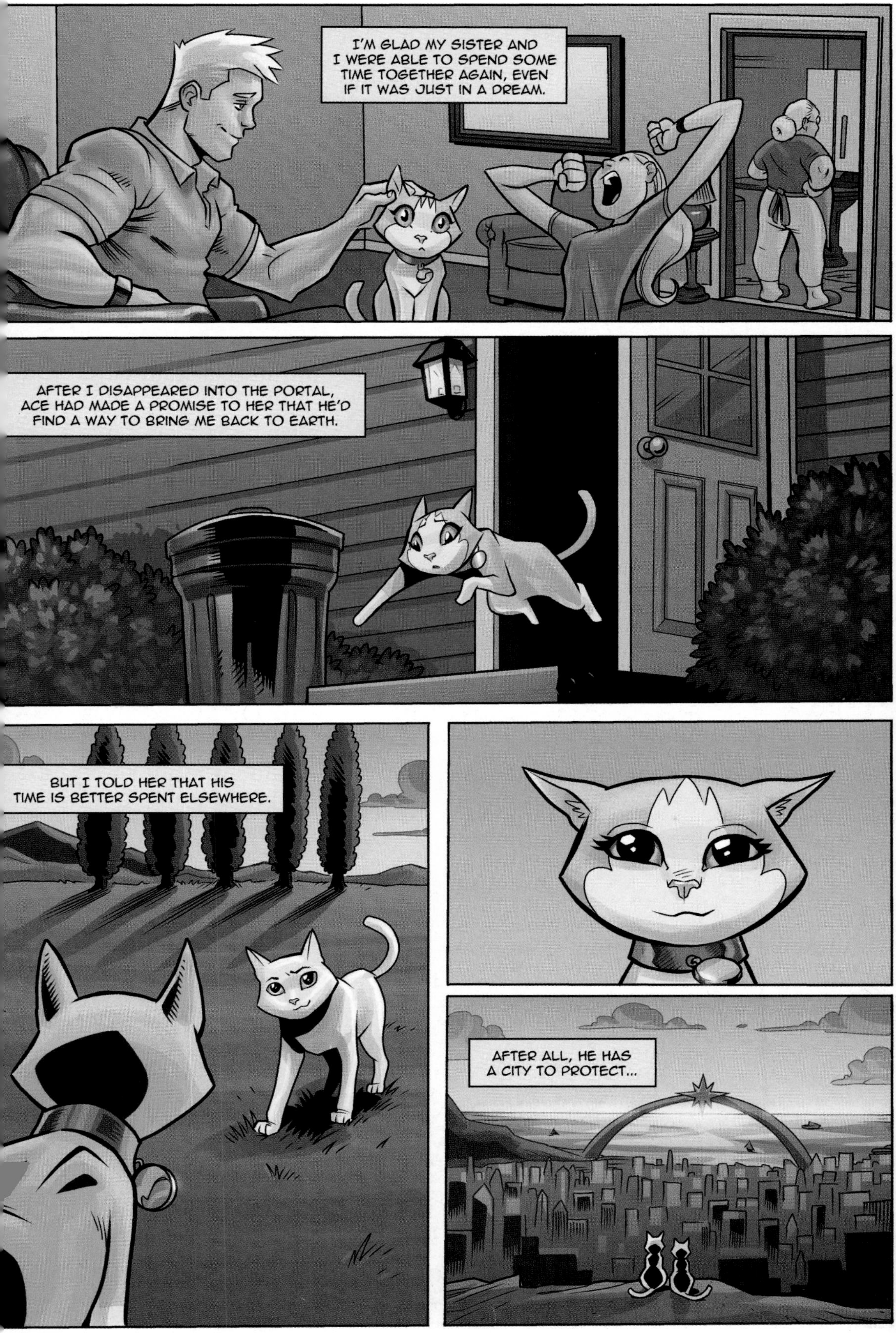
I'M GLAD MY SISTER AND I WERE ABLE TO SPEND SOME TIME TOGETHER AGAIN, EVEN IF IT WAS JUST IN A DREAM.
AFTER I DISAPPEARED INTO THE PORTAL, ACE HAD MADE A PROMISE TO HER THAT HE'D FIND A WAY TO BRING ME BACK TO EARTH.
BUT I TOLD HER THAT HIS TIME IS BETTER SPENT ELSEWHERE.
AFTER ALL, HE HAS A CITY TO PROTECT...

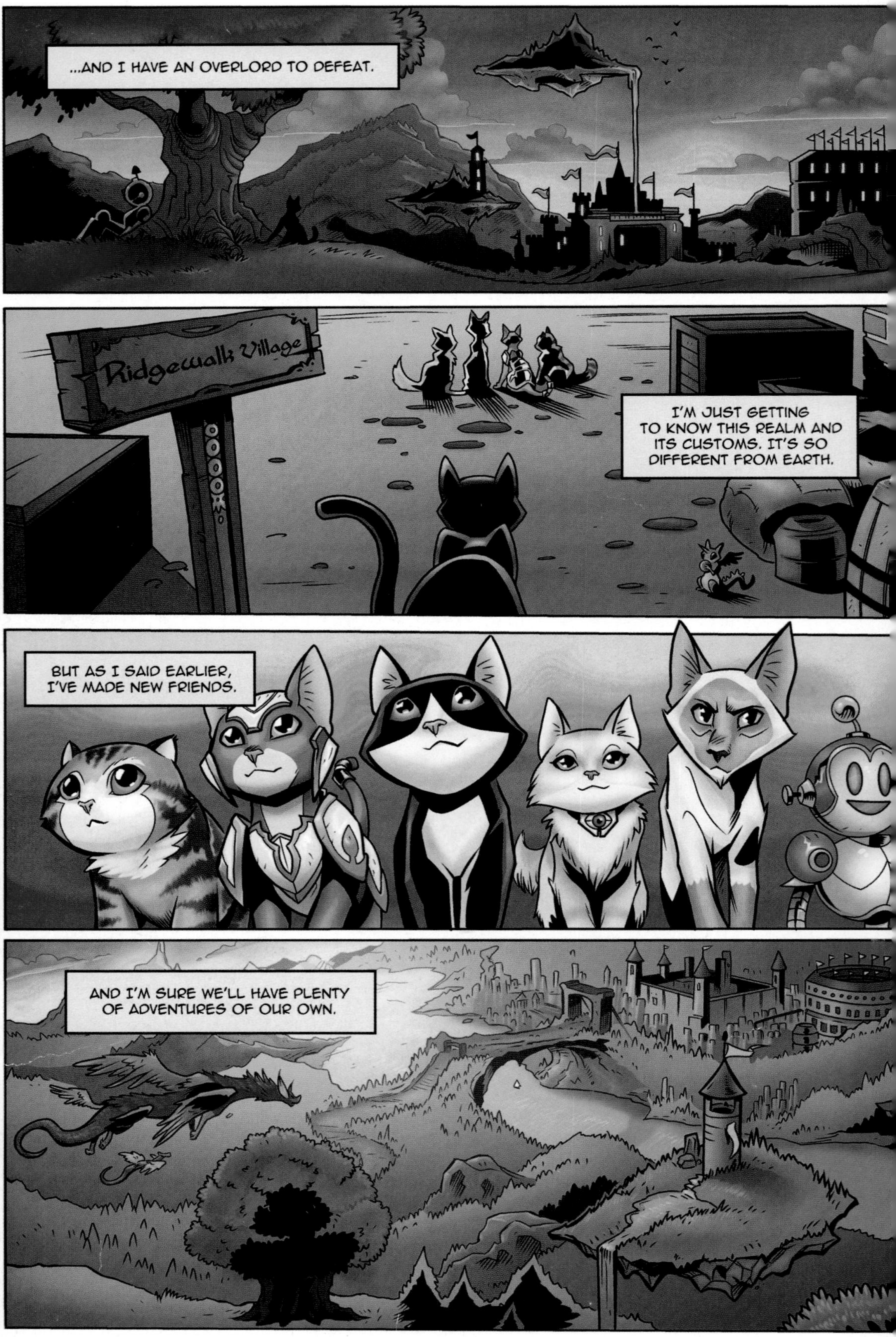
...AND I HAVE AN OVERLORD TO DEFEAT.
Ridgewalk Village
I'M JUST GETTING TO KNOW THIS REALM AND ITS CUSTOMS. IT'S SO DIFFERENT FROM EARTH.
BUT AS I SAID EARLIER, I'VE MADE NEW FRIENDS.
AND I'M SURE WE'LL HAVE PLENTY OF ADVENTURES OF OUR OWN.

HEROCHAT

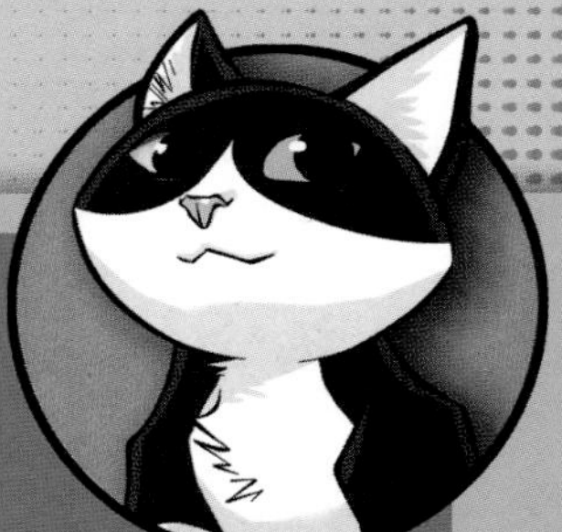

WE DID IT! WE STOPPED THE CROW KING AND HIS INVADING ARMIES! STELLAR CITY IS SAFE ONCE AGAIN. THAT WAS QUITE A SURPRISE APPEARANCE BY MIDNIGHT. WHEN HERO CATS WORK TOGETHER, WE CAN DO ANYTHING.

I HOPE TO RETURN TO EARTH ONE DAY, BUT FOR NOW I'VE GOT MY OWN MISSION ON SKYWORLD. I WONDER WHAT NEW FRIENDS I'LL MAKE. A TALE TO BE TOLD SOME OTHER DAY I SUPPOSE. UNTIL THEN, HAVE FUN AND DRESS UP AS YOUR FAVORITE HERO.

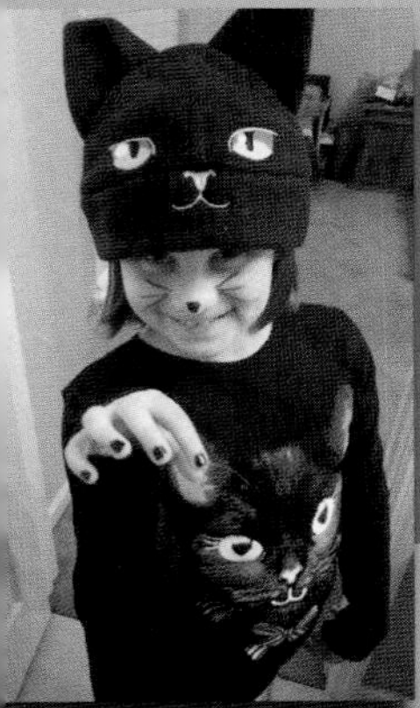

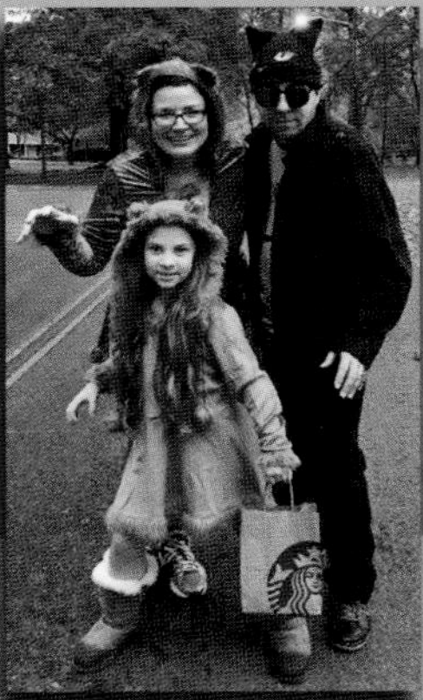

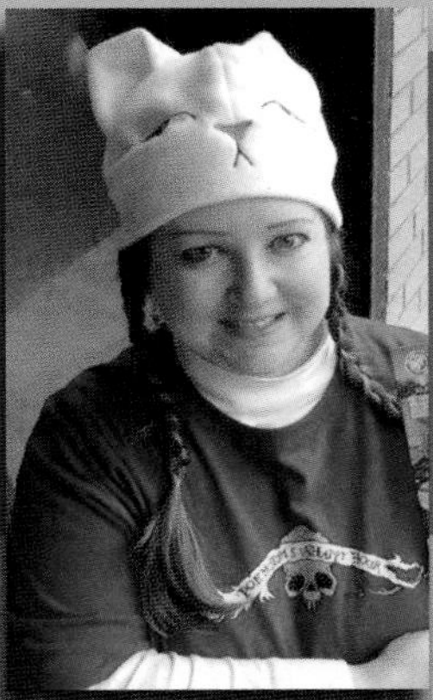

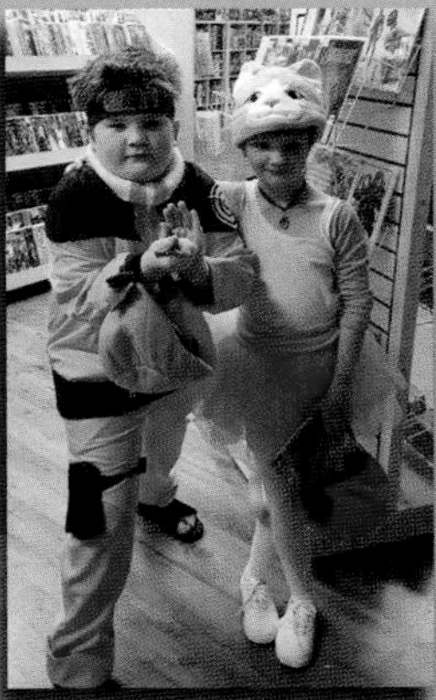

NOW IT'S YOUR TURN! COSPLAY THE CATS

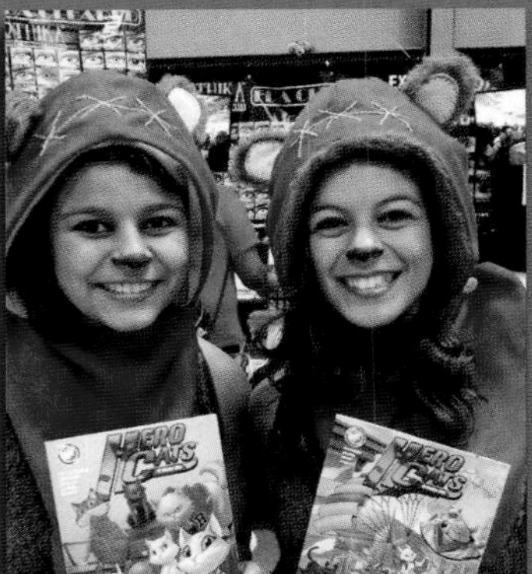

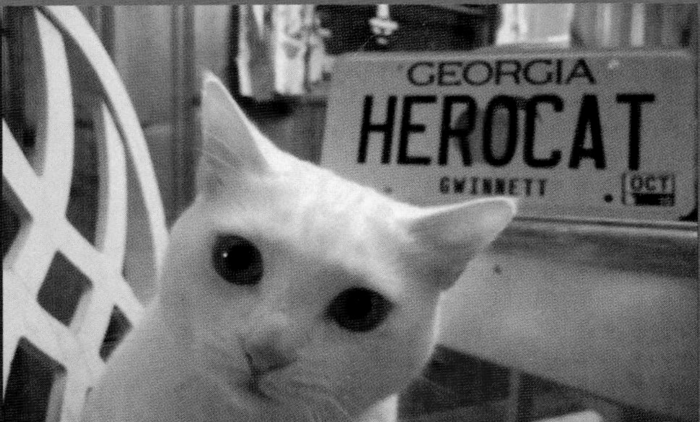
GEORGIA
HEROCAT
GWINNETT
OCT

COMING SOON!

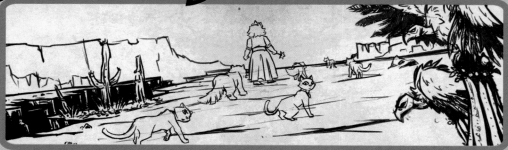

AFTER SUCH AN EPIC ADVENTURE, WHAT'S NEXT?! HOW CAN WE POSSIBLY TOP THE THAT? THE HERO CATS SAVED THE WORLD, SO NOW IT'S TIME TO TOUR IT.

THE NEXT TALE WILL BE TOLD WITH SPECIAL ARTWORK FROM OUR VERY OWN OMAKA SCHULTZ. YOU'VE ENJOYED HIS COLORS ON THE SERIES, NOW WATCH AS HE TAKES US TO

THE WILD, WILD WEST.

HERO CATS
#10
$3.99
PUTTKAMMER
SCHULTZ
SELLERS
BARCLAY

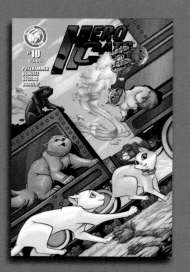

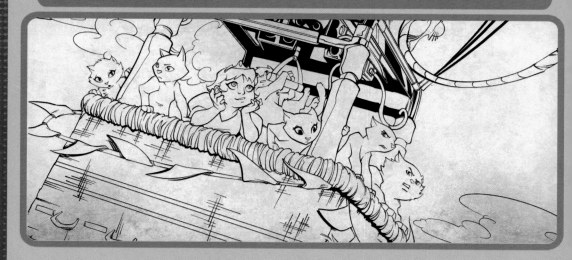

COLLECT THE TRADE PAPERBACKS!

HERO CATS
Of Stellar City
PUTTKAMMER
WILLIAMS
SELLERS
SCHULTZ
VOLUME 1

HERO CATS
Of Stellar City
PUTTKAMMER
WILLIAMS
SELLERS
SCHULTZ
HERMS
NEW DISCOVERIES

HERO CATS
Of Stellar City
PUTTKAMMER
WILLIAMS
SELLERS
SCHULTZ
PAGE
THE CROW KING SAGA

MIDNIGHT VS. GALAXY MAN!

CAN'T GET ENOUGH OF THE CROW KING SAGA? YOU'RE IN LUCK. MIDNIGHT CONTINUES THE FIGHT IN MOSC #3.

AS IF THAT'S NOT ENOUGH, MIDNIGHT FINALLY CONFRONTS GALAXY MAN. BRING THE LIGHTNING! BRING THE THUNDER! IT'S HERO VS HERO!

MIDNIGHT

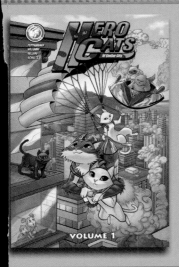

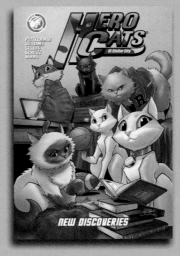

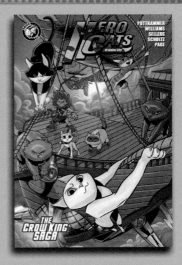

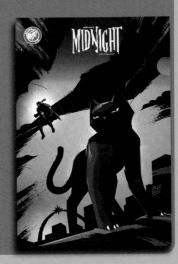

Bryan Seaton - Publisher
Kevin Freeman - President
Dave Dwench - Creative Director
Shawn Gabborin - Editor in Chief
Jamal Igle - Director of Marketing
Jim Dietz - Social Media Director
Jeremy Whitley - Education Outreach Director
Chad Cicconi & Colleen Boyd - Associate Editors

Herocats over Stellar City #9, January 2016

Printed in Canada.

First Printing

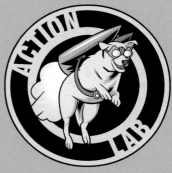

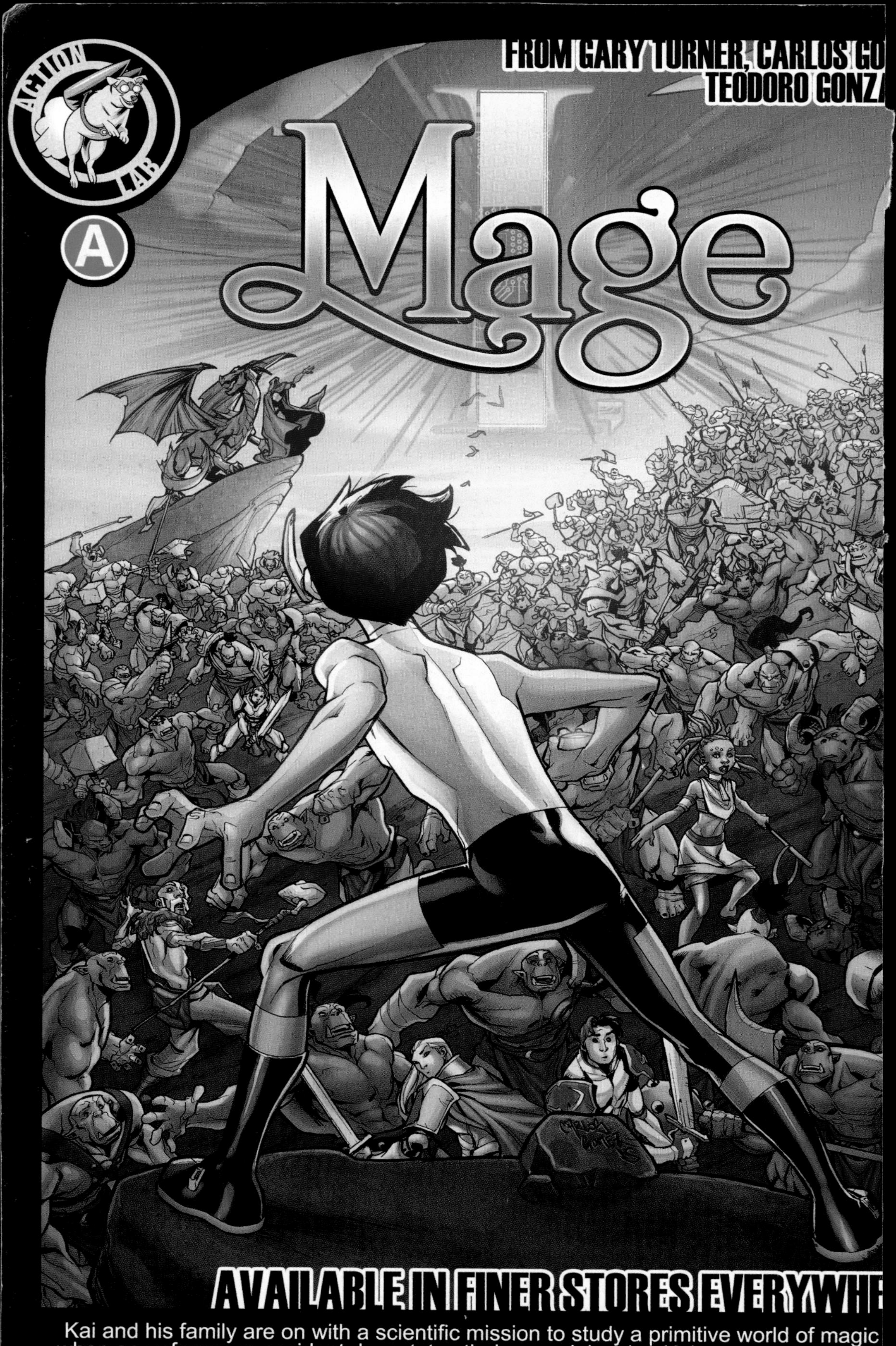
ACTION LAB
A
FROM GARY TURNER, CARLOS GO
TEODORO GONZA
Mage
AVAILABLE IN FINER STORES EVERYWHE

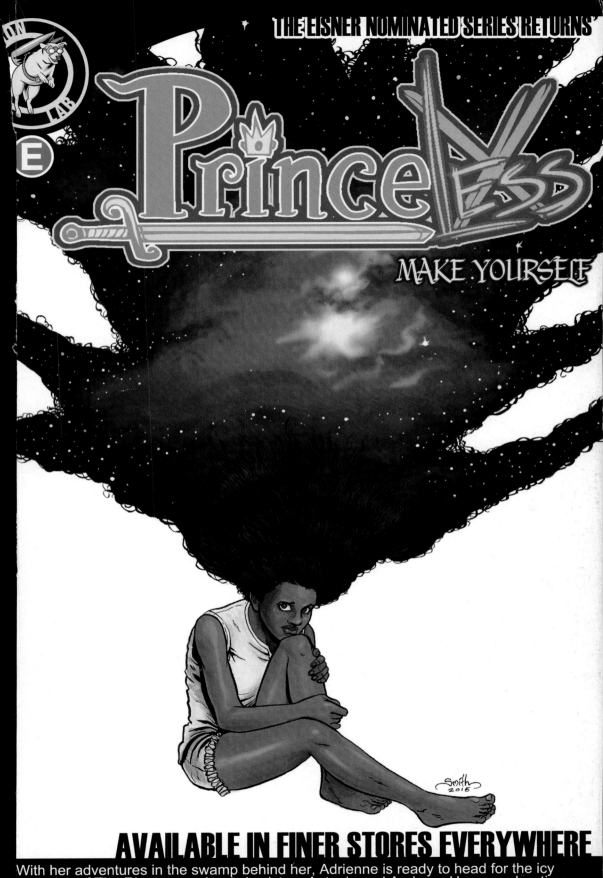

With her adventures in the swamp behind her, Adrienne is ready to head for the icy mountains of The Rim to save her twin sisters Antonia and Andrea. However, her time in Grimmorium Swamp has left a lasting effect on her - especially on her hair. Now, it's time for Adrienne to make a change. Join us for a special zero issue of the new chapter of Princeless with series creator Jeremy Whitley and special guest artist Alex Smith.

CYRUS PERKINS
AND THE HAUNTED TAXI CAB

AVAILABLE IN FINER STORES EVERYWHERE

...rus is on the fast track to solving Michael's murder, but there's an unexpected curve ...e road ahead. The killer is hunting him, and Death is sure to follow. Jump in to what ComicBastards.com is hailing as "One of the best breakouts of the year!"

Action Lab

READ MORE NOW

Hero Cats - Action Lab
www.actionlabcomics.com
00911
7 00465 77241 1

ACTIONLABCOMICS.COM